THE GHOSTS AT PEMBERLEY

Kitty Bennet travels to Pemberley to live with the Darcys and become a companion to Miss Georgiana — but her happy days at the grand stately home are soon overshadowed by the unexpected appearance of the spectral inhabitants of the ancient east wing. Their evil purpose becomes all too evident as a series of attacks ensues, with Kitty seemingly their favourite victim. And when they reveal to her the only condition upon which they will leave, she is horrified. Pemberley will have to be permanently abandoned, the Darcy family and their friends and servants fleeing for their very lives — unless the ghosts' thirst for revenge is satisfied . . .

THE ULVERSCROFT FOUNDATION
(Registered UK charity number 264873)

was established in 1972 to provide funds for research, diagnosis and treatment of eye diseases. Examples of major projects funded by the Ulverscroft Foundation are:-

- The Children's Eye Unit at Moorfields Eye Hospital, London
- The Ulverscroft Children's Eye Unit at Great Ormond Street Hospital for Sick Children
- Funding research into eye diseases and treatment at the Department of Ophthalmology, University of Leicester
- The Ulverscroft Vision Research Group, Institute of Child Health
- Twin operating theatres at the Western Ophthalmic Hospital, London
- The Chair of Ophthalmology at the Royal Australian College of Ophthalmologists

You can help further the work of the Foundation by making a donation or leaving a legacy. Every contribution is gratefully received. If you would like to help support the Foundation or require further information, please contact:

THE ULVERSCROFT FOUNDATION
The Green, Bradgate Road, Anstey
Leicester LE7 7FU, England
Tel: (0116) 236 4325

website: www.foundation.ulverscroft.com

Fenella J. Miller was born on the Isle of Man. Her father was a Yorkshireman and her mother the daughter of a Rajah. She has worked as a nanny, cleaner, field worker, hotelier, chef, secondary and primary teacher, and is now a full-time writer. She has had over twenty-five Regency romantic adventures published, among other stories. Fenella lives in a pretty riverside village in Essex with her husband and ancient Border Collie. She has two adult children and two grandchildren.

Visit her website at:
www.fenellajmiller.co.uk

FENELLA J. MILLER

THE GHOSTS AT PEMBERLEY

Complete and Unabridged

ULVERSCROFT
Leicester

First published in Great Britain in 2014

First Large Print Edition
published 2016

A catalogue record for this book is available
from the British Library.

ISBN 978–1–4448–2832–0

Published by
F. A. Thorpe (Publishing)
Anstey, Leicestershire

Set by Words & Graphics Ltd.
Anstey, Leicestershire
Printed and bound in Great Britain by
T. J. International Ltd., Padstow, Cornwall

This book is printed on acid-free paper

MY THANKS TO
FAY CUNNINGHAM,
MONICA FAIRVIEW
&
RACHEL BEVAN

1

The carriage rocked violently as it traversed yet another rut in the road. Miss Kitty Bennet, despite her hold on the strap, was flung painfully to her knees in the well of the vehicle. Her sister, Mrs Jane Bingley, exclaimed in horror.

'Kitty, my love, have you sustained any injury from your fall? Allow Mr Bingley to assist you to your seat.'

'I am unhurt, thank you, Jane. I can recover my place unaided.' With these words she scrambled to her feet, taking care not to reveal her ankles in the process. Once Kitty was comfortably settled and the rug snugly around her knees, her sister spoke again.

'This journey is beyond tedious, Charles. I had quite forgotten just how far away Derbyshire is from Netherfield. I know it was my suggestion to escape from my mother's constant interference, but I should have considered the parlous state of the roads in December.'

Mr Bingley smiled and squeezed his wife's mittened hand. 'The journey has taken far longer than I had anticipated, my dear, but I believe us to be within a few miles of Pemberley. Despite the discomfort of the past three days, I am looking forward to seeing Darcy and spending Christmas in such wonderful surroundings.'

'I believe this road to be in poor repair, which is why we are being jolted so unpleasantly,' Kitty stated unnecessarily. 'I am black and blue all over, and when I tumbled from the squabs just now I landed on the brick I was given to keep my feet warm this morning.'

'How unfortunate!' said Jane. 'Ah, I do believe the road is smoother here and we have picked up our pace at last.'

The carriage was travelling more quickly, but Kitty was concerned the coachman had sprung the horses without having sufficient knowledge of the locality. What if there was a second patch of road with potholes? 'Mr Bingley, we could overturn if a wheel drops into a rut at this speed,' she said.

'I shall ask Tom to reduce the pace — better to arrive late than not arrive at all.' Mr Bingley checked his beloved Jane was comfortable before pushing himself upright. 'I shall open the window and call out, for I doubt he would hear us over the wind and rain if I do not do so.'

Just as he was struggling with the leather

strap that held the window firm, the coach veered sharply to the right in order to negotiate a turn in the lane. Mr Bingley lost his balance and fell backwards and his head hit the floor with a sickening thud. The window dropped open and Kitty's scream was heard by the coachman.

'Kitty, we must do something to stem the blood,' said Jane. 'Quickly, tear some strips from your shift, and I shall use mine to make a pad to press against the gash in his head.' She was made of sterner stuff than Kitty, and was already on her knees beside her husband. As the coach rocked to a standstill both ladies raised their skirts and began to tear off sections of cotton. There was a prodigious amount of blood and Mr Bingley remained unconscious, which was decidedly worrying.

The coachman clambered down from the box, causing the vehicle to rock violently. Kitty heard him shout to the groom. 'Billy, get to the horses and hold the team steady. They're like to bolt in this storm.'

'I have the strips here, Jane,' said Kitty. 'Are you sure you know what to do? Lizzy was always the one to handle any accidents for us.'

Jane was almost as pale as her husband, but showed no sign of succumbing to a fit of the vapours. 'I am going to lift his head and put this folded material against the gash at the back. When I do so you must wind your strips around in order to hold it tight. I pray this will be enough to stem the bleeding until we can get him to a physician and have sutures put in.'

Together they managed to apply the makeshift bandage, and Kitty was in the process of tying it together when the coachman threw back the door. A gust of icy wind blew through the carriage.

'I reckon there's a grand big house no more than one hundred yards ahead, madam. Shall I take us in there?'

Jane looked up, her face tear-streaked and her mittens quite ruined. 'Do that. Mr Bingley requires the attention of a doctor immediately. He hit his head on the brick when he fell and I fear he has concussion.'

Tom pulled the window closed, fastened the leather strap and then slammed the door. Moments later they were in motion again, but this time they travelled at a snail's pace. Kitty scrubbed her eyes dry with her sleeve. 'I should have moved the brick when I fell on it. This is all my fault . . .'

'Nonsense, my love. The accident was no one's fault. We must use all the rugs to wrap Charles in — he has lost so much blood his skin is becoming cold to the touch.'

There was no room in the well of the carriage for both of them. Indeed, Kitty's legs were in the way. She handed down the furs that had been covering her knees and then swung her legs onto the squabs in order to give Jane sufficient room to tend to the patient.

'I believe we are turning into a drive, Jane. It is too dark to see much of the house, but the drive appears to be smooth and I can see lights in the windows.' She almost fell off the seat when Tom sounded the horn used to warn other vehicles of their approach on the narrow lanes.

By the time the carriage was stationary Kitty could see the front door was open, and several figures were running down the front steps towards them. 'Someone is coming to our assistance, sister. Poor Mr Bingley will be in the warm and taken care of very soon.'

The coach door was flung open and a dark-haired gentleman thrust in his head. 'I am Adam King, the rector of this parish.' He turned and shouted to a figure behind him. 'Jim, take Bess and ride for Doctor Bevan.' He then issued instructions to other minions to fetch a trestle upon which they could place Mr Bingley. 'Ladies, allow me to assist you from the carriage. My housekeeper, Miller, will take care of you.'

'I shall not move from here until my husband can come with me,' Jane replied.

Kitty scrambled along the seat, intending to place her feet back on the floor and then descend, thus leaving the rescuers more room to manoeuvre within the vehicle. Unfortunately she was unable to extricate her legs from the voluminous material of her travelling gown and remained, her cheeks scarlet, stuck on the seat.

'Allow me, miss. You appear to be in some difficulty.' Without a by your leave, Mr King reached in, gripped her around the waist, and lifted her as if she weighed no more than a bag of feathers. As her skirts settled around her ankles, Kitty could not help but notice that the gentleman who had so kindly assisted her was a handsome man. He lived in a house far bigger than Longbourn and had more than a dozen servants at his disposal, which was another thing in his favour. The rain continued to pour down on them but he seemed unbothered by it.

Despite the inclement weather she gave him her most charming smile. He, however, appeared unimpressed and rudely gestured that she make her way to the house. She was escorted by a parlourmaid and handed over to a statuesque woman dressed in dark green bombazine. This lady had grey hair scraped back in an ugly bun at the back of her head and a set of keys attached to her belt.

'If you would care to come with me, miss, I will have a chamber prepared for you upstairs. Do you have your dresser with you?'

'I do not; the carriage containing our baggage and our staff went ahead, and will already be at Pemberley. My sister, Mrs Darcy, will be most anxious at our delay.' Kitty thought it would help with her prestige if she mentioned the family connection to Fitzwilliam Darcy.

The housekeeper was suitably impressed. 'I shall have a message sent to Mrs Darcy immediately, informing her of the accident and saying that you will be remaining here overnight. Will you require a fresh gown, or has your cloak kept you dry?'

Kitty checked her gown was wearable. 'Thank you, I believe I shall do very well in this one. The gentleman who has received the injury is my brother-in-law, Mr Charles Bingley. He is a very close friend of Mr Darcy.'

Miller's expression changed to one of horror. 'Mr Bingley has been injured? How dreadful! He and Mr Darcy are well-known in this neighbourhood and very highly thought of.'

If that was indeed the case, then why had Mr King not recognised Mr Bingley? She could hardly enquire from the housekeeper; gossiping with the staff was not something a well-brought-up young lady would stoop to.

'Kindly excuse me, Miss Bennet. Sally will show you to your chamber. I must see what assistance I can offer downstairs.'

Before Kitty could think of a suitable response, Miller was hurrying downstairs. She followed the parlourmaid to her designated room. She was amazed that a household so remote from Hertfordshire knew to whom Mr Darcy had become affiliated.

'Hot water has been sent up, miss, and there will be two girls to assist you.' The maid curtsied and vanished through a hidden door in the fine wooden panelling that covered the walls, leaving Kitty to enter her temporary accommodation alone.

She looked around the bedchamber with appreciation. The hangings on the tester bed were of a pretty floral pattern and the chaise longue was upholstered in matching fabric. Upon the boards was a dark green, deep pile rug which complemented the furnishings admirably. Kitty was impressed. This room was more than adequate; indeed, she rather thought it quite as good as her own bedchamber at Longbourn — although obviously, not as fine as she expected to find at Pemberley.

Her only complaint was that the chamber was a trifle chilly, as the fire had not been burning long enough to make the room warm. However, the luxurious appointments just served to confirm her initial impressions. Mr King might be the vicar, but he was not reliant on his stipend, and must be independently wealthy.

She frowned. If this were the case, why would he have chosen to study divinity at university and become a man of God, when he could have remained a gentleman of means without the bothersome duties of a cleric? This was a conundrum she was determined to unravel. There was nothing she liked more than solving a puzzle. Indeed, her interest in officers and parties had dwindled since Lydia had run away to marry the objectionable Wickham.

Two chambermaids were waiting to attend to her needs, neither of them much older than herself. The slightly taller girl curtsied. 'Miss Bennet, there is hot water for your ablutions in the dressing room if you would care to follow me.'

★   ★   ★

Adam had no time for frivolous young ladies and was unimpressed by Miss Bennet's flirtatious manner, especially in the circumstances. He returned his full attention to the injured man within the carriage. 'Mrs Bingley, the trestle is arriving and it will be impossible to remove your husband whilst you remain within the vehicle. Please allow me to assist you to descend.' He didn't wait for her agreement but reached in and gripped her firmly about the waist and lifted her to the ground. 'Go inside, madam. There is little point in staying out here and becoming saturated.'

She shook her head. 'A little rain is of no concern to me, Mr King. I shall wait here until my husband is inside with me.'

He had instructed his head gardener to fetch a tarpaulin with which to cover the injured man so at least he would be dry, even if his wife was soaked. Both doors of the carriage were wide open in order to remove the patient. 'It will be easier to remove Mr Bingley head first. Take the trestle to the other side of the carriage, if you please.' He hurried to join his men in order to supervise the operation. 'I shall take his shoulders. Sam, Jethro, climb inside and lift his legs. Hold steady, men; I have no wish to make matters worse by dropping Mr Bingley on the gravel.'

Between them they were able to extricate the injured man without doing him further harm or causing the bandage to slip from his head wound. Adam was concerned that Mr Bingley was still comatose — in his experience the longer a person with a head wound remained unconscious the more dangerous the situation. With the tarpaulin held over the trestle protecting the man beneath, he directed his men up the steps and into the vestibule. 'Miller, have you prepared the apartment that old Mr King used in his dotage? We cannot take Mr Bingley up the stairs; he must remain on this floor.'

'I have, sir, and one message has gone to Pemberley as well as one to fetch Doctor Bevan.'

'Excellent. Send word to the kitchen to have refreshments ready for our visitors. Nothing elaborate — dinner must go by the board tonight. I believe soup and meat pasties would be ideal in the circumstances.'

Fires had been lit in all the rooms in the downstairs apartment and the bed was turned down and waiting. Mrs Bingley nodded to him. 'I thank you for your assistance, Mr King, but I can take care of my husband until the physician arrives.'

It was hardly his place to remind her that she was dripping upon the carpet and likely to catch a morbid sore throat if she remained in her saturated garments. Then common sense overrode his sense of propriety.

'Madam, I insist that you go upstairs and change into something dry. You will not be of any use to your husband if you contract a fever yourself.'

'Very well. I shall do as you suggest, but I shall come down again immediately.' She turned to the waiting footmen. 'Make sure you do not dislodge the bandage when you undress him. I shall be back directly.'

Adam stepped aside and nodded to his butler, Vernon, who was hovering outside. 'Have someone take Mrs Bingley to her apartment. Leave a footman outside the door to escort her back here when she is ready.'

As soon as she was gone he returned to the patient. He intended to supervise the removal of his clothes himself. Undressing Mr Bingley was more difficult than he'd anticipated, and removing his boots almost impossible. Eventually the patient was in a borrowed nightgown and snugly encased in blankets and red flannel. Warm bricks had been put on either side of him, and the fire stoked up with extra coals. They had just settled him when the physician was announced.

'I shall leave you to attend to Mr Bingley, sir,' said Adam. 'His wife will no doubt join you soon.' Satisfied he could do no more, he strode off to take care of himself. He was drenched through to his Undergarments, and he was as much in need of fresh clothes as Mrs Bingley. He met her hurrying down as he reached the upstairs landing. She was wearing a plain rust-coloured gown that had obviously been borrowed from the housekeeper.

'Madam, your husband is comfortable and the doctor is with him. Word was sent to Mrs Darcy, and I expect someone from Pemberley will arrive before long.'

'Thank you. I trust that our luggage will also be fetched here. We much appreciate your kindness in offering us accommodation.' With a small smile she continued her journey to be at the side of her injured husband.

Mrs Bingley was exactly the kind of wife he would like to find for himself; he had always had a preference for fair-haired young ladies. Not only was she beautiful, but also kind, intelligent and gently spoken. Even in a borrowed dress she looked every inch a lady. An image of her younger sister flicked into his mind. He frowned. Although attractive enough, with nut-brown hair and a trim figure, she lacked the refinement and elegance of Mrs Bingley.

His valet, Hobson, was waiting for him. 'I have put out fresh garments for you, sir, and there is hot water waiting.'

In less than a quarter of an hour he was freshly garbed and on his way downstairs. As he reached the landing that overlooked the entrance hall, the butler and two footmen were bowing in Mr and Mrs Darcy. He paused to examine his illustrious guests. He had yet to meet either of them, as they did not attend his church, having their own chapel and chaplain at Pemberley. Mrs Darcy was dark-haired like Miss Bennet, but there the resemblance ended. Mrs Darcy was taller and, even enveloped in a blue worsted travelling cloak, he could see she was the epitome of elegance and good breeding. Mr Darcy was as tall as he, and his shoulders as broad — but there the resemblance ended. Whereas his own hair was nut-brown, his visitor's was as dark as Lucifer.

He must not lurk like an urchin gawping at his betters, but go down and greet his guests.

2

Elizabeth Darcy looked around the spacious entrance hall with interest. Since she and Fitzwilliam had returned from their wedding trip last week there had been no time to gallivant about the countryside meeting her neighbours. Mr King had arrived less than a month ago to take up the position as rector to the parish of Bakewell. She was surprised that his home was so luxurious and elegant — hardly the establishment one would expect a man of God to reside in. The butler bowed deeply.

'Mr Darcy, madam, do you wish to speak to my master or shall I conduct you directly to Mr Bingley? The doctor is with him now.'

Mr Darcy answered for both of them. 'Take us to the sick room. I wish to ensure that everything is being done correctly for my friend.'

A slight sound above them made Lizzy look up. She saw a handsome brown-haired gentleman bounding down the stairs. This must be their missing host. Mr Collins, a distant relation who would inherit Long-bourn on her father's demise, was a cleric,

15

but he bore as much resemblance to this gentleman as chalk did to cheese.

'I apologise for not being here to greet you in person, Mr Darcy, Mrs Darcy. I was drenched and obliged to change my raiment.' His smile was charming and she warmed to him. 'I take it the rain has eased?'

'It has.' Her husband didn't offer his hand, but merely nodded. Dear Fitzwilliam still found meeting strangers an uncomfortable business, although he was slightly less taciturn than he was before they were wed. Mr King looked somewhat surprised at this omission, but not particularly put out.

'Come with me. I have had Bingley installed in the downstairs apartment. Mrs Bingley is with him now.'

'Thank you, sir,' said Lizzy. 'We much appreciate your kindness towards our family. Is my youngest sister with them or elsewhere?' She smiled, hoping her friendliness would compensate for the lack of it in her husband.

Mr King returned her smile in good measure but refrained from making a response. Instead he set off across the hall and led them down a wide passageway to a pair of double doors standing open at the far end. 'In here. I shall leave you now, but if you require anything further please don't hesitate to ask any member of my staff.' He nodded politely to her but ignored Fitzwilliam, and left.

Her husband half-smiled. 'I believe I shall like King. He will be an intelligent addition to our circle of acquaintances.'

The sitting room was well-appointed, although somewhat old-fashioned in appearance. Jane must have heard them enter as she burst from the bedchamber looking distinctly dishevelled, but smiling, which was a good sign. Lizzy ran across the chamber and they embraced fondly.

'Lizzy dearest, thank you so much for coming. Charles has just regained consciousness and the doctor is sanguine that he will make a full recovery. However, he must remain where he is for a few days as he lost a great deal of blood and is very weak.'

Her sister then turned, walked over to Fitzwilliam and curtsied. There was no need for this formality, but her husband was a formidable man and not relaxed in company. Lizzy hoped in time her dearest partner would become less stiff in his dealings with others. Indeed, already he smiled more readily and had even laughed out loud once or twice in company.

'Mr Darcy, you will be pleased to know that Charles is in no danger and Mr King is taking care of everything satisfactorily.' She wiped her eyes on her handkerchief before continuing. 'He has concussion, but it does not seem to be too severe.'

'Is he ready to receive a visitor? I should like to see him for myself, if you have no objection.'

A feeble voice called from the bedchamber. 'Come in, Darcy old fellow, and tell everyone to stop fussing as I am perfectly well apart from a few stitches in my head.'

Fitzwilliam smiled and stepped past Jane without allowing her to comment. He vanished and could be heard questioning the unfortunate physician in his usual forceful way.

'Jane, how did the accident occur?' Lizzy asked. 'Did the carriage overturn?' When she heard the story she shook her head in disbelief.

'To be so sorely injured by a brick — it hardly seems credible. However, Mr Bingley's in no danger and we can take Kitty back with us today. Georgiana is so eager to meet her that she will fall into a decline if we do not bring her.'

'I have asked for our luggage to be brought back here. I wasn't sure if you would quite like to have her foisted on you in this way. I can honestly say that she is greatly improved in temperament and has become a good friend to both Charles and me. However, she is still inclined to be flighty and might prove a bad influence on your sister-in-law.'

'Georgiana is a delightful young lady, as intelligent as her brother but not so dogmatic in her views. Unfortunately, she is too quiet. I'm sure they will bring out the best in each other. I'm hoping Kitty will, in fact, lead Georgiana into mischief — I don't believe she has ever misbehaved in her life.' She stopped as she recalled the unfortunate episode two years ago when Wickham had attempted to elope with Georgiana. By chance Fitzwilliam had been visiting Brighton and was able to prevent disaster. 'It was I who suggested to Fitzwilliam that Kitty make her home with us. He was reluctant at first, as he had not seen her in the best light — but there is a tender-hearted man hidden inside that brusque exterior, and he only wants the best for those he loves.'

Jane nodded. 'He apologised most handsomely for keeping Charles and me apart. Although we understood his motivation, I'm forced to admit that we disapproved of his actions. However, that is in the past and we are all good friends now.'

★　★　★

19

Kitty viewed the garment that was laid out for her with horror. There was no doubt in her mind that this gown had been intended for a servant. The material was rough cotton and of an unpleasant beige colour. However, it had never been worn, and she must be grateful to have something dry to put on in the circumstances. She schooled her features into what she hoped would pass for delight in the nasty garment. 'I should like my own clothes to be dried and pressed and returned to me as soon as possible,' she said.

One of the girls bobbed. 'It will be done at once, Miss Bennet. There's a grand fire in the laundry room and they will dry in no time.'

Fortunately her underpinnings were not so wet that they required replacing; and soon Kitty was dressed, if one could call it that, in the drab gown which made her look like a parlourmaid. Her hair had been rearranged and she was as ready as she would ever be to appear in her dreadful garments. She was tempted to remain hidden until her own clothes were ready, but she wished to know how Charles was doing and could not bear to wait another minute to find out.

The young footman gave her a cheeky grin and she was grateful he didn't sneer at her appalling ensemble. 'Follow me, miss. It's like the village fair down there, what with all the coming and going.'

One was not supposed to converse with a servant, but it would seem uncivil not to reply. 'I take it that Mr and Mrs Darcy have arrived. Is the doctor still with Mr Bingley, do you know?'

He scratched his head, knocking his half-wig askew. 'Not rightly sure, miss, but I don't reckon Mr and Mrs Darcy are aiming to stay long as they ain't had the carriage unharnessed.'

Kitty was enjoying the informality of the conversation and was about to reply when her companion changed his demeanour. She looked up to see Mr King frowning at her from the spacious landing. She sailed up to him as if she were an elegant young lady. 'Thank you so much for finding me this delightful gown, Mr King. Such a pretty colour, don't you think?' It was quite apparent from her tone that she thought nothing of the sort. 'I gather my sister and her husband have arrived from Pemberley.' Botheration! She had intended to ask how Mr Bingley was, but his supercilious stare had irritated her and pushed her into this silliness.

'Mr Bingley has recovered consciousness and is expected to make a full recovery, just in case you were concerned for his well-being. You, miss, are to return with Mrs Darcy to

Pemberley.' He viewed her with opprobrium. 'No doubt my housekeeper will find you a cloak of some sort to wear, as your own garments will not be dry in time.'

This was the outside of enough. Kitty barely restrained an impulse to stamp her foot. She looked at him disdainfully. 'I am delighted to hear you say so, sir, as I have no wish to remain here any longer than I have to.' She straightened her shoulders and marched past him as if he were invisible. The helpful footman had made himself scarce, and when she reached the vestibule she had no idea in which direction to go.

'Do not dither, Miss Bennet, or you might well be mistaken for a parlourmaid if you remain there much longer and be given instructions to make up the fire in the drawing room.'

Incensed, she spun, only to see Mr King laughing down at her. Reluctantly her mouth curved and her anger slipped away. 'You are outrageous, sir. I was doing my best to pretend I had on my finest gown and you have brought me sharply down to earth.' He held out his arm and she placed her hand on it. 'Is Mr Bingley really going to be well? Jane loves him so much. I do not know how she would manage if anything were to happen to him.'

'He is concussed and has lost a deal of blood, but nothing life-threatening, Miss Bennet, I do assure you.'

Something prompted her to ask the question that had been bothering her. 'Forgive me if I am being impertinent, but you do not look like a reverend gentleman; and this establishment, I do declare, is far grander than Longbourn.' No sooner were the words spoken than she regretted them. She expected to receive a sharp set-down, but to her astonishment he chuckled.

'You are being impertinent, my dear, and I do forgive you.'

She waited for him to answer her questions, but instead he patted her hand and, still chuckling, guided her to the rear of the building, leaving her to be greeted with enthusiasm by her older sisters.

'Kitty, my love, welcome to Derbyshire,' Lizzy exclaimed as she embraced her fondly. 'I'm hoping I can persuade you to come back with us tonight, as I don't think Georgiana will survive another night without meeting you.'

'Jane, how is Mr Bingley? I shall not go if you would like me to stay and help you nurse him.'

'Dear Charles will not be able to leave his bed for a week at least, but he is in no danger and requires no more than myself to take care of him. You must go to Pemberley, and we shall join you as soon as he is well enough to travel.'

'In which case, Lizzy, if you are quite sure you wish to have me come tonight then I shall be delighted to accompany you,' said Kitty. 'I am as eager to meet your new sister as she is to meet me. We are the exact same age and I am certain we will become bosom bows in no time.'

She glanced around and saw that Mr King had abandoned them. She had not quite made up her mind about this gentleman. He was prodigiously handsome, but a trifle disagreeable, and reminded her strongly of Mr Darcy. The first thing she would do on her arrival at her new home would be to discover more about the rector, as she could not fathom how he came to be a gentleman of God. From their brief acquaintance she would have thought him more suited to the army than the saving of souls.

'I believe that Mr King has gone in search of a suitable cloak for me. No doubt it will be something else from the servants' hall.' She held out the skirt of her drab gown and giggled.

'We are similarly garbed, dearest Kitty, but

I believe my gown to have come from the housekeeper's wardrobe.'

The bedchamber door opened and Mr Darcy emerged. Kitty thought at first that he was nonplussed by their appearance, and then she realised he was struggling to hide his amusement. Impulsively she turned and curtsied to him. 'I bid you good afternoon, sir. Is there something I can fetch you from the kitchen?'

His shout of laughter filled the room. She believed this was the very first time she had ever heard him laugh. He smiled at Lizzy all the time, and was obviously devoted to her; but he was not given, as far as she was aware, to such outbursts of merriment.

'Miss Bennet, my sister is going to enjoy your company, as will Lizzy and I. Do you have a cloak? Although the journey to Pemberley is no more than two miles, in this weather the journey can be tediously long.'

'After travelling from Longbourn, Mr Darcy, I shall never consider anything else of any moment. Unfortunately I do not have a cloak of my own . . . '

Mr King spoke from behind her. 'Indeed you do, Miss Bennet. I have found you something. Hardly elegant, but I do assure you it will complement your gown perfectly.' He was smiling and his eyes, a deep cerulean blue, twinkled down at her. She could not help responding and returned his smile.

He held out a spotlessly clean but well-worn cloak of an indeterminate colour that could once have been green. Instead of putting it in her hand he swirled it open and placed it around her shoulders. Although he was careful not to brush her skin with his fingers as he did so, she could not help but notice the quizzical look Mr Darcy directed to Lizzy.

With glowing cheeks she hurriedly stepped away from Mr King and rushed across the room to embrace Jane. 'I am so glad that Mr Bingley is not seriously injured. I blame myself for not removing the brick when I fell upon it earlier.'

'Nonsense, Kitty. As I told you before, accidents are just that. Whatever happens, I promise that we will be with you in time for the Christmas festivities.'

'Good God, I should hope so, for they are yet three weeks away,' said Mr Darcy. 'If you and Bingley are not at Pemberley within a sennight I shall come and fetch you myself.' He was not impressed.

Kitty flinched but neither of her sisters reacted. Indeed, Lizzy smiled at him. 'Being cross, my love, will not make Mr Bingley recover any more quickly. He is in the best of hands here, and you must contain your impatience for a while longer.'

Immediately his expression changed. He was as variable as a weathercock, and Kitty understood that she would have to tread warily if she was not to be in constant dread of a bear-garden jaw.

A footman approached Mr King and spoke quietly to him. 'Ladies and gentleman, your carriage awaits. The wind has abated and the rain has ceased, but I fear we are in for some snow tonight.'

In a flurry of farewells they departed, and Kitty had no time to speak to her host again before being handed into the carriage by Mr Darcy. The interior was cold; but in her thick, serviceable cloak she was warm enough. The vehicle rocked alarmingly, and then the door was slammed and the horses given the office to move.

She found being closeted with such a formidable gentleman unnerving, and had no wish to be involved in any conversation, even with her dearest sister there to protect her from a stinging rebuke. She settled into the far corner, pulling the rug and her cloak around her face so they would imagine she was sleeping.

In fact the bumping and jolting made it impossible to relax, but then the road unexpectedly improved and the journey became more comfortable. Forgetting her nervousness, Kitty sat up. 'Thank goodness. I was feeling decidedly unwell with all that jouncing and bouncing.'

Lizzy answered from the darkness, 'All the lanes around Pemberley are in good repair, my love, as it is the responsibility of the local parish to keep them in good order. We will make better time now, and shall be turning into the drive shortly.'

'Is not Mr King's parish part of Lambton or Kympton?'

Mr Darcy answered Kitty's question. 'No, he comes within the parish of Bakewell, and they do not appear to have funds to keep the lanes as they should be.'

Emboldened by his friendly tone, she decided to risk asking him a further question. 'The rectory is a grand house; one would have thought Mr King might repair the roads himself. He is obviously a gentleman of private means.'

There was an uncomfortable silence for a few seconds, and then Mr Darcy answered. 'Is he indeed? How observant of you, my dear, to have come to that conclusion on so short an acquaintance.'

He had neither confirmed nor denied her statement and left her squirming with embarrassment, grateful he could not see her scarlet cheeks. She did not dare to venture any further remarks and wished she could disappear entirely.

3

After a remarkably brief time, the carriage rocked gently to a halt and Kitty removed the rug from her face. She was astonished to find the interior of the vehicle brightly lit from flambeaux being held by too many footmen to number. The flames were flickering wildly but still illuminated the magnificent building she could see through the window.

She forgot her embarrassment and leaned forward eagerly to stare at the hundreds of twinkling windows that appeared to stretch for miles in both directions. 'Pemberley is even more beautiful than I expected. I fear I shall be sadly out of place here. I'm not used to living in a palace.'

'Kitty, we do not use the whole of it. Indeed, the east wing is old-fashioned, unsafe, and under holland covers. The staff are accommodating, and you will have Georgiana as your guide. We have put you in an apartment next to hers, although if you prefer, you could share.'

There was no time to answer, as the carriage door was opened and the steps let down. Instead of allowing the ladies to descend first, Mr Darcy stepped out and then reached in and swung Lizzy to the ground. Kitty shrank back, terrified he would attempt to do the same to her. He glanced in and grinned at her, an expression that sat strangely on his aristocratic features. 'My sister is already on her way to greet you, Miss Kitty. Do you intend to remain hiding in here indefinitely?'

'I beg your pardon, sir. I am coming directly.' She scrambled across the squabs and almost fell from the door, but his strong hand steadied her.

'You must not be afraid of me, my dear. I am not as curmudgeonly as you might think. My darling Lizzy is slowly changing me from a proud and disdainful gentleman into a more approachable fellow.'

This speech was as astonishing as his home. She found herself returning his grin and for the first time in their acquaintance saw him as a gentleman she could like very well indeed. 'I should love to share an apartment with your sister, but I think it would be best if we got to know each other first. Thank you so much for inviting me to make my home with you. I give you my word that I will . . . '

He chuckled and raised his hand. 'No, do not promise me anything. I want you to become a sister to Georgiana, who has spent far too much time without the companionship of young ladies her own age. You have my consent to do as you wish, as long as you remain within the grounds of Pemberley.'

Before Kitty had thought up a suitable response a beautiful young lady, tall and slender and the image of her brother, threw herself into her arms. 'Welcome! I cannot tell you how delighted I am to have you come to live with us — ' Georgiana stepped back and her mouth dropped open. 'My stars! That is certainly an unusual ensemble. I sincerely hope you have something more colourful in your wardrobe.'

'I was drenched to the skin and this was all Mr King's housekeeper could muster. My own garments should have arrived in my absence. If you would care to take me to my room, I shall change into something more acceptable.'

Her new friend giggled and grabbed Kitty's arm. 'I was funning. I guessed immediately what had happened. Lizzy has found you an excellent dresser; her name is Annie. She has been with us this age and has been well-trained in all the duties necessary to keep you looking your best.'

'I am to have my own abigail? I shall scarcely know myself, and before long will think that I am truly a lady of means and not a poor relation.' This statement was not intended to be taken seriously but Georgiana immediately looked concerned.

'You must never call yourself that. You are my sister and part of my family.' She looked around to make sure Mr Darcy and Lizzy were not close enough to overhear her next remark. 'I heard my brother tell your sister that he intends to settle a substantial dowry on both you and your sister Mary. I should not be telling you this, but it means that you are no longer a *poor* anything. You are an eligible heiress, and we shall be presented at court together next year.'

This was indeed news to Kitty. Six months ago she would have been cock-a-hoop and wish to immediately write to her younger sister, now Lydia Wickham, and boast of her good fortune. However, she hoped she was as changed as Mr Darcy. She no longer spent her days reading such romantic novels as *The Romance of the Forest, The Mysteries of Udolpho* or *The Midnight Bell* and dreaming of the day when she would meet a handsome red-coated officer. In future she intended to spend her time improving her playing of the pianoforte (Lizzy had told her Georgiana was a virtuoso on this instrument), painting watercolours, and learning from Lizzy how to run a large household. She had no intention of rushing into matrimony as Lydia had, only to regret her choice within a week or two of the wedding.

Papa had married impulsively, blinded by the beautiful young lady who her mama had once been, and had discovered to his detriment that they had little in common. Kitty smiled as she recalled her father telling her he intended to escape to Derbyshire in the New Year and make a prolonged visit to Pemberley. Mama refused to travel in the winter; even the thought of visiting such a prestigious place would not prise her from Longbourn until the weather was more clement and the roads less hazardous.

Fortunately Georgiana did not appear to need a reply to her standing statement, as she bustled Kitty into the huge black-and-white chequered entrance hall. 'There is a central passageway that leads from one end of the house to the other, so really it will be impossible for you to get lost. Do not you admire the great staircase? When we are away from here folk come from all over the country to be shown about this house, and the staircase is particularly well spoken of.'

The staircase was indeed very handsome, being made of polished white marble and wide enough to drive a carriage up, if one should have wished to do so. 'The carving on the outside is beautiful,' Kitty replied. 'I'm not surprised visitors are impressed.' She stopped to stare in awe at the ceiling, upon which were carved garlands of fruit, flowers and palm branches.

They ran up the stairs arm in arm and Kitty was all but dragged down a wide passageway, noticing as she passed that the walls were covered with boring brown portraits of long-gone ancestors. Kitty did not care much for these. They dashed across the vast gallery and along a wide corridor that was illuminated by a row of tall windows at the far end.

'We have adjoining apartments, Kitty, but I am hoping once we are better acquainted you will wish to share with me. I shall show you your rooms first — you have a pretty sitting room, a bedchamber and a dressing room. There is also a small side room for sewing and suchlike.' She clapped her hand to her mouth. 'The room is not for you, of course; it is for your maidservants to work in.'

'I am quite content to sew, but I cannot abide embroidery. Making a garment that someone will eventually wear seems a sensible use of my time, but not embroidering flowers and animals on a cushion cover.'

Everything about the Darcys was confusing. Lizzy had been at great pains to explain to her that Georgiana was a quiet, shy young lady who rarely spoke, and Kitty knew from her own experience that Mr Darcy himself was taciturn and not renowned for his good humour. Now everything was topsy-turvy, and she was so excited she believed she might burst.

Despite the plethora of footmen downstairs, on the first floor there were none. Her companion threw open the door and stepped aside to allow Kitty to walk in. 'Do you like it? I chose the hangings myself. I think that yellow is such a happy colour, and far better than burgundy and green.'

'It is everything I could have dreamt of, Georgiana. I love the peacocks strutting across the curtains and on the cushion covers.' She ran from one item of furniture to another, exclaiming in delight. 'I have an escritoire and it is fully stocked with pens, paper and ink. I do believe I see an easel in the corner, and a box of paints and brushes to go with it.' She turned and embraced her new sister. 'As soon as I am changed I shall go downstairs and thank Lizzy and Mr Darcy. I am going to love it here! We are going to have such fun together.'

'Do you ride?'

Kitty shook her head. 'No, I had no opportunity to learn; my sister Jane is the only horsewoman in our family. However, I should dearly love to start, if that is possible.'

'Our head groom, Sam Roberts, taught me and he shall do the same for you. We cannot explore all the park on foot; there are hundreds of acres surrounding the house. However, that is a pastime for the better weather. Until then we have the whole of Pemberley to enjoy.'

The bedchamber was as delightful as the sitting room with a large tester bed, a chaise longue, and all the necessary drawers and cabinets. A diminutive girl dressed in a smart grey cotton gown and pristine white cap and apron curtsied politely. Hovering behind her was a taller, plumper girl dressed identically. 'I am Annie, Miss Bennet. I am your dresser and Jenny is your chambermaid. I have unpacked and pressed your clothes. Would you like me to select something for you?'

Kitty turned to her companion. 'At what time do you dine? I have no wish to change more often than I need to.'

'Fitzwilliam prefers to keep town hours. We eat at seven o'clock, so you have no need to put on your evening gown at the moment. Have you something similar to mine you can wear?' Georgiana's simple gown was in heavy damask-rose cotton with a pretty spencer in a darker shade.

'Annie, would you find me something?' Kitty asked. 'I also require a fresh chemise and petticoats.'

'I shall accompany you, Kitty, and help you choose,' Georgiana offered.

In a remarkably short space of time, Kitty was freshly gowned in a jonquil cambric with a gold sash tied under the bosom. As this gown had long sleeves there was no need to add a spencer. Her boots had been removed and she was now wearing matching indoor slippers.

She was desperate to ask Georgiana what she knew about Mr King but could not do so until they were alone. It did not do to gossip in front of the servants. The housekeeper she had discovered was called Reynolds, the butler was named Peterson, and Mr Darcy's steward was a Mr Ingram.

'What exactly does Mr Ingram do?' Kitty asked. 'My papa has no need of one.'

'He takes care of the finances of the house and then reports to Fitzwilliam. There is an estate manager as well, but I misremember his name. I have no wish to discuss such tedious things; I have something far more exciting to impart.'

They were now curled up on a comfortable

sofa in front of a roaring fire in Kitty's sitting room. The bedchamber door was firmly closed and both maids busy somewhere behind it. 'Before you embark on your news, I wish to have all the information you know about Mr King. How is it a rector lives in such lavish circumstances? Also, why does he look more like a soldier than a man of the cloth?'

'I can tell you what I know, but it is not much as the gentleman in question only moved into the vicinity at the beginning of the month. The previous incumbent was his uncle, and a man of means. I believe he was highly thought of in the area.' She frowned and closed her eyes for a moment. 'His grandfather was a nabob, and made a massive fortune with the East India Company. Therefore, even though Mr King is the youngest son, he is a wealthy man and has no need to work for a living.'

Having her speculations confirmed in this way gave Kitty pause for thought. 'You must think me a flighty miss to be taking such an interest in a single gentleman so soon after my arrival in Derbyshire.'

Georgiana shook her head and her dark ringlets bounced on either side of her face. 'Indeed I do not, Kitty dearest. Although I have not yet seen him myself, I understand him to be a prodigiously handsome gentleman. And you were not far wrong in your assessment; he was indeed a soldier with Wellesley in India. He attended Oxford University and obtained his degree in divinity, but originally he chose to serve his country in a different way.'

Kitty was agog. She leant forward, eager to hear what had changed Mr King's mind.

'I believe he was sickened by the violence and loss of life and, when his uncle passed away, he resigned his commission and took holy orders.' For someone who had professed to know very little about her handsome neighbour, Georgiana was remarkably well-informed.

'I did not like him very much,' Kitty said. 'He reminded me of Mr Darcy . . . ' She stopped, horrified, and her hands flew to her mouth as if intending to push the words back in.

Instead of being offended by her rudeness, Georgiana giggled. 'I know exactly what you mean. Although I love my brother dearly, he can be rather arrogant and proud. Are you telling me that Mr King is of a similar character?'

'He is a formidable gentleman, not at all what one would expect in a pulpit. At least, being a wealthy man, he will be able to alleviate the suffering of his parishioners in a way that is not normally available to a vicar. I believe a rector has access to a small estate as well as the church tithes, so one would expect Mr King to donate this money to the parish poor.' How pompous and silly she sounded — more like her older sister Mary than herself.

Georgiana jumped to her feet and grabbed Kitty's hand. 'Now it is my turn to tell you something. Pemberley is vast and we do not use the whole of it, even when we have house guests. However, the east wing is abandoned and nobody ever goes there.' Her eyes were sparkling with excitement. 'In all my life I have never ventured in; just accepted the chambers were derelict and unsafe.' She paused for dramatic effect. 'However, four weeks ago I came across a journal written more than one hundred years ago by an ancestor of mine. This girl talks of the east wing and says her grandfather had decided to abandon it because of the ghosts.'

'Ghosts? Do you mean Pemberley is haunted? How wonderful! Shall we be intrepid ghost hunters and uncover the truth in this story?' Kitty was beside herself. Never in all her days had she expected to share a house with spectres. They would be like the

41

heroines in a Gothic novel. Not that she truly believed in such nonsense. Papa had told her that those who thought they saw them owned an overactive imagination and that there was always a logical explanation for any so-called supernatural event.

'We must not divulge our intentions to your sister or my brother, or they will put a stop to it,' Kitty said.

'Actually, Mr Darcy gave me permission to go anywhere and do anything that I wished to, so long as we are together and remain within the grounds. So we will not be breaking any rules by exploring there.'

'There is no time today, but I am going to take you on a tour of the house and we will pass by the entrance. Although the doors to this wing are kept locked, the keys are left in full view in Fitzwilliam's study. If we borrow them to unlock the communicating door on the nursery floor and then return them immediately, nobody will be any the wiser.'

Together they wandered through the upstairs portion of the house, with Georgiana pointing out the salient features: which doors led to the linen cupboard and which to bedchambers and sitting rooms, and so on. The family occupied the central portion of the house; and the guests, when there were any, resided in the west wing. After an hour

Georgiana led Kitty up a flight of stairs to the nursery floor.

'Good heavens!' exclaimed the former. 'I have not been up here for years and remembered it quite differently.' She ran forward and opened a door which led into the schoolroom. 'I thought this room far bigger, but had forgotten how small the windows are and that they have bars across them.'

To Kitty the room seemed as extravagant as all the others she'd been shown. 'If you were taught on your own it must indeed have seemed enormous. Our schoolroom was half the size and had to accommodate twice as many noisy girls.'

'I should have much preferred to have been with siblings. For me, being sent away to school when I was older should have been a pleasure rather than a penance, as it was the first time I had the opportunity to make friends.' She sniffed and rubbed her eyes on her sleeve. 'However, Mama had just passed away and I was distraught. Arriving so miserable and withdrawn meant that I was always considered an outsider and never became friends with my peers.'

Impulsively Kitty threw her arms around her friend. 'I am sorry for your loss and your sadness, Georgiana, but things are different now. You are a woman grown and now have a plethora of sisters to be your friends.'

'I wish that my brother considered me an adult too. Both he and Lizzy tend to treat me as a schoolroom miss with no opinions or wishes of my own. I love them both dearly, but having a sister of my own age is so much better.' She had recovered her good humour. 'I expect that Lizzy told you how eagerly I had been anticipating your arrival.'

'She did mention it in passing. Ever since the invitation arrived I have been in high spirits; my father, for the first time that I can recall, gave me his approval. Lizzy has always been his favourite, you know, then Jane, but he has little time for the rest of us. I expect you know that my youngest sister, Lydia, ran away with Wickham. I believe she is already regretting her decision.'

For some reason her companion became subdued when she mentioned this disgraceful episode. Kitty hoped Georgiana was not shocked to find herself related, even remotely, to someone who had behaved so badly.

'There is just time enough for me to show you the door through which we will enter the east wing. It is at the far end of the passageway, and I believe it must have been used by the nursery maids once upon a time.'

'How old is that part of Pemberley? The front of the building is obviously of recent construction. You told me that the central passageway was put down in 1610, so that must make the east wing even older.' Kitty could hardly credit she was walking about in a building that had been constructed many hundreds of years ago. Longbourn was not nearly as venerable, although she believed it to have been built a hundred years ago.

Upon the subject of her ancestral home Georgiana was both knowledgeable and enthusiastic, and regaled Kitty with facts and figures all the way back to their chambers. 'I shall be wearing a white evening gown; unfortunately none of my evening gowns are coloured,' Kitty said. 'However, they have embroidery, lace, beads and suchlike as well as pretty sashes of bright colours, so I cannot complain.'

'Mama allowed me to select pastel shades. I would much prefer a vibrant green or red, but those must be left to married ladies and the demi-monde.' Kitty had little notion who *these* ladies were, but was fairly sure they were not respectable. 'I have a delightful gown in the palest yellow, with a golden sash and matching slippers. Shall I wear that, as it's the closest thing I have to white?'

The matter of their ensembles having been settled to their satisfaction, Georgiana all but skipped into her own apartment and Kitty into hers. She could scarcely credit that she had only been in Derbyshire for a few hours and already had embarked upon an adventure.

4

Mr King was unsurprised to be obliged to dine alone as usual. Mrs Bingley, although she now had her own garments, had politely declined his invitation, saying she would have a tray with Mr Bingley until he was well enough to join them.

Was it the hand of God that had caused the accident and introduced the Darcys and Bingleys to him? Although he did not regret his decision to sell his commission and take over the stipend vacated by the death of his uncle, he had been finding life in this quiet backwater of Derbyshire rather lacking in excitement. He had expected to be able to use his considerable wealth to alleviate the sufferings of the poor, but as far as he could see there were no such beings in his parish and he would have to go further afield to spread his largesse. Uncle Benjamin had had the same idea and his flock was well taken care of.

Then his lips curved as a possible project occurred to him that would benefit everyone in the neighbourhood. There would have been no accident this afternoon if the road

47

had been properly repaired. He would ride to Pemberley tomorrow with news of the patient's progress and discuss the matter with Mr Darcy. This was a courtesy only; he had no need to ask for permission from anyone to do his duty.

Before he retired he made his way to the rear of the house and knocked on the door of the apartment in which Mr Bingley was recovering. An unfamiliar maid answered his summons and bobbed.

'I beg your pardon, Mr King, but Mr and Mrs Bingley have retired for the night.'

'I have no wish to intrude. I am just here to enquire how the patient is doing.'

'The master is sleeping and the sickness is abating.'

He strolled back to the drawing room but had no interest in reading the *Times*. He wandered restlessly around the room, disliking the emptiness and the way his footsteps echoed everywhere he went in this huge house. He had spent most of his life with others — first at boarding school, then at Oxford University, and for the past five years as an officer fighting shoulder to shoulder with his comrades. To his chagrin, he was discovering he did not enjoy his own company. He missed the camaraderie of the mess and the constant bustle of army life.

When tending to a mortally wounded friend there had been an epiphany, and in that instant he had known he must dedicate his life to the service of God and not to killing.

So here he was, an ordained minister of the church full of good intentions and eager to minister to his flock; but there was little to do apart from writing his sermons and taking two services on Sunday. There would, of course, be baptisms, burials and marriages to perform, but so far no one in his parish had required any of these offices. He scowled into the fire, wishing there were some way to alleviate his loneliness and give him back his vocation.

It wasn't the prerequisite of a priest to be a devout Christian. Many of the young men he had studied with were only interested in living the lifestyle of a gentleman, and viewed the trappings of the church as a necessary evil. Indeed, only today he had seen an advertisement in the newspaper announcing there was to be an auction, by Hoggart & Phillips of Old Broad Street in London, for what they called 'the most valuable living in one of the finest sporting counties'. No doubt this living would fetch a pretty price if it were put on the open market. Uncle Benjamin had rebuilt the rectory using his own funds, and it was as grand as any manor house in the

49

district — apart from Pemberley, of course.

Repairing the lanes in the parish was a worthy cause, but it did not fill him with excitement. When his uncle had heard his nephew was taking holy orders, he had immediately written to ask him to take over the parish when he died. Adam had not hesitated to accept this generous offer, but with hindsight he realised he would have been better to go into an urban parish where his ministry could have made a difference.

He retired to his bedchamber in a black mood. As he said his nightly prayers, he asked for the Almighty to guide him and give him the strength of character to undertake whatever task he was given with humility and good grace.

★　★　★

Georgiana stood back to admire Kitty's ensemble. 'You look delightful, dearest. Although we are not related by blood, I do believe we could be taken for siblings.' She moved to stand beside her and Kitty was obliged to agree.

'You are half a head taller than me and slightly more slender, but we both have dark hair and ringlets and large brown eyes.' Kitty giggled and curtsied to her image. 'La, Miss

Darcy, I do declare we shall be the belles of the ball tonight.'

Arm in arm, they strolled from her sitting room and began to make the long journey along the corridors until they eventually reached the great staircase. Kitty felt like a princess gliding down to dine in such a splendid house. Halfway she stumbled, almost sending both of them head first.

'Botheration! I must learn to master the demi-train and hold up my skirt at the front if I'm not to break my neck. Falling down marble stairs would no doubt prove fatal.'

'You will soon become accustomed to them; I think nothing of it now.' Georgiana ran her hand across the smooth banister. 'I have never dared to slide down this, but maybe if Fitzwilliam and Lizzy go out one day, we should both do so.'

Kitty was astonished and excited by the suggestion. The more she got to know her friend, the more confused she became. Georgiana was proving to be not a shy, well-behaved young lady but someone as lively as herself. 'I should love to slide down the banisters, but I think it best if I don't attempt it until I am more settled here. If I should be caught I am certain that Mr Darcy would send me packing, and I do so want to stay here with you.'

'I promise you, Kitty, my brother shall not send you away whatever mischief we get up to. Now, we must traverse this chamber and go into the great hall, for we always meet there before dinner.'

The closer they got to joining her sister and her terrifying husband, the more nervous Kitty became. Whatever Georgiana might say to the contrary, she was convinced that Mr Darcy would not tolerate any wild behaviour on her part. It might be best if she remained silent during dinner; that way she would not give him a disgust of her. She had often seen her father's dismay when she had rattled off ill-thought-out comments at the table.

They crossed the acres of highly polished floor, then went through the double doors at end of the room on the left into the great hall. Kitty gazed around in wonderment at this magnificent chamber; she believed that it must be fully sixty feet in breadth and half as much again in length. The plasterwork on the ceiling had been done by a master craftsman, and the crystal chandeliers were breathtaking. The hundreds of candles made the glass sparkle and added to the splendour.

Mr Darcy and Kitty's sister were standing in front of the fire and turned to greet them. 'You both look enchanting,' said the former. 'Far too splendid for an informal meal.' He turned to Lizzy with a smile. 'As soon as Jane and Bingley are with us, you must organise a party to welcome our visitors and introduce you to my neighbours. We have not had an event of this sort since we returned last month from our wedding trip, and it is long overdue.'

Kitty curtsied politely but he shook his head. 'No, Kitty my dear, you are one of the family and I do not expect you to behave like a guest. Can I get you a glass of champagne, or would you prefer orgeat?'

Kitty's heart settled into a more acceptable rhythm and she was able to answer his question without stammering. 'I am afraid that I am not partial to either of those, sir. Perhaps I could have lemonade, if that is not too much trouble?'

He snapped his fingers, and a footman who had been standing like a statue against the wall jumped to attention and hurried off. Only then was she aware there were four other servants placed about the vast room just in case the master or mistress required something.

'I hear that you have been taken on a tour of the upper floors, Kitty,' Lizzy said with a smile. 'What did you think?'

'If I do not become lost and starve to death it will be a miracle.'

Georgiana squeezed her hand affectionately. 'I give you my solemn vow that I will not let you meet a grisly end in Pemberley. I shall give you a large ball of wool that you can unwind in your perambulations, like the hero in the Minotaur story, and thus return safely to the bosom of your family.'

Everybody laughed at this riposte. Kitty saw Mr Darcy's eyebrow rise, and his beloved Lizzy nodded. The butler arrived to announce that dinner was served and the four of them strolled down the hall, across the central flagstone passageway, and into the small dining room.

For a small dining room it was prodigiously large, and Georgiana whispered to Kitty that in fact it was the only dining room and could seat fully fifty people around the massive central table. Fortunately they were seated at one end and not obliged to yell at each other down the expanse of mahogany.

The meal was served à *la française*, with all the dishes being placed attractively in the centre of the table. Kitty was scarcely aware of what she ate, but she knew it was all delicious and perfectly prepared. Conversation was light-hearted, and on a few occasions either Darcy or Lizzy actually addressed her directly.

When the final cover was removed, Kitty

expected her sister to stand and lead Georgiana and herself into the drawing room whilst Mr Darcy remained with his port. However, they stood up together and arm in arm strolled back through the great hall out into the cavernous vestibule which contained the staircase, and into the chamber they referred to as the saloon or music room. It had taken fully five minutes to reach this room, and Kitty was glad she had a warm shawl to cover her bare shoulders. At the far end of the room was an enormous pianoforte, a large golden harp, and various music stands. There was also a collection of spindly gilt chairs upon which anyone wishing to listen to the music could seat themselves. There were two fireplaces halfway down, one on each side of the room. The chandeliers and fires made the space delightfully warm. Mr Darcy suggested Georgiana play to them, and then wandered up to stand beside her and turn the music sheet.

This gave Kitty and an ideal opportunity to talk to Lizzy without being overheard. The room was so vast that people conversing by the fire could not possibly interfere with the musicians at the far end. 'Lizzy, I cannot tell you how much I love Georgiana but how surprised I am to find her so lively and full of fun. From your correspondence I understood that she was a quiet girl, more like Mary than myself.'

'Fitzwilliam and I are equally surprised at the change in her. We hoped that your arrival would help her to come out of herself in time, but within a few hours of your companionship she is so much more animated. And, my love, from what Jane has told me, you too have changed in the past few months. I declare that you and Georgiana are now the perfect match for each other.'

Kitty was unused to receiving praise from any of her family and her heart swelled with pride. In the past she had been a follower of her younger sister, Lydia, heedless and giddy, and thinking only of officers and new gowns. Since Lydia had been marooned somewhere in Northumbria with the militia, she knew herself to be a changed person. Spending so much time with her older sister, Jane, at Netherfield had taught her good manners and given her a respect for other people's opinions. However, she rather feared that her former wildness was likely to influence Georgiana in a detrimental way. For the first time in her life she wished to be approved of, and was determined to behave with propriety and not do anything outrageous.

'Thank you for your kind words, sister. I

shall endeavour to live up to your expectations. When the weather is clement I intend to learn to ride so Georgiana and I can explore the park together. Until then there is this enormous house to explore. Would you have any objection if we poked about in the attics?'

'The attics? Good heavens, I have not been anywhere near them myself and have no intention of doing so.' She beckoned to Mr Darcy, who abandoned his position by the pianoforte and strolled towards her.

'Yes, my love? How can I be of assistance?' His smile was tender and made him look years younger.

'It would appear Kitty and Georgiana intend to occupy their time scrambling about in the attics. Is there any reason why they should not do so?'

He seemed somewhat surprised by this remark. 'I can think of more productive ways for you girls to spend your time, but as I already gave you my permission to roam about the house at will I suppose the attics are included in that consent.' He smiled warmly at her and Kitty basked in his approval.

'I suggest that you wear your oldest clothes, my dear, and take oil lamps, not candles, as they will be safer. If you find anything interesting you must let us know. I don't believe I have ventured as far as the nursery floor in years, let alone the attics.'

'I thank you, sir,' said Kitty, 'and I promise we will not spend all our time poking around in the dust. I'm hoping to improve my skills on the pianoforte and paint some watercolours of the grounds. I believe there is an impressive library which I have yet to visit.'

Lizzy laughed. 'I should do your exploring before Jane and Mr Bingley arrive, as when they do we shall start entertaining and preparing for the Christmas festivities, and I shall require you and Georgiana to help.'

'There is nothing I enjoy more than making Christmas garlands.' Kitty turned eagerly to Mr Darcy. 'Do you have a ball at Pemberley to celebrate the New Year?' No sooner had she spoken the words than she regretted her impulsive question. 'Although as Lizzy knows, I do love to dance, my enquiry was for another reason. I would like to be involved with the preparations — writing invitations, decorating the great hall, or anything else that might be of assistance.'

'We do intend to hold a ball, Kitty, as it will be an excellent opportunity to introduce my wife and her family to my neighbours,' said Mr Darcy. 'I am sure that Lizzy will be delighted to have you and Georgiana assist her.'

The lovely piano music that had been filling the room came to an end and Georgiana beckoned her over. 'Pray excuse me; I am going to speak to your sister.' She all but ran to join her friend, eager to impart the interesting information she had gleaned from Lizzy and her husband. 'You play so beautifully, Georgiana. I wish I was half as proficient as you. Will you teach me to play like that?'

'I can try, but virtuosity is a God-given talent. If you do not have it you will never be any more than proficient. Come, play something for me and I will tell you if I can help you to improve.'

Kitty looked nervously at the couple who were seated together and conversing head to head. She would hate to have Mr Darcy find her wanting in her musical skills. 'I do not require any music. I can play you a sonata from memory by Pleyel.'

She slid onto the piano stool beside her new friend and ran her fingers across the keys before settling herself to play this delightful piece. Although not as technically accomplished as Mary, or with the verve and liveliness of Lizzy, she believed she had some talent. Hours of practice on the expensive instrument at Netherfield had, she hoped, made her better.

When the final note died away she sat for a moment with her head bowed, still lost in the music. The sound of someone running across the boards jerked her from her reverie. She opened her eyes and looked round to see Lizzy, her skirts gathered in one hand, arriving with more speed than decorum. Kitty scrambled from the seat to meet her.

'Kitty dearest, when did you learn to perform so well? I have never heard that piece before. You played it superbly.' Lizzy opened her arms and Kitty moved forward to be embraced.

'I am so glad you liked it. I have been working hard on my music these past weeks.' She smiled at her friend, who positively bounced with excitement next to her.

'I can certainly teach you some new pieces, Kitty,' said Georgiana. 'I do believe that in time you will play as well as I do.'

'If I can be half as good as you, I shall be more than satisfied. Perhaps we could work on some suitable songs to play together at Christmastime?'

From the far end of the chamber a deep baritone voice boomed. 'When you three butterflies have finished fluttering around the piano, would you consider returning and playing a hand or two of cards?'

'Kindly refrain from shouting, Fitzwilliam,'

said Lizzy. 'Poor Kitty almost fainted from the shock.' She turned her back on her husband. 'We prefer to play whist, Kitty. Do you know the rules?'

'I do. Mr Bingley taught me and I have been playing frequently with him. I shall partner Georgiana. I am certain that we will be trounced, but the experience will be salutary, no doubt.'

5

Kitty had never spent a night in such luxury. The sheets on her bed were of the finest cotton, and the comforter satin-covered and as pretty as any she had ever seen. Despite the comfort she awoke early, far too excited to remain in bed when there was so much to look forward to.

She had always been considered the sickly sister, succumbing to winter colds and coughs, but since Lydia had left her health had improved as had her character. Jane had insisted this was because Kitty no longer spent her days dashing about the country in a flimsy muslin dress hoping to flirt with officers from the militia. Whatever the reason, in the past few months she had been in the best of health, and every morning she got up eager to fill her day with interesting pastimes. She scrambled out of bed and, by the embers in the fireplace, was able to make her way across and light a candle. The mantel clock told her the time was a little after five, far too early to ring for assistance.

The dressing room was unpleasantly chilly, but she quickly discovered the necessary undergarments and her plainest and warmest gown. This was a morning dress, loose-fitting, with long sleeves and a high neck, and would be ideal for scrambling about in the attics or wherever they actually went. It took her far longer than she'd anticipated to tie the various tapes and make herself presentable.

There was a full-length glass in her bedchamber and she took advantage of it. Even in the flickering light from a single candle she could see her image well enough. Her gown, once a pretty damask-rose, had faded to an indeterminate shade of pink; but nevertheless she was satisfied with her appearance. Her eyes were sparkling and despite having crammed her hair under a cap, she looked respectable.

Her stomach growled; nervousness had prevented her from eating more than a small portion of the sumptuous dinner put before her last night. Breakfast would not be served until ten o'clock at the earliest, and she did not think she could survive without sustenance for so long. Did she dare to creep through the house and find her way to the kitchens to help herself to some bread and butter?

Today she would definitely ask Georgiana if she could move in with her. She was not accustomed to being on her own, having always shared with one of her sisters, and the apartment was far too large for her ever to feel comfortable in.

Should she tap on the door just in case her friend was awake? She shook her head. Better not to wake anyone else so early in the morning. There was an oil lamp on the central table in her sitting room and she removed the glass chimney, trimmed the wick and lit it from her candle. The last thing she wished to do was leave a trail of wax behind her.

Her chest felt tight, her pulse was racing, and she almost changed her mind as she stepped into the pitch-dark, echoing passageway outside the room. Then her stomach rumbled again and hunger gave her the necessary courage to continue. She closed her eyes for a moment in order to visualise the route she had taken to reach this apartment.

Satisfied she would be able to make her way safely to the great staircase, she set off, feeling like an intrepid explorer. She held the oil lamp aloft, not liking the way the eyes of the gloomy ancestors followed her down the passage. She wished she had put on her cloak and gloves, as she might as well be outside it was so cold. There were no fireplaces in the corridors and she supposed that such a vast establishment would inevitably be cold everywhere apart from the rooms that had fires.

She ran down the marble staircase, through the great hall, and out into the central corridor. As she stood shivering in the pool of light made from her oil lamp, she realised she had been foolish to venture downstairs when she had no idea in which direction the kitchens might be. She would return at once to her apartment and wait until seven o'clock, when her maid would hopefully appear with a jug of chocolate and some warm rolls.

She retraced her footsteps and was in the gallery at the top of the stairs when a sudden stream of icy air snatched the cap from her head. The white scrap of material appeared to have developed a life of its own and spun violently towards the east wall. It skittered to a halt in front of a sumptuous velvet curtain.

Kitty ran after it and, as she bent down to retrieve it from the boards, noticed there was a door hidden behind the curtain. Was this another entrance to the east wing? Georgiana had not mentioned there was a way in on the first floor. Something prompted her to step behind the material and examine the door more closely.

She reached out her hand to touch the doorknob and, to her horror, it turned beneath her fingers and the door swung inwards. Her feet were rooted to the floor but her arm was at full stretch. For some reason she could not remove her hand. If the door opened any further she would be pulled headlong into the darkness.

The lamp fell from her fingers, the glass smashed, and oil spilled onto the curtain. With a hideous roar it was aflame. She was trapped. Fire behind her and darkness and danger in front. She screamed, tumbled forward, and her world went black.

★ ★ ★

Lizzy was jolted awake and prodded her husband urgently. 'Fitzwilliam, I am sure I heard a scream.'

He did not wait to argue but rolled smoothly out of bed, snatched a candlestick from the bedside cabinet and, in his nightgown and bare feet, raced across the room to ignite it in the fire. 'I shall investigate, my love. Remain where you are; I do not wish you to get cold.'

Lizzy ignored him and scrambled out of bed, pushed her feet into her slippers, snatched up her négligée and rushed after him into the corridor, quite forgetting to bring a candle of her own. The master suite at

Pemberley overlooked the park at the rear of the house and shared a wall with the abandoned east wing. Georgiana had her rooms on the west side and Kitty was staying in an adjacent apartment.

Fitzwilliam was standing, alert, listening and sniffing. 'God dammit! I can smell fire. Rouse the house, Lizzy. We need water up here and we need it now. We must not take any chances.'

Together they raced down the passageway, the smell of burning becoming more pronounced as they reached the gallery. There was a sheet of flame on the east side of the space and this was being fanned by an icy blast from somewhere behind it.

She didn't stop to investigate but hurtled down the staircase, skidded into the great hall and reached the dinner gong. Snatching up the padded hammer, she began to bang as hard as she could, and the noise boomed down the corridor. After a few minutes she rushed into the hall and tugged at the bell-strap in the hope that someone in the servants' quarters might hear it.

The sound of running feet approaching meant somebody had heard. Peterson appeared, his nightshirt collar visible beneath his waistcoat, followed closely by half a dozen footmen almost correctly dressed.

'There is a fire upstairs, a curtain is alight, and Mr Darcy wants water there immediately. He said we are to rouse the house just in case the conflagration spreads.'

The words were scarcely out of her mouth before the men vanished at full pelt the way they had come. Content that she had done as she was bid, she ran back through the house with the intention of waking Georgiana and Kitty and getting them to safety.

When she arrived at the gallery, the fire was beginning to take hold of the panelling. Fitzwilliam had vanished but she met him returning with two chamber pots full of water, and he threw the contents onto the walls. 'Get the girls out, Lizzy! I fear the situation is deteriorating. Unless we get water up here fast, we could lose the house.' His nightshirt was soot-smeared and his hair in disarray.

'They are coming with the buckets. I shall get the girls downstairs. Take care, my love; you are not properly equipped for fighting a blaze.'

There was no need for candles, as the fire lit the area like day. Lizzy dashed to Georgiana's bedchamber and hurried in. 'Georgiana, get up at once! There is a fire in the gallery and we must go somewhere safe,' she yelled.

Immediately there was a response from the huddled shape in the bed. 'I am awake. I shall be out in a moment. Wake Kitty; she will not know where to go.'

Confident the girl was alert and doing as she was bid, Lizzy raced into Kitty's bedchamber. She saw at once she was not there. The white sheets showed an empty bed and, if she were not mistaken, there was a nightgown draped across a chair.

Her heart plummeted and her throat closed. She had not imagined the scream which had woken her. Her beloved sister had been trapped by the fire. For a second she was unable to move, her mind refusing to take in the enormity of the situation.

She flew back to the gallery, where there was now a chain of men passing wooden pails of water up the huge staircase and across the expanse of boards to be thrown at the fire. Then the man at the head of the line raced away with the empty bucket. The air was full of choking, damp smoke and Lizzy could barely see. Her eyes were streaming by the time she reached Fitzwilliam. 'Kitty is behind the curtain. We must save her!' She was about to fling herself forward in a desperate attempt to reach the blaze, but he threw his arms around her and lifted her bodily from the floor.

'Darling, there is nothing we can do. If your sister was indeed behind that curtain then we must pray she found refuge in the east wing. There is nothing we can do until the flames are doused.'

She struggled and attempted to wriggle free from his restraint. 'I cannot bear to wait! How could this have happened? What was she doing wandering around so early in the morning?'

He held her tight and slowly her panic subsided. 'Lizzy, I am almost certain she has not perished in the fire. Look, my dear: the fire is almost out, the curtain completely destroyed, and we would be able to see her remains.'

He set her back on her feet but kept his arms around her. The men continued to throw water but there were no longer flames, just smouldering wood and blackened panelling. 'I can see broken glass and the twisted remains of an oil lamp,' Lizzy observed. 'Kitty must have dropped it and that was what started the blaze.' Then something else occurred to her. 'I thought that all the doors to the east wing are kept locked? She cannot have gone through there. Where on earth can she be?'

★ ★ ★

Kitty remained on the floor, stunned. There was no light, no sound, nothing but inky blackness. Her heart was beating so hard she could hear it in her ears. She didn't dare to move, to even attempt to sit up. It was as if ice flowed through her veins and not blood.

Several minutes dragged past before she was able to begin to think coherently. Her limbs still refused to obey her commands, but her mind appeared to be functioning normally again. She sniffed and blinked a few times. She could smell no smoke, see not the slightest flicker of light from the flames, and could hear none of the hideous crackling. But surely if she was just the other side of the door then she should be able to hear or smell the fire she had caused by dropping her lamp. Too terrified to sit up, she forced her hands to inch slowly away from her. Yes — these were definitely boards beneath her fingertips.

A wave of relief washed over her. For a few seconds she had almost believed she had been pitched into hell, but she was fairly certain Satan's domain would not have wooden boards to walk on. Emboldened by her discovery, she decided to get to her feet, as remaining flat on her face was both undignified and uncomfortable.

Still puzzled by the silence and blackness, but fairly sure she had somehow become trapped on the wrong side of the door, she rolled onto her back and drew her knees to her chin. She must be facing forwards, away from the door; perhaps that was why she could not see or hear the flames. Reluctant to risk standing up when she could see nothing, she slowly pushed herself around until she was facing in the opposite direction, toward the door through which she must have fallen.

The black was as impenetrable in this direction as in the other. There was nothing for it: she would have to stand up and creep forwards, with her arms outstretched, until she touched the door. She closed her eyes, finding moving about in this fashion far easier than staring into total darkness. She tried to remember exactly what had happened before she found herself wherever she was.

She had gone behind the curtain, the door had opened mysteriously beneath her touch, and then she had dropped the lamp. The curtain had burst into flames, and she must have somehow managed to escape from the danger through the open door. Therefore she could be no more than a few steps from where she had entered. Finding her way across such a short distance would surely present no problem, even in the darkness.

The impenetrable black was unnatural. So was the silence. Her panic returned and her knees all but buckled beneath her. Perhaps if she shouted someone might hear her. She tried, but her first attempt failed; her words stuck behind her teeth and refused to emerge. After a few steadying breaths she opened her mouth and screamed as loudly as she could.

Icy chills flickered up and down her spine. She was quite certain she had screamed, but she'd heard nothing. Had she somehow become deaf? She put her forefinger in each ear and wriggled them vigorously, and she heard the noise quite clearly inside her head.

Thoroughly alarmed, she shouted again and again for assistance, but her cries were silent. With a whimper she collapsed in a heap and buried her head in her knees, praying for divine intervention. A strange whirring and rustling enveloped her and she knew nothing more.

★ ★ ★

Georgiana arrived at Lizzy's side and clutched her hand. 'What is wrong? Where is Kitty?'

Fitzwilliam put his arm around his sister and kissed the top of her head. 'We were rather hoping you could tell us that, my dear. We believe her oil lamp started the blaze, but there's no sign of her here. I am about to initiate a search.'

'As the fire is all but out, Fitzwilliam, do you still require us to go outside?' Lizzy did her best to sound unbothered by the mystery of Kitty's disappearance.

'No, my love. We must return to our chambers and get dressed.' He grinned, looking almost boyish as his teeth flashed in his soot-blackened face. 'If I do not get into something more respectable, I fear my staff might never recover from the shock of seeing their master attired only in his nightgown.'

'You do look rather singular,' said Lizzy. 'I should think this is the first time in the history of Pemberley the owner has been seen in bare feet outside his bedchamber.'

This light-hearted exchange had the desired result and Georgiana relaxed her rigid stance. 'Kitty must have fled. We will find her hiding somewhere. You are quite terrifying, Fitzwilliam, when you are enraged, and she will be so distressed that she has caused this disaster. I am going to get dressed and help with the search.' She stared up at her brother and he smiled.

'I am not at all cross with her, my dear, but I am concerned that she could have been injured and is in need of urgent assistance.' He snapped his fingers and his steward arrived at his side. 'Make sure the panelling is sodden, and that the fire is completely out. Then send every available member of staff to search the house for Miss Bennet.'

The man nodded and Lizzy heard him issuing brisk instructions to recently arrived footmen. These were correctly attired in their livery and demi-wigs, unlike those in the bucket chain who had been in breeches and shirts, some without stockings, and their bare feet pushed into clogs.

A fire, even in the most solid and luxurious of houses, was a most dangerous and destructive thing. There was so much wood in an ancient house like this that the flames could take hold in minutes; if you did not get to it immediately the whole building could be destroyed.

When they returned to their suite Fitzwilliam's valet and Lizzy's dresser were waiting to attend to them. This morning Lizzy was ready before her husband, as he had to wash away the remains of the fire before he could dress. As soon as she was ready, she joined him in his dressing room. They stood on no ceremony in this respect and freely wandered from one room to the other as they wished.

'There is something I must do, Fitzwilliam. I shall wait for you to join me in the gallery.'

Not hesitating for his answer, she hurried into the passageway. She recoiled at the unpleasant odour of smoke and water. The sconces had now been lit, and in the flickering light she could see the walls were smut-smeared and the family portraits also. This entire passageway would have to be redecorated, and goodness knew how they would get this done before their Christmas guests arrived in two weeks' time.

There were maids on their knees with cloths and buckets, mopping up the water that had been thrown at the flames. The floor was awash, the water running up to the marble staircase and down the stairs. Lizzy held her skirts aloft and picked her way carefully to the site of the conflagration.

There was no longer even any smoke; the fire was well and truly out. The men who had dealt with the blaze had vanished, no doubt to get into their livery before coming back to deal with the mess. She walked up to the door that had been concealed by the velvet curtain and reached out to touch the doorknob. Her breath hissed through her teeth — the brass was still too hot to touch.

Without hesitation she wrapped her hand in a bunch of material from her skirt and grabbed the knob. It did not turn. The door was locked. This meant that Kitty had not gone into the east wing but, as Georgiana suggested, had run away to hide from her brother-in-law, who she must imagine would be incensed with her carelessness.

6

Kitty could hear voices calling her name, but she was too far away to reach them. She was trapped inside a Stygian darkness, held there by an unseen force. She closed her eyes and said the Lord's Prayer over and over until suddenly someone's hands were gently touching her.

'Kitty, dearest girl, open your eyes. Everything is all right and nobody is cross with you.'

It was as if her eyelids were glued together; they refused to open. But she could hear Lizzy speaking to her and feel a light touch on her shoulders. She wanted to speak, wanted to open her eyes, but for some reason was unable to. If she could hear her sister, why was her world still black?

A deep, familiar voice spoke to her firmly. 'Kitty, I'm going to carry you to your chamber. You are unwell and I have sent for the physician to attend to you. Doctor Bevan will be here directly.'

Although she could hear Mr Darcy speaking to her and understood every word he said, she was powerless to respond in any way. Her limbs remained slack and her eyes closed. She was aware of being lifted and could hear the murmur of anxious voices in the background as he carried her from wherever she was to her bedchamber.

She wanted to tell him to take her in with Georgiana, that she didn't want to sleep alone anymore, but she was trapped in her dark solitude and must allow herself to be transported from place to place. She was carried downstairs and along the passageway and then through the door.

'Here we are, little one. You are in your own chamber. Lizzy will stay with you until you wake.'

Her arms were raised and lowered, her clothes removed, and a fresh nightgown pulled over her head. She was as helpless as a rag doll and could do nothing to indicate to her family that she was able to hear them but could not reply. All she could do was pray, and the only prayer she could think of was the Lord's Prayer.

Kitty was becoming weaker. However much she fought against the powers that were holding her captive, however much she prayed, she was losing her fight to stay in this world. Her ability to follow the conversations of those around her was lessening. She was sure Dr Bevan had been at her bedside and that he had examined her, but she had been unable to make out what he said to Lizzy or Mr Darcy.

★ ★ ★

Mr Bingley was so recovered in the morning that Dr Bevan pronounced him well enough to sit in a chair. Mrs Bingley was radiant; even with dark shadows under her eyes she was still a beautiful young woman.

'I am relieved your husband is feeling so much better,' said Mr King. 'The physician has said you will be able to continue your journey to Pemberley tomorrow.'

'We are sorry to have put you to so much trouble, Mr King. No doubt you will be delighted to see the back of us.'

'Not at all, Mrs Bingley. I have enjoyed the unaccustomed activity. This house is far too large for one person, and I find myself rattling around in here in a most unpleasant way. I was eagerly anticipating having you and your husband dine with me before you leave. Will your husband be well enough to join me this evening?'

'I am not hard of hearing, you know,' a cheerful voice shouted from the bedchamber. 'I intend to get dressed this afternoon and look forward to dining this evening.'

Adam exchanged glances with Mrs Bingley. He decided not to yell back but go in and speak to his guest. 'Good morning, Bingley. I'm pleased to see you looking so well. What a difference a good night's sleep has made.'

Apart from the spectacular bandage around his fair head, the patient appeared perfectly fit. He was sitting in his dressing robe and devouring a substantial breakfast. He grinned. 'I know an invalid should only eat gruel and sops, but I no longer feel nauseated and my headache has almost gone. I don't believe I have concussion at all; and if my wife would allow me, I would be up and about already.'

The physician had listened to this exchange in silence but now spoke up from his position by the window. 'You took a nasty blow to the head, Mr Bingley, and it is always wise be cautious. I am not so slow-witted that I cannot see you no longer require my services. I shall come to Pemberley to remove your stitches six days from now.'

Adam nodded. 'We thank you, sir, for your prompt and efficient attention.' As he led the way through the house he heard someone hammering on the front door. He increased his pace and arrived in the vestibule to find a groom in the Pemberley livery waiting on the doorstep.

'Is Doctor Bevan within? He is needed most urgently at Pemberley.'

'Yes, he is here. Tell me at once what the emergency is.' Adam stepped aside to allow the doctor to dash past and scramble into his gig. He snapped the whip and his horse took off at a canter with tail flying and ears pricked. No doubt the beast was used to racing around the countryside in this way. Fortunately the lane between the rectory and Pemberley was without potholes, unlike the stretch in the other direction to Bakewell.

The groom seemed reluctant to speak, but Adam pressed him for an answer and he eventually divulged the reason the physician was needed. Miss Bennet had been taken seriously ill, but the man appeared to know nothing more.

Bingley and his wife must not know about this second disaster, at least not until he had discovered for himself exactly what was wrong. He roared at his butler: 'Have my horse brought round immediately. No word of this must reach my guests — is that quite clear?'

Vernon nodded. The man was not stupid and understood that, like the rest of the staff Adam had inherited, he was still on trial and could lose his position if he did not fulfil his duties efficiently. 'I shall be back in time for dinner,' Adam told him. 'There is no need for Cook to delay on my account.'

He was already dressed in breeches and boots; all he had to do was don his riding coat, beaver and gloves, and collect his whip, and he would be ready. He took the stairs three at a time and erupted into his apartment, half-scaring his manservant to death. Hobson rose to the occasion and within a minute or two Adam was ready and hurtling back downstairs. A waiting footman flung open the front door as he approached, and he was delighted to see his horse prancing at the bottom of the steps. The reins were already over the animal's head. He grabbed them and vaulted into the saddle; then he too was cantering down the drive and out into the lane.

It would be quicker to go across country — jump hedges and ditches and then gallop, which he could not do on a public highway, however remote it might be. He turned Courtier's head towards the gate at the side of the lane, kicked him, and his stallion soared over with feet to spare.

The fact that he would arrive mud-spattered and dishevelled from his ride was of no concern. For some reason he knew his presence was needed. His urgency was not because of any warm feelings he held towards

Miss Bennet — she was a stranger to him — but because he sincerely believed he would be able to help in some way.

He sailed over the final gate and galloped across the park that surrounded Pemberley, dislodging huge black divots from the pristine grass. He sat back in the saddle and his horse skidded to a halt. A startled stable boy rushed out to greet him. Adam had arrived before the doctor or the groom. He tossed his reins to the lad and ran beside the brick wall that he hoped would lead to the side door.

He paused before knocking to quickly rub the worst of the mire from his boots. His summons was answered immediately, and the footman who admitted him showed no surprise at his unorthodox and precipitate arrival.

'Adam King to see Mr Darcy, if you please.' The man bowed, and without further ado led him down the passageway and into a flagstone corridor that after a while opened into an even more spacious stone passage that appeared to bisect the house. They turned right, and then his guide halted in front of some tall double doors. They were open and he could hear voices inside.

'Mr King to see you, sir,' the footman announced in a loud voice.

Adam stepped into a vast chamber that

must have been all of forty yards in length and thirty yards in breadth. Good grief, one could entertain a regiment in here. Darcy stepped forward to greet him, accompanied by a young lady who could only be his sister, Georgiana.

'My word, we did not expect anyone from the rectory to be here so soon. Is the doctor on his way?' Darcy nodded politely. The man looked drawn. If Adam was not mistaken, there was a distinct smell of smoke about the place.

'I came across country. Bevan will be here shortly. Has there been a fire? Is Miss Bennet burned?' The thought of such a pretty girl being disfigured filled him with horror.

'Yes, we had a small fire but it is put out and the damage not too serious. Kitty was not injured by the flames but has suffered some sort of collapse and is in a coma.'

'What happened?'

'We are not exactly certain, but from the evidence it would appear she dropped the lamp and this ignited a curtain, causing the blaze. We are at a loss to understand why we found her collapsed in the schoolroom on the nursery floor.'

Miss Darcy was red-eyed and obviously bitterly distressed but said nothing, although she caught his eye as if she wished to speak to him in private. Was he misreading the signs? He raised an eyebrow and she gave an almost imperceptible nod.

'I am here in my capacity as a minister. If I can offer my prayers or support in any way, please do not hesitate to ask. By the by, Bingley has made a remarkable recovery and will be able to travel here tomorrow.'

'Excellent news,' said Mr Darcy. 'I can hardly comprehend that within twenty-four hours my family has been entangled in two catastrophes. I am bracing myself for the third event.' He summoned up a weak smile to accompany his attempt to lighten the mood.

'Miss Darcy, perhaps you would be kind enough to direct me to the chapel so that I might pray for Miss Bennet's speedy recovery.'

The girl glanced at her brother for permission and the look bestowed upon her demonstrated his deep affection for his sibling. 'Go with Mr King, my dear. I think a while spent in contemplation and prayer would be beneficial for all of us. I shall join you in the chapel as soon as I have spoken to Doctor Bevan.'

'If you would care to come this way, Mr King, our chapel is on the west side of Pemberley.'

Adam nodded to Mr Darcy and followed her down what seemed like hundreds of yards of passageways and through a dozen doors until they reached their destination. She had made no attempt to talk to him, just hurried him along.

He pushed open the heavy door and stepped into an ancient and peaceful place. He paused for a moment to drink in the atmosphere. There were two handsome stained-glass windows; a dozen tall, ornately carved chairs set out on either side of the chapel; and a raised stone altar upon which stood a tall golden cross.

After a few moments of quiet prayer he was ready to discover why the girl had wished to speak to him. She was sitting quietly beside him with her head lowered and her hands clasped in her lap. 'Miss Darcy, how can I be of assistance?'

Immediately she swivelled on her chair, her expression earnest. 'I must tell you something about this place that you might not know, as you have so recently arrived in the neighbourhood. The east wing is abandoned and has been so for a hundred years or more. My brother told me Pemberley is so vast the family has never had any need for those three floors with their low-ceilinged rooms and inconvenient staircases.' She fidgeted in her chair and plucked at her skirt as if reluctant to continue.

'You can tell me anything, Miss Darcy. I give you my word it will go no further.'

Reassured by his words, she swallowed and for the first time raised her head and looked him directly in the eye. 'A few weeks ago I discovered an old diary written by an ancestor of mine, a girl of about my age, in which she gives another reason entirely for the empty east wing. She says this wing was abandoned because of ghosts.'

Whatever he had expected her to say, it had certainly not been this. 'Ghosts? Are you trying to tell me that the events here have been caused by supernatural powers?'

She nodded vigorously. 'Indeed I am, sir. Kitty and I had decided to investigate these claims. I think that somehow she encountered one of these spectres and the shock has sent her into a trance. Please, I beg you, come and pray over her.'

'I shall do so — but pray for her, not over her. What makes you think she has had contact with a spirit?' He could hardly credit he was discussing something so ridiculous, as if the existence of the supernatural were a fact; but in his capacity as a priest he must do his best to comfort and not criticise.

'I believe something drew her to that door.

It leads to the east wing. Then, terrified by what she saw, she dropped the lamp, which caused the fire. I cannot fathom how she ended up in the schoolroom.'

'Miss Darcy, I think you are correct in your assumption that she went to investigate behind the curtain and then dropped her lamp. However, is it not more likely that being so upset by the accident, she fled and somehow struck her head?'

She jumped to her feet so suddenly her chair crashed noisily to the flagstones. 'You must come at once and see her for yourself, and then you will understand why I am so certain it is terror that holds her in a coma.'

When she ran from the chapel he had no option but to follow her. This time she took him by a different route and across the central passageway, which he recognised, then through the vast hall in which their feet echoed on the polished floor.

'Kitty is in her chamber, which is on the first floor. I expect the doctor is with her by now, but no one will think it odd of you to wish to offer your prayers for her recovery.'

He followed her through a large double door at the far end that led into another huge room holding the most ornate and elaborate marble staircase he had ever set eyes on. He was given no time to admire the ceiling paintings, the frescoes or anything else as she dashed up ahead of him. With her skirts flying about her ankles and no regard for decorum, she scurried along the corridor and straight into what was obviously a private sitting room. Dr Bevan was conversing gravely with Mr Darcy while Lizzy stood by the window. Matters must be serious indeed to cause such long faces.

'I beg your pardon for intruding,' said Adam, 'but Miss Darcy wishes me to pray with her for Miss Bennet's recovery.'

They barely acknowledged his presence. Darcy gestured towards the bedchamber and Adam took that as permission. There were two maids hovering by the bedside, who curtsied and stepped back into the shadows.

Miss Darcy spoke. 'Leave us; we wish to be private with Miss Bennet.' Once they had done so, she said to Adam: 'Quickly, you must exorcise the spectre before they come back in.'

Adam had no intention of doing any such thing, but he would pray for the girl and hope the Almighty would hear his words. He stepped to the end of the bed and for a moment was too shocked to do anything but stare. This girl looked nothing like any patient he had ever seen — and he had seen plenty of those in his years as a soldier.

It was as if a block of ice had formed around his heart; a malevolence pervaded the room. Without conscious thought he raised his hands above his head and asked for God to intervene. His prayer was silent, but his words were heartfelt. His fingers tingled and he pointed them at Kitty. Slowly her colour returned and she was no longer a living corpse but a being of this world.

★ ★ ★

Kitty was aware someone else had entered the chamber. She strained to hear who the new visitors were. For some strange reason she was now able to recognise Georgiana, but her companion had yet to speak.

Something was changing: the darkness was fading; a greater power was bringing her back into the light. The evil that had held her captive slipped away and she was free. She opened her eyes and sat bolt upright in bed. She was not surprised to see a man of God praying next to her. 'Mr King, you have saved my life. How can I ever repay you?'

7

Kitty's sudden awakening sent Mr King backwards as if stabbed by a sharp hatpin; and Georgiana, who had been standing beside the bed, shrieked with excitement. The resulting noise and confusion brought the doctor, Lizzy and Mr Darcy running into the room.

'Dearest Kitty, I cannot believe you are so suddenly recovered!' Lizzy exclaimed as she dropped beside her on the bed and took her hands.

'Mr King did it, Lizzy,' said Georgiana. 'He prayed for Kitty and there was a miracle.' She had tears trickling down her face. Indeed, when Kitty looked around, everyone apart from Mr King appeared overwhelmed with joy at her recovery. Why was he staring at her in a most particular way?

'I dropped my lamp and started the fire, Mr Darcy. I am so dreadfully sorry to have caused — '

'We shall not say another word about it, my dear girl. The fire was put out quickly and the damage can soon be repaired.' He moved closer, not looking at all forbidding or austere at this moment. 'How did you get up to the schoolroom? Was it fear that caused you to run away?'

Dr Bevan cleared his throat noisily. 'I think Miss Bennet has had more than enough excitement for one day. It would be wise if she was left to rest, and questions and answers kept until tomorrow.' He smiled at her. 'You gave us quite a fright, young lady. Never have I encountered a patient so deeply unconscious, and I have certainly not seen anyone recover so quickly.'

Lizzy took charge. 'The doctor is right; we must leave Kitty to rest. Is there anything you need before we go?'

What Kitty really wanted was for them all to stay; for some reason she had no wish to be alone. Then inspiration struck. 'I should like Mr King stay and pray with me — I believe that I should give thanks to the Almighty for my recovery.'

He nodded as if pleased by her suggestion. 'I should be delighted, Miss Bennet, as long as your family is happy for me to do so.'

Mr Darcy replied for all of them. 'I never cease to be amazed at the power of prayer. Perhaps you would be so kind as to lead us in a short service in the chapel when you have done here, Mr King?'

After a chorus of wishes and farewells the

bedchamber emptied, although Lizzy had carefully left both the door leading into the passageway and the one that led into the sitting room wide open. Even the rector must observe the proprieties.

He waited until the sound of voices and footsteps had faded before fetching a chair and placing it beside the bed. From his expression he had no intention of praying, but of asking difficult questions. 'Miss Bennet, can you tell me exactly what transpired? However extraordinary, however unbelievable, I wish to know.' His expression was deadly serious, and he looked determined to get answers.

She closed her eyes and clenched her fists, trying to still the rapid beating of her heart. She didn't want to talk about it; but having him sitting there, so calm and strong, gave her the confidence. Once she started, the words tumbled out and she described exactly what she had experienced, missing out not a single detail.

When she finished her tale she was shaking, but relieved she had shared her terror with someone else. To her astonishment he took her hands in his, and the warmth and strength of his grip calmed her. She raised her eyes to find him watching her sympathetically.

'Did I imagine it? It is too fantastical to be true.'

'Miss Bennet, I'm quite certain that you believe what you experienced is genuine, but in your terror the actual incident has become confused.'

Kitty snatched her hands back. He was humouring her; he thought her a silly, hysterical young lady. She was about to remonstrate with him but then recalled how, a few moments ago, he had called her back from the brink of oblivion. Her head swam and his image blurred. She could not fight the waves of blackness that were swirling around her.

* * *

Adam cursed under his breath. His maladroit handling of the situation had caused the poor girl to swoon. She was not comatose as before; her colour was good and her breathing regular. There was no need to alarm her family this time. Better to leave her to rest.

He sat up and bowed his head. He had been asked to pray, and would do so before he left. He believed in the power of the Lord; that there was both good and evil in this world; that there was a heaven and hell; but before today he had never considered there might be a third state of being.

Today he had come across indisputable proof that there were indeed spirits inhabiting a place somewhere between heaven, hell and this world. Logically one must assume that, as in reality, there would be both benign and evil spirits in this place.

His intention had been to reassure the girl, try and allay her fears, give her time to recover from her appalling experience before she was obliged to adjust her perception of this world — as he had just done. Instead she now thought he had dismissed her story, and that was definitely not the case.

Although he believed her version of events, he was still of the opinion that she had not actually been behind the door and then magically transported to the schoolroom. The evil miasma must have invaded her mind and, in trying to escape from the terror, she had taken herself to the nursery floor before succumbing to the black spirit in her head.

He quickly murmured a fervent thank-you to the Almighty and asked for guidance and support in his fight against the dark powers. For he was in no doubt at all that Satan was directing whatever lurked in the east wing.

The others were waiting a few yards down

the passageway, not near enough to eaves-drop, but within earshot if they were needed. The physician was no longer with them; he must have gone about his business. Adam had no wish to alarm Mr and Mrs Darcy further with his disturbing discovery, so decided not to reveal what he had been told.

'Miss Bennet is sleeping, but she has had an uncomfortable experience.' He hesitated, not sure if they would take it amiss if he made suggestions as to the disposition of their household. 'Perhaps she might feel more comfortable if someone were to stay with her. I believe she might well suffer from night terrors if she is on her own in a strange place.'

'We had already decided Kitty should move in with me today,' Miss Darcy said.

Mrs Darcy nodded. 'Kitty has always been frail, although these past few months she has been much recovered. After her collapse this morning I should be much happier if she was sharing with you, Georgiana.'

'Georgiana, can you arrange for her belongings to be transferred?' asked Mr Darcy. 'Do we need to have a second bed moved into your chamber?'

'Absolutely not. We shall share. After all, we are sisters, and that is what sisters do, is it not?' Miss Darcy looked at her sister-in-law for confirmation.

'Indeed it is, my love. Jane and I were together until our marriages three months ago. Kitty shared with Lydia until she left Longbourn. I am certain she will be more comfortable with you at her side.'

'Then I shall transfer her immediately,' Mr Darcy said decisively. 'Thank you for coming, King. As soon as Bingley is here and fully recovered, I should like you to dine with us.' With no more than a nod he vanished into Miss Bennet's bedchamber, closely followed by his wife and sister, leaving Adam stranded in the passageway.

He sniffed. The pungent smell of smoke would lead him to the great staircase, and from there he was sure he could find his way to the front door as it was in the same chamber. Life was exciting once more; he no longer regretted his decision to move to Derbyshire. Fighting the supernatural was more to his taste than fighting the French.

★ ★ ★

Kitty thought she was scooped out of her bed and carried to another chamber by a gentleman with a distinctive aroma of lemons and the outdoors. Perhaps she was dreaming, but it was certainly a very pleasant dream. She sighed and settled into a cocoon of soft pillows and goose-down mattress, vaguely aware that there were people moving about in the room, but they were being so circumspect that they did not really intrude into her slumber.

She awoke some hours later feeling fully restored and ravenously hungry. Although she remembered in every ghastly detail her experience in the east wing, she was no longer unsettled by it. She knew herself to be safe from whatever it was as long as she remained on this side of the locked doors.

On sitting up she stared around the bedchamber with surprise. This was not the room she had fallen asleep in — she was somewhere else entirely. She fell back on the pillows, feeling her pulse accelerate and cold sweat trickling between her shoulder blades. Had she once more been transported by supernatural powers?

Then a familiar voice spoke from the other side of the room. 'Kitty, you are awake at last. Fitzwilliam has moved you in with me. Is that not absolutely perfect?'

'Georgiana! I was wondering where I was. I intend to get dressed immediately. I am sharp set, as I have not eaten since I don't know when.' She threw back the covers and tumbled from the bed. 'Have my clothes been moved as well? I care not what I put on as long as I can go somewhere I can eat.'

'I shall ring for a tray to be sent up at once. There is no need to put on more than your négligée; we shall remain in my sitting room until it is time to change for dinner.'

Kitty was surprised her friend had not already begun her interrogation, for if she were in Georgiana's shoes she would already have been pressing for information about the extraordinary events of the morning. Would it be more sensible to keep what she knew to herself? When she had told Mr King he had not believed her, and she had no wish to be thought a young lady given to telling falsehoods.

'I must find the commode before I do anything else. I beg you, dearest friend, send a girl down to fetch me something to eat.'

By the time Georgiana returned from giving her instructions to one of the maids, Kitty had made the necessary visit and found her wrap and slippers. The chamber she was now sharing was identical in size to the one she had been in before, though the furnishings were more luxurious and the furniture of the highest quality.

She surveyed the room with pleasure. Indeed, the bed she had been in could happily sleep half a dozen; but she was certain if she requested a second bed, it would be fetched for her. She had not shared since Lydia had run away with Wickham, but after her harrowing experience she would feel more comfortable having a companion at her side when night fell.

'I cannot believe you look so well,' Georgiana exclaimed when she returned from her errand. 'I have strict instructions not to tire you, so you must come at once and sit down next door. Your belated luncheon will be here soon. Pemberley is so vast it takes fully five minutes to get from the kitchen to the dining room, and even longer to bring a tray upstairs.'

The sitting room was equally delightful, and Kitty observed that a daybed had been drawn close to the roaring fire. Obediently she settled herself and allowed her friend to fuss with pillows and rugs without comment. In the past she had enjoyed being the centre of attention when she succumbed to one of her frequent illnesses, but nowadays she was made of sterner stuff and no longer liked being an invalid.

'There, dearest Kitty. I have done all I can.' With a sigh, Georgiana curled up in the armchair on the opposite side of the fire. 'Lizzy insisted that I make you rest, but I think that is the last thing you must wish to do.'

'I shall remain here until I have eaten, but then I shall put on a morning gown and go and inspect the fire damage. Hopefully, Lizzy and your brother will be safely ensconced downstairs and not know about my perambulations.'

'I knew that was what you would wish to do, for it is what I would do myself in your situation. I shall not pester you with questions until you have eaten, but then I am hoping you will tell me exactly what happened.'

The rattle of crockery was heard from the bedchamber — there must be a servants' exit on that side of the apartment — and Kitty's stomach rumbled disastrously. 'I beg your pardon. How indelicate of me.'

Two maids came in from the communicating door, one carrying a laden tray whilst the other rushed ahead to open the door and place a small table by Kitty's side. They bobbed and vanished in a whisk of white aprons.

'There is enough for three people on this tray! I shall never eat it all. Would you like to share it with me?'

Georgiana shook her head. 'If I do I shall not be able to eat my dinner, and Fitzwilliam will look disapproving and Lizzy will want to know if I am sickening for something.'

Kitty devoured cold cuts, bread and

cheese, apple pie and plum cake with relish. The lemonade that accompanied this delicious repast was drained to the last drop. 'I assume there are hothouses at Pemberley? I should dearly like to visit them.' Her friend had been unable to resist the temptations on the tray and had eaten almost as much as she had.

'We grow everything on the estate: lemons, oranges and pineapples in abundance, but also berries and other fruits. This household is quite self-sufficient; we even have our own farrier to take care of the horses.'

Eventually replete, Kitty replaced her napkin and used cutlery on the tray and kicked off the rugs. 'I am feeling absolutely splendid. I shall put this table out of the way and then I will be ready to go to the gallery.'

'Are you quite sure you wish to go back there so soon? Something dreadful must have happened to you there, and I shall quite understand if you wish to remain here for the moment.'

Kitty sat down again. 'I'm going to tell you what happened, but you must promise never to mention it to anyone else.' She had no intention of revealing everything and cause Georgiana unnecessary distress. She gave her Mr King's interpretation of events and even that was almost too much.

'There are truly evil spirits living in the east wing? No wonder it has been left abandoned. I have no wish to investigate further; after your experience I think it would be better to leave well alone.' Georgiana had lost colour and was plucking at her skirt.

'We now know that the diary is correct. It is all we wished to confirm, is it not? Until today I had not truly believed there could be such things as ghosts, but now I know they are real I have no wish to further my acquaintance with them. I thank the good Lord that we did not actually open the door on the nursery floor.'

'Do you think they will remain in the east wing?' Georgiana glanced nervously over her shoulder as if expecting to see a spectre in the shadows.

'I see no reason why they shouldn't. I inadvertently disturbed them by my meddling, but if we stay away from the connecting doors I am quite certain they will remain in their domain.' This was fustian, but she could hardly reveal her true feelings and tell her friend that she believed the opposite.

Whatever it was that lurked in the darkness of the east wing had come out to find her, not the other way round. An icy chill slithered down her spine and this time *she* looked fearfully over her shoulder. 'Actually, Georgiana, I think I should prefer to stay here and not go exploring after all.'

When the hour came to begin changing for dinner, Kitty was reluctant to leave the warmth and safety of the apartment. 'I am so full, Georgiana, I could not eat another morsel. Please will you convey my apologies to Lizzy and Mr Darcy, but I shall not be joining them for dinner tonight.'

'In which case, I will not go down either. I shall go and tell Lizzy immediately. She will understand in the circumstances that I wish to keep you company. I shall not be long; do not look so worried, Kitty dearest.'

The door closed behind her friend and immediately the sitting room seemed less welcoming, the shadows in the corner darker and the flames in the fireplace smaller. Kitty pressed herself into the chaise longue. Her heart was attempting to escape from her bodice and her hands were clammy. There was something in the room with her and she did not dare turn her head to see what it might be.

8

Mr Bingley insisted he was well enough to dress for dinner, and Adam was delighted that for the first time since he'd arrived three weeks ago he would not sit on his own in the dining room. He took longer on his appearance than usual, ensuring that his neck cloth was tied immaculately, his shirt front sparkling, and his grey silk waistcoat uncreased. He had adopted the modern fashion of pantaloons and evening shoes, relieved not to be forced to wear knee breeches and stockings at such an informal occasion.

He had given his guests an abbreviated version of the events at Pemberley. They knew there had been a small fire, and that Kitty had collapsed from the shock but was now perfectly well. A note had been sent to Mrs Darcy informing her that the Bingleys would be arriving first thing tomorrow morning. Adam was determined to accompany them, as he wished to speak to Miss Bennet again and put matters right between them.

The meal was going to be simple, with few

removes and only two courses, as Mr Bingley would probably not enjoy a rich repast so soon after his injury. Adam waited impatiently in the drawing room for his guests to arrive. The sound of tinkling laughter and voices told him they were on their way.

Mrs Bingley walked in on her husband's arm, looking quite enchanting. Her glorious golden hair was piled casually on top of her head and her eyes sparkled in the candlelight. Her gown was a deep buttercup-yellow, held under the bosom by a gold sash. What the material was, Adam had no idea, but it sparkled and flowed as she moved and he thought it very attractive.

'Good evening, Mrs Bingley, Mr Bingley. I am delighted you can join me tonight.' He half-bowed. Mr Bingley did the same, and his wife dipped in a small curtsy. Then they all laughed.

'Good grief, how ridiculous! I believe we could consider ourselves friends, even after so short an acquaintance. Such formality is not necessary,' Mrs Bingley said gaily.

'I am relieved to hear you say so, madam, for I am in sore need of friends. Would you like a drink before dinner? I have orgeat, ratafia, or sherry wine.'

She shuddered dramatically. 'I dislike all three, thank you, but I shall certainly take a glass of wine with my meal.'

He quirked an eyebrow at Mr Bingley, who shook his head and smiled. This was the first opportunity Adam had had to look at this gentleman. He was as fair as his wife and his eyes were almost as blue as hers; they could almost be siblings rather than husband and wife. They made a handsome couple and were obviously deeply in love. Apart from the bandage around his head, Mr Bingley looked well.

'I shall be sorry to see you go tomorrow, but shall come with you as I wish to speak to Miss Bennet,' said Adam. 'I fear I offended her today and wish to put matters right.'

'I love my sister dearly, Mr King,' said Mrs Bingley, 'though she is a volatile young lady and can be quick to take offence. But I assure you she will have forgotten about it within an hour, and I am sure she will be pleased to see you.' She tilted her head and scrutinised him closely. 'Kitty will appreciate your interest, sir. She has always enjoyed the company of a handsome officer.'

Was this a warning that Miss Bennet was not to be trifled with? 'I am no longer a soldier, Mrs Bingley. My battles are now with good and evil, and I thank God I no longer fight with steel, but with prayer.' Even to his ears this sounded pompous and trite, but it was too late to repine.

Fortunately Vernon announced dinner was served, and he sincerely hoped they would both forget his injudicious remark. Over dinner, conversation was light-hearted and he learnt a lot about the Bennet family, where they lived and in what manner. All in all dinner was an enjoyable occasion and, by common consent, he and Mr Bingley refused to wait behind to drink port and accompanied Mrs Bingley to the drawing room. They did not remain long, as Mr Bingley decided he needed a good night's sleep if he were to travel the next morning.

'We shall leave as soon as it is light enough to do so,' Mrs Bingley said. 'We shall not need to break our fast before we go, Mr King, thank you. I have sent word already to my sister, and they will be expecting all three of us to join them for breakfast.' She smiled and he was struck once again by her charm and beauty. Small wonder Bingley had fallen in love with her.

'If you are quite sure I will not be intruding on a family occasion, I shall be delighted to accompany you, even so early in the morning.' He chuckled. 'Fortunately, departing at first light in December will not be too early. I shall be ready at eight o'clock.'

Mr Bingley took his wife's arm and they

prepared to retire. He nodded at Adam. 'No doubt you are well used to getting up at dawn — although I dare say a soldier of God does not have to rise quite so early as a soldier of the King.'

Adam could hear them laughing as they returned to their apartment and his cheeks flushed. He liked Bingley; he was a fine fellow and obviously had a sense of humour — not something he was famous for himself.

★ ★ ★

Kitty clenched her fists, and the sudden bite of pain as her nails cut into her palms steadied her. She would not be cowed by her experience. She sprung to her feet, turned and shouted into the shadows. 'Go away! You are not wanted here. Return from whence you came immediately.'

'Good heavens! What have I done to offend you that you wish me to go away again?' Georgiana assumed she was referring to her.

'I am so sorry. My nerves are in rags. I imagined there was a ghost hiding in the corner and it was to that I was speaking.'

'You poor thing, I should never have left you on your own.' Her friend rushed across to the offending corner and shook the curtains fiercely. 'I am certain you imagined it, Kitty, for there is nothing untoward over here.'

'What would you have done if a supernatural being had actually been there?'

Georgiana grinned. 'I should have screamed and run away exactly as you did. We are not suited to ghost hunting, I fear. Neither of us has an aptitude for it.'

'I agree with you. However, I should love to spend a few days rummaging through the attics looking for treasure, which is what we were supposed to be doing anyway.'

'That will have to wait a day or two. Lizzy told me Jane and Mr Bingley are coming first thing tomorrow morning. I have not seen Jane for this age, and I am eager to become reacquainted.'

'That is good news, indeed. If I am honest, I am reluctant to go anywhere that is either dark or isolated at the moment.'

The matter settled, they spent the remainder of the evening chatting about the weather, the latest *on dits* from London, and anything else that took their fancy.

The chamber was no longer threatening; if there had been an evil presence, it had gone. Kitty rather thought she had imagined it. Whatever dwelt behind the locked doors — and she was in no doubt something malevolent did live there — it had remained where it was for a century or more, and she could see no reason why it should now interfere with those who lived in the real world.

Although they had not requested a supper tray, it appeared at nine o'clock and they discovered they were indeed hungry enough to do it justice. They retired soon after and their respective maids left them comfortably ensconced in the huge tester bed.

'Shall I blow out the candles, Kitty? We can leave them burning if you would prefer.'

Kitty was tempted to agree, but did not wish to appear weak in front of her new sister. 'Annie got the chambermaid to make up the fire and there will be sufficient light from that, so please, do blow out the candles.'

They settled back in the comforting glow from the flames, but sleep eluded Kitty. She stretched out her arm but was unable to touch Georgiana, who was already asleep. After a while the comforting sound of her companion's rhythmic breathing helped her to relax. She was safe and warm, and as she drifted off to sleep she almost believed she had imagined her horrific encounter.

When she awoke the next morning it was to find Annie smiling beside her. 'Good morning, miss. I have your jug of chocolate and sweet rolls. If you would care to sit up I shall place the tray on your lap.'

Kitty glanced across the expanse of coverlet, shocked to see Georgiana had vanished. 'What time is it? I must get up at once.'

'It is a little after nine o'clock. Miss Darcy always rises at half past seven and didn't wish to disturb you so took her chocolate next door. Would you like me to take it in there instead?'

'Yes, that would be excellent. Is Miss Darcy still there, or has she gone down?'

The communicating door swung open and her friend stepped in. 'As you can see, I am still in my négligée. I have been reading and I'm in no hurry to get ready. We are to join everyone in the breakfast parlour at ten o'clock. Jane and Mr Bingley are already here.' She paused and her mouth curved. 'You will never guess who has come with them.'

'Mr King — it could be no other at this time of the morning. Is it not unusual to receive visitors so early?'

'A stranger perhaps, but Mr King is now considered a friend of the family. After all, he took in Jane and Mr Bingley after their accident, and then brought you back from your coma yesterday.'

'In which case it behoves us to make an

effort with our appearance, does it not? One cannot appear looking shabby when there is a handsome and wealthy gentleman present.' She pouted and placed a finger on her lips and Georgiana giggled.

'You are incorrigible, Kitty, and I am so pleased you have come to live with us. Life is going to be so much more interesting in future.'

Annie had taken the tray next door, and Kitty rolled out of bed and snatched up her wrap. 'I am not a flirt, although I believe I could have been called one a year ago. I shall enjoy wearing my new gowns and dancing whenever I get the opportunity, but I shall not do anything untoward, I promise you.'

'I am sure that you will not. Fitzwilliam would not have allowed Lizzy to invite you if he had thought that you would misbehave.'

'Anyway, where Mr King is concerned, I owe him a huge favour, but that is the extent of my interest. I find him quite disagreeable and dictatorial, and have absolutely no intention of favouring him with my interest.' She skipped across the room and danced her friend around in a circle.

Breathless and laughing, they fell onto the bed and conversation turned towards more important matters, those of selecting an appropriate ensemble. Kitty's chocolate was forgotten in the excitement of getting ready.

'We need to be elegant but not formal, and I am unsure what to choose, Georgiana.'

'I know exactly what we should wear. I have two gowns identical in every way apart from that one was made too short for me. It should be a perfect fit for you. Shall we dress alike, as we are now sisters?'

At five minutes to the appointed time they were both ready. The gowns were in sprigged muslin, the delicate floral embroidery in pastel shades and the sashes a deep rose silk. Kitty had decided not to have her hair dressed in the same style as Georgiana, as that would be taking the jest too far. They stood side by side, admiring their reflections in the long glass.

'I love this gown,' said Kitty. 'Thank you so much for giving it to me. My mama placed no restrictions when we were selecting our ensembles, and I fear that I used to dress in most unsuitable garments. Lydia took all my old gowns with her when she visited, as I no longer intended to wear them.' She lifted the hem to admire the pink petticoat and then dropped the muslin. 'Jane paid for my new wardrobe — though I suppose I should say Mr Bingley did, as it was his money that paid the bills — and she assisted me with my choices. I am confident I will not look out of place in so grand a home as this.'

'In future my brother shall pay for your gowns and for your come-out in town. Mind you, if Lizzy is in an interesting condition or has produced an infant, then I am not sure what will happen.'

'I am in no hurry to find myself a husband, Georgiana. My sisters did not marry until they were in their twenties, and no one can say that they did not make splendid matches.'

They strolled arm in arm along the passageway, and Kitty was astonished to see there was little evidence of there having been a fire the previous day. The walls had been scrubbed clean of smoke and soot and the panels that had been burned were now covered by dark blue velvet curtains.

She had expected to be nervous when she crossed the gallery to the great stairs, but felt perfectly secure. 'Did anyone recover my pretty lace cap? When I went to peek behind the curtain it came off, and when trying to pick it up I dropped the oil lamp. I don't remember anything else very clearly after that.'

'I expect it was incinerated. Was it a particular favourite of yours? I have several; you can borrow any one of those whenever you want to.' Georgiana halted halfway down the stairs and her expression was serious.

'Although I sincerely hope you will not wander off in the middle of the night again.'

'I give you my solemn vow that I shall remain in our apartment until a respectable hour. Later today I want to spend time in the ground-floor rooms examining the frescoes on the ceilings and all the splendid carvings and sculptures. Pemberley is like a palace to me after Longbourn.'

'I am sure that you are exaggerating; you will become accustomed to its luxuries and think of it as home in no time at all. Hurry up! We must not tarry; we are shockingly tardy. There is one thing that Fitzwilliam dislikes above any other, and that is unpunctuality.'

The double doors leading into the breakfast parlour were guarded by two footmen. Kitty hoped they were not intending to announce them — that would be quite ridiculous. Her friend ignored them as if they were wax figures from a museum.

Kitty's stomach lurched unpleasantly as conversation ceased at their appearance in the doorway. Mr Darcy and Mr King were standing together, and she was struck by their similarity of build and colouring. Lizzy and Jane were already seated at the central table, and Mr Bingley was in the process serving his wife from the dishes that filled the sideboard.

Kitty was unused to seeing so much food for breakfast; at Netherfield there was never more than toast and conserves, and perhaps a dish of coddled eggs and field mushrooms. Here there was a veritable banquet spread out for them.

'Good morning, everybody. I apologise for arriving late . . . ' She had been about to fabricate an excuse but instead she smiled. 'I have no excuse apart from taking far too long to get ready.' She curtsied politely. Mr Darcy smiled and Mr King seemed inordinately pleased about something.

'Lizzy, Jane, please don't get up,' said Georgiana. 'I also apologise for keeping you waiting and also offer no excuse.' She steered Kitty to the buffet. 'We are spoilt for choice this morning. I think I shall be exceedingly greedy and have a slice of ham and a griddled egg, and then come back for something else.'

The custom was for the gentlemen to serve the ladies, but Kitty decided she would help herself. She had no wish for Mr King to feel obligated to fetch her food. The atmosphere was relaxed and informal, and she was pleased to see she and Georgiana were dressed appropriately. Mr Darcy turned to the sideboard and began to select items for his wife. He seemed to know exactly what she would like as he did not ask her opinion on the matter.

Georgiana already had what she wanted, which left Kitty and Mr King alone together. Kitty found his proximity unnerving and clumsily dropped a silver serving spoon with an embarrassing clatter. Before she could pick it up one of the footmen had pounced on it and then returned to his sentry duty.

'Good morning, Miss Bennet. I'm pleased to see you looking so well. I wish to apologise if my — '

'There is no need, sir. I wish to forget that yesterday ever happened. As far as I'm concerned, everything I told you was a figment of my imagination, and there are no such things as ghosts.'

His hand came out as if he were going to touch her, but then fell back to his side. 'A wise decision, Miss Bennet, but I want you to promise me you will not go into the east wing under any circumstances.' His voice was low, his expression sombre. They both knew that something evil and dangerous lurked behind the locked doors.

'Pemberley is more than big enough to explore without venturing into the aban-doned wing. We intend to turn our attention to the attics and see if we can discover any interesting artefacts abandoned up there.'

Satisfied with her response, he turned away and began to fill his plate with tasty morsels. Strangely, Kitty's appetite had deserted her; she took no more than a slice of toasted bread and a pat of butter to her place beside Georgiana at the table.

9

There was no time to visit the attics, as Lizzy and Jane wanted Kitty and Georgiana's help to plan the decorations for Christmas. Lists had to be made, and ribbons and glass baubles fetched, which filled most of the day.

'If the weather is clement tomorrow, girls, Fitzwilliam and I have decided we will attend the church in Bakewell,' said Lizzy. 'Our chaplain has a severe head cold and we do not wish to drag him out of his bed if at all possible.'

'Is that where Mr King preaches, Lizzy?' Kitty asked as she carefully rolled the last of her ribbons and put them in the basket.

'Yes, that is quite correct. Although it is but a few miles from here, the previous incumbent passed on all his parish duties to a curate of dubious abilities, so most of the parishioners have been going elsewhere to pay their respects to the Almighty.'

Georgiana added the gold ribbons she had been rolling to the basket. 'My brother told me that the King family own the incumbency, so Mr King does not owe his living to anyone. He is an independent gentleman who happens to be a man of the cloth.'

Kitty had no wish to discuss this any further. Just the mention of his name brought back the horror of her experience. He would be forever associated with what had happened, and she would never be comfortable in his company. 'Will there be many house guests for the festivities, Lizzy?' she asked.

'We have invited three families to join us. There will be ten young ladies and gentlemen, including you and Georgiana. That will make a grand total of twenty adults here from three days before Christmas Eve until Twelfth Night.'

'How exciting!' Georgiana exclaimed. 'I don't believe I can remember a time when we had so many staying. Fitzwilliam does not like to entertain . . . That is to say, he *did* not like to entertain; but since you married him, dearest Lizzy, he is a changed man.'

'You are right. One might almost call him sociable nowadays.'

The gentleman in question strolled in with Mr Bingley at his side. He must have heard Lizzy's remark but made no comment. 'What a hive of industry it is in here, my love. Have you quite finished sorting out the garlands? Is it safe for Bingley and me to join you, or will we be dragooned into helping you?'

Lizzy reached out and took his hand. 'We

have finished, so you may sit down with impunity. I was just telling the girls of our plans for the Christmas period. Are we not to have a party next week as well?'

He perched on the edge of her chair, draping his arm along the back of it. 'I shall have Ingram send out the invitations on Monday. I wish to introduce you to my neighbours.' He looked across at Kitty. 'I have booked a trio of musicians, so neither you nor Georgiana will have to play for us.'

'Good heavens!' exclaimed Kitty. 'Are we to have dancing as well as dinner? How exciting! I do hope you will feel up to it, Mr Bingley. I know how you and Jane love to dance together.'

'I am already feeling fine, apart from a slight headache. I am having my sutures removed next week, and Darcy has kindly postponed the party until after that. Thursday will be a bang-up do, and I have every intention of dancing with my darling wife as often as she will permit me.'

'We have not danced together since the ball at Netherfield, Charles, and that is more than two years ago. No doubt you have partnered other young ladies, but not me.'

'That is not strictly true, Jane my love. We have stood up together at least three times since then.' The candlelight gleamed on his hair, making it seem like a golden halo. 'However, I will agree that we have not danced at a ball or formal occasion since then.'

Something prompted Kitty to mention the infamous assembly at Meryton, where they had all first met. 'I recall the first time you danced. Do you remember the occasion, Mr Darcy?'

For a second he looked nonplussed and then he chuckled. 'I do indeed, Kitty. You and Lydia behaved quite disgracefully by chasing after officers all evening. Bingley monopolised Jane, and I was insufferably proud and inexcusably rude to my darling Lizzy.'

The company parted in good cheer, and Kitty was thrilled to be included in this happy family. She and Georgiana returned to their apartment to change for dinner and discuss their plans for the morrow.

★ ★ ★

Lizzy ascended the staircase with her husband's arm around her shoulders. They had just reached the gallery when unaccountably she shivered and a wave of dizziness and nausea made her knees buckle. As she was slowly collapsing to the boards, Mr Darcy instantly reacted and was able to keep her upright.

'Are you unwell, Lizzy? I shall carry you to our chambers and send for Doctor Bevan at once.' Keeping one arm around her shoulders, he slipped the other beneath her knees and she was hoisted into the air.

Strangely, the further she got from the gallery the better she felt. 'I am feeling fine now, my dear. You may put me down. I have no wish to be transported about the place like a parcel.'

He ignored her request and shouldered his way into their bedchamber, marching past two startled maids to deposit her gently in the centre of the bed. 'You certainly do look less pale than you were a few moments ago. Perhaps fetching the doctor would be a little premature.'

The girls had disappeared, knowing without being instructed that they were unwelcome when their master and mistress were together in their bedchamber. Lizzy sat up and smiled shyly at her beloved. 'Actually, darling, I believe I have an explanation for my fit of the vapours. I think it could be possible I am increasing. I had not intended to mention it just yet, as I cannot be certain, but I have missed two monthly cycles, and dizziness and nausea are not uncommon when a woman is in this condition.'

This was not a fabrication, but neither was

it the reason she had felt unwell. What she had just experienced was quite different from the morning sickness, but she was not going to tell Fitzwilliam that. There had been quite enough unexplained goings-on at Pemberley recently. There was definitely something amiss in the gallery, and she for one was going to make quite sure she never walked there in the dark, or on her own.

'We are having a baby? I cannot believe you are pregnant so soon. We have only been married three months.'

'If I correctly understand the mechanics of the process, my dear, it can take less than a minute to conceive a child. I think we can safely say we have been enjoying the married state as often as possible.'

His eyes darkened and he reached for her; then seeing her hesitation, he smiled and kissed her tenderly. 'I think you should rest for an hour before you change for dinner. I shall return downstairs or there will be little rest for either of us.'

'I expect Mr Bingley would enjoy a game of billiards. I cannot tell you how happy I am to have Jane and Kitty here with me. My younger sister has changed so much that I scarcely know her. Jane was not exaggerating when she sung her praises. I can see a difference in Georgiana already, cannot you?'

He nodded. 'Apart from the fact that she seems to attract disaster to her like a magnet, I find her a delightful young lady. Spirited and intelligent, exactly what my sister needs to bring her out of her shell.' He paused at the door. 'Are you sure you will be all right?'

'Absolutely certain. Fitzwilliam, we must not announce our news until after the New Year. By then I will be far enough along to be certain I am in an interesting condition. I have no wish to be treated like a delicate flower, and that goes for you too, my darling. I am as healthy as a horse; I am sure I can bear any number of children without risk to the infant or myself.'

'I fear that in ten years' time this place will be overrun with children and you quite exhausted by bearing them.'

At first she thought him to be making a jest, but then she saw the worry in his eyes. 'I believe there is a way to interfere with nature that does not involve you sleeping in a separate bedchamber. I have no intention of having a child every year; in fact I have no wish to have more than three or four children altogether.'

'So few, my love? And here was I, anticipating a regiment of little ones. I shall be happy, as always, with whatever the good Lord provides.'

Her snort of laughter was echoed by his chuckle. He raised his hand in farewell and wandered off to find his friend. Lizzy settled back into the pillows and closed her eyes. Her lips curved as she considered just how lucky she was in her choice of partner. Not only was Fitzwilliam intelligent, witty and kind; he was also the most handsome man she had ever set eyes on. The fact that he was also the wealthiest was an added bonus, but not an essential part of his attraction. He was everything a husband should be, and she thanked God every day that somehow they had found each other despite the interference of Miss Bingley, who had done her best to keep them apart. Neither Caroline Bingley nor her married sister had been invited to Pemberley. No doubt when Mr Bingley found a suitable property in Derbyshire they would be obliged to see his unpleasant sisters occasionally, but Lizzy would not worry about it until then.

Her mind drifted back to the strange feeling she had experienced when walking through the gallery earlier. Had Kitty, in fact, been frightened by something similar? Was that why she had dropped her lamp and caused the fire?

Lizzy would go at once and ask her sister if there were something strange going on; then she had every intention of discovering what it was and setting matters right. She jumped up from the bed, but her head swam and her stomach lurched. She flopped down again, annoyed at her physical weakness. Perhaps she would leave her investigation until she felt more the thing; she had no wish to collapse in an ignominious heap in the corridor.

★ ★ ★

'I'm not sure that I am content with this evening gown, Georgiana,' Kitty said as she held out the insipid pink silk skirt for inspection. 'However, as I am no longer the flighty young miss whose only interests lay in fashion and officers, I shall wear it without further complaint.'

Her friend patted her arm. 'You look delightful as always, but I do think it could do with a brighter sash. I believe I have a long length of scarlet ribbon somewhere.' Georgiana smiled at her maid, who curtsied and vanished into the dressing room to return triumphantly a few moments later. She handed the ribbon to Annie.

'Annie,' Kitty asked, 'do you think threading some through my hair as well would be acceptable?'

Her dresser smiled and curtsied. 'I shall do

so at once, miss. It will look ever so jolly.'

When the changes had been made, Kitty was satisfied. 'Thank you. All I need is to push a piece of holly into my bodice and I shall look positively festive.'

Her friend was wearing a pale yellow satin gown with pretty embroidery around the hem and neckline and looked, as always, quite lovely. Together they made their way downstairs, and when Kitty quickened her pace Georgiana did not complain. They almost ran through the gallery and down the stairs, not slowing to a more decorous pace until they were halfway down.

'Are there to be guests joining us tonight, do you know?' asked Kitty.

'No, just family. Will you play for us after dinner, Kitty?'

'I only have one other piece off by heart, and I am not sure that is suitable for a family gathering. Tomorrow we must spend time at the pianoforte and you can begin your instruction. I would love to be able to play some Christmas tunes with you.'

Dinner was uneventful, and Kitty could not help but notice that Lizzy and Mr Bingley both looked tired. She and Georgiana were playing a game of spillikins in front of the fire. 'Shall we retire? We will have to be up early for church tomorrow.'

Her companion followed her glance and understood immediately. 'Lizzy, Kitty and I are going to retire. We will not wait for the tea tray.'

'Goodnight, girls. I think if no one has any objection that I will retire also.' Immediately Darcy was on his feet and offering his arm.

Her objective successfully achieved, Kitty embraced both her sisters, curtsied to the gentlemen, and arm in arm with her bosom bow left the drawing room and walked briskly through the hall and into the chamber which held the great staircase.

Each time she approached the marble stairs she experienced a flutter of fear. 'I do not like going this way. Can we use another route?'

'Yes, of course we can. How thoughtless of me to take you past the place where you had such a horrible experience. Come, in future we shall use the oak staircase on the other side of the dining room. Indeed, I cannot understand why I did not think of it before.'

The route to this secondary staircase involved crossing the central flagstone passageway and cutting through the dining room. These stairs were as commodious as the main staircase at Longbourn. Kitty had wondered if they were for staff use only, but was reassured when she saw them.

Finding their way to their apartment was a little more complicated, but as long as it did not require Kitty to pass through the gallery she was quite prepared to walk an extra half-mile. Eventually they emerged on the west side of the house that was used exclusively by guests, as the family occupied the central portion, and the least said about the east wing the better.

Once they were safely ensconced in their bedchamber and their maids dismissed, Kitty broached the subject she had been mulling over for some time. 'I think the gallery is haunted. I would like to ask Mr King to pray there in the hope that his words will have the power of God behind them. I know, without a shadow of doubt, that his intervention brought me back from the brink of oblivion.' No sooner had she spoken than she wished the words unsaid, as she had no wish to alarm Georgiana. But her friend merely nodded in agreement.

'I think you might be right, and Mr King's prayers had a miraculous effect on you. We cannot creep about the house without attracting notice. It is all very well to use the back stairs occasionally, but either my brother or Lizzy are bound to comment if we refuse to use the main staircase.' She frowned. 'Perhaps it would be better to explain to

Fitzwilliam before we enlist Mr King's assistance.'

Kitty shuddered at the thought. For all his smiles and compliments, she lived in dread of being on the receiving end of one of his famous set-downs. 'A leopard cannot change its spots' was a saying that must have a grain of truth in it.

'I would much prefer to try and sort this out without involving either Lizzy or your brother, if you don't mind,' said Kitty. 'Only if Mr King refuses to help us, or his ministrations are ineffective, should we embroil anyone else in this mystery.'

'If we are fortunate we should be able to speak to Mr King after the service tomorrow. I believe that Fitzwilliam has taken a liking to him, and should not object if he visits on Monday.'

'I am not sure it would be advisable to ask him directly, especially not after the service and in a place we might be overheard. I had thought I would write him a note; it should be far easier to slip it into his hand without being observed.'

Georgiana looked unconvinced. 'Think about it, Kitty dearest. If you were to be seen handing him a letter, would not people believe you were making a clandestine arrangement to meet?'

'Good grief! Do you think so? He is the very last gentleman I should wish to have my name associated with — far too austere. And he must be almost the same age as your brother.'

'I am sure he is not past five-and-twenty, and Fitzwilliam will be thirty years old on his next name day.'

'That is by the by. All I wish him to do is agree to exorcise the Pemberley ghosts so we can all sleep easily in our beds.'

★   ★   ★

The next morning was bright and frosty and Kitty was looking forward to attending church. Mr Bingley had declared himself fit enough to ride with Mr Darcy so that the ladies could fit more comfortably into the carriage for the three-mile drive to Bakewell. He had now removed the bandage and his sutures were hidden by his hair.

If Mr King was surprised to see them, he hid it well. He greeted them affably, but with no more deference than he gave his other parishioners. Kitty and Georgiana walked demurely behind the others into the darkened interior of the church.

'I am glad we have on our warmest cloaks; it is perishing in here. I believe it could be warmer outside,' Kitty whispered.

'No doubt it will be better once everyone is inside. Look, there is an empty pew on the right. Fitzwilliam will find it strange not sitting in pride of place today.'

The well-to-do in the congregation took the seats and the space behind them was filled to capacity by those less fortunate. Presumably the missing Bakewell congregation had returned now his uncle was dead. Everyone joined in the hymns lustily and Kitty was relieved Mr King kept his sermon to a reasonable length. Her toes were frozen solid in her boots and she could no longer feel the tips of her fingers. She had taken Georgiana's advice and not written a note to give to Mr King, as she was going to attempt to speak to him privately after the service.

After they had been blessed, the congregation was free to go. Those at the rear of the church remained politely standing until those at the front has made their way down the aisle and out into the December sunshine. Mr Darcy and Lizzy stopped to speak to Mr King for a moment, as did Jane and Mr Bingley, but it was obvious there was going to be no opportunity for Kitty to do the same. He nodded and she curtsied as she passed, but that was all.

As they made their way back to the

carriage, Lizzy waited for them. 'I have invited Mr King to join us for dinner tonight, and his curate is going to take evensong for him; Fitzwilliam suggested he might like to play billiards, so he is coming some time this afternoon.'

Kitty exchanged a triumphant glance with Georgiana but was unable to do more. If he was to be with them for several hours, there must be an opportunity to waylay him with her suggestion.

10

After breakfast Kitty and Georgiana returned to their apartment in order to decide how to spend the remainder of the morning.

'I thought I might start your instruction this morning, Kitty, unless you would prefer to go for a walk whilst the sun is shining.'

'I should dearly like to examine the parterre. I know there is nothing apart from the box hedges to look at, but the patterns are fascinating. Also, I should like to see the view of the lake from the terrace.'

'Then that is what we shall do. In the summer months we put cushions on the stone benches enclosed within the wall and take tea there, or read a book.'

'I can hardly credit I shall be here to experience that myself. To think that a year ago the height of my ambition was to marry a handsome officer, and now I have become part of your family. I am a very lucky young lady and appreciate my good fortune.'

A short while later they were on their way once more. 'Are we to take the back stairs again?' Georgiana asked.

'No, I want to walk around in the gallery to

see if my conjectures are correct. Perhaps I am being overly fanciful after my nasty experience; I should not wish to involve Mr King on a fool's errand.'

Their chatter faded as they approached the end of the passageway. Georgiana moved closer to her and put her arm through hers. Kitty decided she must be brave and ignore the feeling of dread that was creeping towards her along the boards as if it were a physical thing and not a figment of her imagination.

They stepped into the gallery, and Kitty was held fast by force she did not understand. It was as if the breath were being sucked from her lungs; as if she were somehow being emptied of life. Georgiana screamed; the sound echoing around the empty space and the terror in her voice jerked Kitty from her trance.

'Run, run with me back to our apartment! Don't stop until we are inside.' Kitty's friend grabbed her hand and half-dragged her away from whatever it was that lurked in the space. They were hurtling along with skirts flying when Mr Darcy erupted from the master apartment, his face like thunder.

'What the devil is going on? Lizzy is resting — ' He broke off from his tirade when he saw that his sister was incoherent with tears. Immediately his expression changed to concern. 'What is it, sweetheart? Come in, both of you, and tell me at once what has upset you.'

Georgiana flung herself into his arms and he embraced her, stroking her back and her hair and murmuring words of encouragement as if she were a small child again. With the door closed Kitty was able to recover her composure, the feeling of dread vanishing as if it had never been.

The bedchamber door opened and Lizzy appeared. She took one look at the two of them and her colour faded. Kitty rushed forward and was just able to prevent her from collapsing to the carpet. Mr Darcy abandoned his sister and swept his wife up into his arms and strode back into the bedroom.

Kitty was too shaken to remonstrate with her friend for involving Mr Darcy and Lizzy; she was also concerned that her sister had swooned. Lizzy was the healthiest of them all and had never been ill in her life.

She gathered Georgiana into her arms and offered what comfort she could, but her friend continued to weep and shake like a blancmange.

They were left on their own for five minutes and then Mr Darcy reappeared, his face serious. 'We want to talk to you,' he said to the girls. 'Lizzy must remain in bed, so join us in here if you will.'

Georgiana was gulping and sniffing occasionally and her handkerchief was sodden, but apart from that they had both more or less recovered from the terror of what now appeared to be inhabiting the gallery. Kitty took Georgiana's arm and led her friend into the inner sanctum. Lizzy was resting in the enormous bed, looking like a child in the centre of a silk comforter and heap of lace pillows. However, she had recovered her colour and was looking remarkably well for a lady who had so recently fainted.

'Come in and sit on the bed with me,' she said. 'Fitzwilliam will join us after he has pulled the hangings shut. This is a conversation I do not wish to be overheard.'

Now was not the time to question this extraordinary suggestion. The very idea of sharing a bed with someone so toplofty as Mr Darcy caused Kitty to stumble, and she ended on her knees as if in prayer. Before she could regain her feet he tossed her on the bed, and then Georgiana was similarly disposed of. Whilst she regained her equilibrium and smoothed out her rumpled skirts, he strode around dragging the curtains together and enclosing them in an intimate gloom.

The situation was ridiculous, and exactly

what Kitty needed to dispel the last of her fear. She caught Georgiana's eye, and before they could prevent it they were both helpless with giggles. Then Lizzy joined in, and when Mr Darcy climbed in he looked from one to other in exasperation; then he too began to laugh.

Then as suddenly as the laughter had started, it ended. They sat in silence for a few moments and then he spoke. 'What happened to you the other day, Kitty? Tell me exactly; leave nothing out.'

When she had finished the silence hung heavily between them. Lizzy reached out and took her hand. 'I felt it too, Kitty. There is something evil lurking out there.'

'I feared as much when you were found in a coma, Kitty,' said Mr Darcy, who was leaning against the pillows on the left of Lizzy, whilst she and Georgiana were similarly disposed on the right. 'I should have told you the dark secret that Pemberley holds before I brought you here, my love.'

Kitty trembled and slipped her hand into Georgiana's, finding it was as cold and clammy as hers. She waited in the oppressive quiet for Mr Darcy to continue his revelation.

'I found a diary a few weeks ago, Fitzwilliam,' Georgiana blurted out. 'It was written more than a hundred years ago, and it mentioned that the east wing had been abandoned because of ghosts.'

'Why on earth did you not come to me? Too late to repine — the damage is done. One hundred and fifty years ago, before this part of the house was built, there was only the east wing. My ancestor had several sons, and unfortunately two of them were . . . I do not know how to put this delicately, and apologise in advance for my robust language. They were evil bastards and used the privilege of rank and wealth to destroy the lives of those with whom they came into contact.

'The story goes that one infamous weekend, when the rest of their family was elsewhere, they invited other like-minded devils here and not only brought with them a bevy of light skirts, but also abducted three local girls. They were so engrossed with their debauchery that they failed to notice the villagers had banded together and come to rescue their daughters and seek revenge.

'The details of what happened next are too gruesome to repeat. Let it suffice for you to know that the girls were rescued, and the brothers and their cronies perished in the most horrible way imaginable. The family never returned; they preferred to live on another estate. After several decades the Darcys built a new house around the old —

but the east wing was untenable.'

'What happened to the men who perpe-
trated this murder?' Kitty asked.

'They left nobody alive to stand as witness
— apart from the girls themselves, of course.
The magistrates could do nothing, as the
villagers had returned to their homes as if
nothing untoward had happened. We only
know this story because one of the abducted
girls told the local vicar on her deathbed. By
then the culprits were all dead and there was
nothing that could be done.'

Something about this story bothered Kitty.
'We are talking of the rakes as the evil ones,
but in this case they were the victims not
the perpetrators. They might have been
debauched, but they were not murderers as
the villagers were.'

They were staring at her as if she had
spoken in tongues. 'Are you suggesting, Kitty,
we should be sympathetic rather than
condemn them?' Mr Darcy asked eventually.

'I rather think I am. I do not condone the
way these young men behaved — it was
totally reprehensible — but they did not
deserve to be murdered and the murderers
allowed to get away with their heinous crime.'

'That's as may be, Kitty. However it is not
the villagers we are concerned with now, but
the spirits of the men who are haunting this

143

place,' Mr Darcy said firmly.

Georgiana now had a question. 'Fitzwilliam, surely they did not kill the ladies from London as well?'

He shook his head. 'No, sweetheart; they fled the scene and were not there to be interviewed when the constables arrived.'

'Has it stood empty since then?' Kitty asked.

'It has, my dear. Although I believe that several attempts have been made over the years to reoccupy the wing, each time the family were driven out by unnatural occurrences. Eventually it was deemed best to leave it. I was told the story by my father and believed it to be superstitious nonsense. What has happened these past few days has made me think again.'

'I was hoping to involve Mr King in this, Mr Darcy,' said Kitty. 'The strength of his prayers released me from my captivity and I truly believe he could exorcise these ghosts for you.'

'I think that Kitty is correct, my love,' said Lizzy. 'We do need his assistance. Do you know if anything similar has ever been attempted in the past?'

'My father only mentioned it the once, and that was when I asked why we didn't renovate the wing. He was so abrupt that I never mentioned the subject again. There have been no manifestations of any sort in my lifetime, and I cannot imagine what has brought these evil creatures into our part of the house.'

Georgiana roused herself and joined in the lively debate. 'Could Kitty be the reason? They enticed her to the door by snatching away her cap, did they not?'

'I think it started when we were in the schoolroom and were talking about going into the east wing to investigate,' Kitty said, not wishing to think she might be the cause of the unpleasantness.

Mr Darcy repudiated this. 'I think the diary is the key, Georgiana. Finding that has stirred up the past. Did you read the whole thing?'

She shook her head. 'No, I flicked through it until I saw the mention of ghosts and then put it aside.' Georgiana paused as if thinking hard. 'I can probably find it again if you wish to read it yourself. It is with the other journals. I didn't really want to investigate the east wing, Kitty, but thought it might be something you would be interested in, and I did so want you to be happy here and not be bored by our country life.'

This revelation was greeted by silence; then Kitty pulled herself together. 'I could never be bored in your company. Already you are as close to me as my sisters.' She appealed to her brother-in-law. 'I beg you, sir, to explain to your sister that whatever is happening has nothing to do with either of us. Georgiana, how did you come across the diary?'

'I was looking for a book of local interest for you and noticed the shelf of diaries and plucked that one out at random.'

Lizzy sat bolt upright and her gasp made them all turn to look at her. 'How long ago did this happen, Georgiana?'

'Six weeks ago, no earlier, because I recall we had just heard from Jane that she and Bingley were coming to stay whilst they searched for a suitable property in this neighbourhood.'

'In that case, it would have been exactly the time that I discovered I might be increasing. I think this is the reason the evil spirits are restless.'

Mr Darcy jumped off the bed, threw open the drapes and began to pace the carpet. No one dared speak and interrupt his thoughts. He halted and strode back to the bed. 'I have considered what you said, my love, and at first thought it unlikely that was the cause. There have obviously been other pregnancies in the family over the past century, but no mention of problems from the east wing. Then I remembered that neither of us were born here, but in London. When Mama was expecting you, Georgiana, she told me no Darcy children had been born at Pemberley for generations. The family tradition was to move to town and not return until the infant was a few months old.'

Kitty tumbled from the bed, dragging her friend with her. She stared at Mr Darcy with horror. 'Do you think that as soon as the family knew a baby was expected unpleasantness would begin, so they immediately left for London? Is there any way of checking family records to prove this to be the case?'

'I believe that would be possible. Perhaps you girls would make this your task? I shall get my man of affairs to find the records you require.' His expression changed and he punched his fist into his hand. 'I know for a certainty there have been other women in an interesting condition staying here, but there have never been any problems of this kind. I believe the advent of a Darcy child is what perturbs the spirits. I think it would be best if we removed to London immediately.'

'Fitzwilliam, we cannot go until after Twelfth Night. The invitations have already been sent for the New Year ball and to the house guests joining us. Surely doing so would mean having to come up with a suitable explanation. I am sure you have no wish to advertise the fact that Pemberley is haunted.'

He shook his head vehemently. 'I don't give a damn what anyone thinks. I shall not have my family put at risk.'

'If Mr King is able to intervene, then could we not stay at least until the spring?' Georgiana asked quietly.

He looked as if he was going to refuse outright, but then reconsidered. 'I am sure the family must have tried something similar at some point, but obviously with no success. However, as he's coming here later I shall take him into our confidence and see what he can do. I shall make my decision after that.'

Lizzy smiled at him, and immediately his expression softened and he no longer looked so formidable. 'I think, my love, if he can contain these spirits — push them back from our side of the house — then that will be sufficient for us to enjoy our first Christmas here,' she said. 'If we moved to the downstairs apartment we should not be obliged to come anywhere near the east wing.' She glanced at the far wall. 'Our rooms are closest to the ghosts, are they not? What do you think?'

'I think it an excellent idea, and I shall set things in motion immediately. Those rooms have not been occupied since my father moved there after my mother's demise. As soon as they are prepared we shall relocate.' He stared in turn at each of them, assessing their composure. Satisfied by what he saw, he smiled. 'Next summer I shall have the east wing demolished and all the rubble taken elsewhere. I cannot imagine why it has not already been done.'

He gestured towards the door, and Kitty and Georgiana embraced Lizzy and hurried off. Once secure in their own rooms, and sure no servant was in earshot, the two friends were able to discuss what had happened.

'I shall never go into the gallery again, Kitty. In future we will always take the oak stairs. I am surprised that no member of staff is aware there is something unpleasant living next door. Usually they are the first to gossip about anything that happens here.'

'Perhaps these are very particular ghosts and they only show themselves to gentry.' Her feeble attempt at humour did nothing to alleviate their concerns. 'I suppose we might as well change; it will give us something to do and take our minds off what is stalking this family.'

★　★　★

As Adam would be returning late, he decided it would be unwise to ride as the weather could turn nasty. He sent word to the stable yard for his carriage to be made ready and then faced the perplexing problem of what to wear. He had been invited to remain for dinner, and no doubt the family would change into their evening finery. He could hardly take his evening rig and valet with him, so must either appear overdressed for a game of billiards or underdressed for dinner. For the first time since he had left the army he regretted that he could no longer wear his uniform. He settled for a dark blue jacket, grey silk waistcoat, breeches and Hessians. He added a diamond pin in his impeccably tied neckcloth, gave himself a cursory glance in the glass, and picked up his caped coat, hat and gloves and headed for the front of the house.

A footman opened the door and bowed him out. His carriage was waiting in the turning circle. The coachman and the groom were on the box, the two horses stamping impatiently and eager to be off. He waved a second footman away and jumped into the carriage without letting down the steps.

The carriage rocked and then the horses moved away smoothly. The facilities at Pemberley were excellent; his cattle and men would be well taken care of in his absence. He had informed the coachman he would not be returning until dark, and had been pleased to note that the lanterns were already in place on each corner of the coach.

He settled onto the squabs and let his mind drift over the extraordinary events of the past week. First there had been a carriage accident, and then a haunting. No, more than that — something powerful and demonic had snatched Miss Bennet, and he was at a loss to know how to deal with it.

As he had been about to depart, a sudden impulse had caused him to pick up the gold cross he wore in church and slip it into his waistcoat pocket. There was something evil lurking in that beautiful house — and he was determined to root it out.

11

The great hall, which also was the ballroom, was so large one's voice echoed when one spoke. By common consent it had been decided that it would be safest to congregate in chambers that did not connect to the east wing. This meant that in future the music room and the great staircase would not be in use.

'I am having the pianoforte and the harp moved in here, girls,' Mr Darcy told them. 'For some reason I felt obliged to explain my decisions to Peterson and Ingram. I told them they would be needed here when we entertain and that you two wish to become accustomed to playing in a larger space.'

Who was more shocked by his admission that he had told a falsehood, Kitty was hard put to say. Georgiana was aghast and put her hand over her mouth, and Mr Bingley and Jane exchanged glances, but Lizzy laughed out loud.

'Well, Fitzwilliam, you could hardly tell them the truth. If the staff were to get wind of the fact that this place is haunted — not by benevolent spirits either, they would leave en masse, and where would we be then?'

Mr Bingley ran his fingers through his hair, making him look like an untidy schoolboy. 'Ghosts at Pemberley? If Jane and I had been aware of this I don't think we would have come. I've not had the misfortune to encounter such a thing, and I'm in no hurry to do so now.'

Jane took his hand. 'If what Mr Darcy says is correct, then they have been in residence for generations and nothing untoward has happened to anyone living here. Why should we be in any danger now?'

The Bingleys had not been told the whole; they knew nothing of Kitty's near-fatal experience. Mr Darcy had thought it better that they keep this knowledge to themselves, and neither had he informed them that Lizzy was increasing.

'We are hoping King will be able to placate the spirits and keep them in their own abode until I can have the building razed next year.' Mr Darcy, sounded, as always, in full command of the situation; but Kitty detected a hitherto unseen nervousness in his demeanour. She was certain this was because his beloved wife was at risk, as well as his sister. She doubted he would care one way or another if anything happened to herself, apart from the fact that it would upset both Georgiana and Lizzy.

This was a lowering thought and she pushed it to the back of her mind. Her behaviour last year had been enough to give him a dislike of her, and she didn't blame him one jot. However, she hoped he would come to view her differently as the weeks passed. She was certainly seeing a better side to his character and found him just a little more approachable than he had been before.

Papa was coming to stay in February, though she wished he could come immediately. Although they had not been close (Lizzy and Jane were his favourites), they had become better friends in recent weeks, and he would know immediately how to deal with this situation.

Even with the cavernous grate filled with an enormous fire, the extremities of the hall were too cold for comfort. The six of them huddled in front of the fire, marooned in a sea of polished boards and the occasional island of chairs and sofas.

'This is beyond ridiculous,' said Mr Darcy. 'I refuse to remain in here any longer. We shall remove to the drawing room; it will be warmer and more comfortable there.' He snapped his fingers and the lurking footman scurried over. 'Have Mr King conducted to the drawing room when he arrives.'

Lizzy glided up beside him. 'The doors between the music room and the staircase have been closed. If we also keep the communicating door from the drawing room shut, we shall be perfectly safe. We will be installed in the downstairs apartment by this evening, and Jane, Mr Bingley and the girls intend to use the oak staircase and not go anywhere near the gallery. You must relax, my love. Nothing untoward will occur.'

They all trooped behind Lizzy and Mr Darcy down the central passageway and through the library, to arrive at the drawing room. Kitty was somewhat out of breath: walking about this place was the same as taking a long walk in the countryside. It was certainly as cold away from the fires. Living somewhere so grand was all very well, but she would be much more comfortable in a smaller establishment that did not require a map to get from one chamber to another.

Jane settled on a chaise longue and Mr Bingley flopped down beside her. Mr Darcy escorted Lizzy to a comfortable padded armchair, hovered by her until she was seated, and then resumed his restless pacing. Kitty and Georgiana stationed themselves at a cluster of small tables and chairs a respectful distance from their elders and betters.

'I have never seen my brother so unsettled, Kitty. Even when he and Lizzy were apart and he was so miserable, he was still in command. I don't like to see him so upset.'

'I think it makes him seem more human. Before this I had thought him a godlike figure, not susceptible to everyday emotions and worries. Since I've been here I have seen a different side to him and like him much better. I am sure he is unsettled because of Lizzy's condition — I expect in some ways he is blaming himself for not having looked into the family history more thoroughly before bringing her here.'

Her friend did not seem especially reassured by this remark. Kitty was silent for a few moments and then tried again. 'Mr Darcy has been head of this household for years; he runs the vast estate impeccably, and neither gambles nor drinks to excess. He is respected and admired by all who know him. However, there is not a man in the kingdom who would not be perturbed at having to deal with the supernatural. Indeed, I don't believe any of us thought ghosts were real until now.'

'You are right, of course, but it does not make me any less anxious — not just on his behalf, but on all of ours. We are prisoners in our own house, hiding from these things. Pemberley no longer seems a happy place.'

A footman appeared in the doorway. 'Mr King is here to see you, sir. He's waiting in the vestibule.'

Mr Darcy was not impressed by this information. 'Bring him here immediately. He is expected.'

The unfortunate servant paled at the rebuke and Kitty could hear him running to retrieve the missing guest. Perhaps Mr Darcy had not changed so much after all. She looked around the room and observed that all the occupants were silent, watching the door, as eager as she was for Mr King to arrive. A shiver of apprehension trickled down her spine. What if he could not drive these ghosts back into the depths of the east wing where they could do no harm? What if his intervention made matters worse? She pushed another more alarming thought away. For some reason she was terrified he might suffer the same fate as she, and there would be no one to bring *him* back.

She turned to Georgiana. 'Do you think your brother is going to explain everything to Mr King right here, or will he take him somewhere private?'

This question was answered for her when the gentleman himself strode in through the open door. He bowed. 'Good afternoon. I hope I have not kept you waiting.' His friendly smile faded as he looked at each of them. 'There is something wrong. I believe I know what is troubling you all.' He came fully into the room and waited for the ever-present footmen to close the door behind him before he continued. 'You have ghosts at Pemberley — and they are not of the benign sort, either.'

Mr Darcy seemed unsurprised by his announcement. 'Exactly right, sir, and your knowledge makes what I'm going to say to you so much easier.' He then told Mr King the gruesome story and the repercussions that had followed it throughout the years. He omitted nothing, even his plans to demolish the east wing next year.

He reached the crucial part. 'After what happened first to Kitty, and then to both the girls and Lizzy, I am of the opinion that something urgent needs to be done before we are driven from our home. Can you exorcise them? Your prayers vanquished them once, and I am hoping they can do the same again.'

'I am afraid driving away satanic infestations might not be as simple as you think, Darcy. I have been doing some research over the past few days and have come to the firm conclusion that spirits only remain in this world if they have unfinished business. In order to send them on their way we must somehow discover what they want and fulfil these wishes.'

His extraordinary suggestion hung in the air, and even Mr Darcy was speechless. Lizzy recovered first. 'Are you suggesting that someone must go into the east wing?'

'Out of the question,' Mr Darcy snapped. 'Far too dangerous.'

Mr King seemed unbothered by this reaction. 'I shall go in. I will endeavour to discover what it is they want.'

'I think I know what that is,' Kitty said. She quailed under the combined stare of the three gentlemen, but was determined to speak her mind. 'I believe they want revenge for their deaths. Although these men were bad, they were not murderers, and I think it was wrong that the villagers remained unpunished for their crimes.' She had jumped to her feet in order to deliver the speech, but now her legs refused to hold her upright and she collapsed onto her chair. Being the centre of attention was not pleasant, but she stiffened her spine and raised her head, expecting to see condemnation on the faces of those in the room. Instead Mr Darcy was looking at her with what could only be described as admiration.

'Devil take it! I believe Kitty is right. Though I'm damned if I know how we can put matters right more than a century since the murders took place here.'

She was not sure what shocked her most — that he admired her, or his profanity.

'Fitzwilliam, kindly moderate your language,' Lizzy said firmly, and Kitty approved of her reprimand. Then her sister continued, 'If you and Mr King wish to use barrack-room language then I suggest you go elsewhere, for poor Kitty is about to have a fit of the vapours after hearing such words in our drawing room.'

Mr Darcy raised an eyebrow and his lips twitched, whilst Mr King smiled quite openly. If there was one thing Kitty did not like, it was being a figure of fun. In her opinion gentlemen did not use bad language in the presence of a lady.

With what she hoped was elegance and grace, Kitty rose to her feet and nodded regally. 'I have a megrim, and shall return to my apartment. I shall not be joining you for dinner.' Before they could protest, she spun and made her way to the exit and slipped out through the door. She paused outside in the passageway expecting to hear protests or the patter of feet as Georgiana raced after her, but the doors remained closed behind her. Her departure was obviously of no account to anybody there.

Her eyes filled and she walked blindly in what she hoped was the correct direction for the oak staircase. The usual bevy of footmen were, just when she could do with one, nowhere to be seen. She was not famous for her sense of direction and, after wandering for a considerable time down freezing passageways, she was still no nearer to finding her destination.

Surely she should be somewhere in the vicinity of the second stone passage — the one that led to the oak stairs. She turned left and right but all she saw were closed doors. She peered into each room as she went past but there were not any she recognised. There was a miscellany of anterooms, sitting rooms, sewing rooms and various storerooms, but none were any of the main reception rooms that she sought.

Then she was struck by what she hoped was a solution to her problem. The next chamber she came across that she considered could be used by the family, she would enter and search thoroughly for a bell-strap to pull. She would remain there until a member of staff came to find her, and then they could guide her in the right direction.

She eventually discovered what she was seeking and hurried inside, already thoroughly chilled from her sojourn in the freezing passageways. There was, of course, no fire lit, but at least the chamber was free of drafts. She was delighted to observe there was one laid in the grate, so all she needed to discover was a tinderbox with which to light the kindling.

The room was a small office of some sort. A desk and two chairs occupied the centre, two padded armchairs stood on either side of the fireplace, and a handsome bookcase and sideboard occupied the far wall. The sideboard was the obvious place to search, and she was immediately rewarded by finding a tinderbox. Having lit fires many times before, she had no difficulty in igniting the fluff in the box, transferring the flame to a candle, and then pushing this into the fire.

Until the room was warm she could not concentrate on anything else. Her teeth were chattering and her fingers clumsy and she wished she had brought her cashmere shawl with her. Even with her long-sleeved cambric gown with a high neck and spencer, she was still chilled to the marrow.

As soon as the wood caught she added more lumps of coal and then some logs from the basket standing beside the fireplace. Her hands were grimy; she needed to wipe them. Perhaps there was something she could use in either the sideboard or the desk.

Her search proved futile, but the worst of the dirt had been removed by her rummage through the furniture. There were several ledgers in the desk drawer and she thought she might peruse one whilst she waited. But first she must discover if there was a bell with which to summon assistance.

Even after a thorough investigation of every nook and cranny she had still not found what she wanted. She was unsure what to do next. Should she remain where she was and hope that eventually someone would find her, or venture out again and continue along the icy passageways until she found a way back into the heated part of the house?

Perhaps she would stay here until she was warm and could feel her extremities once more. She took one of the ledgers over to an armchair and curled up with the book in her lap. She might as well read this as she had nothing else to do. Idly she flicked open the book and at once realised this was no recent record but something ancient.

The writing was almost indecipherable, with so many loops and whorls she could hardly distinguish one word from the next. The page she was studying appeared to be about expenditures of some sort, as there were figures amongst the words.

As she read, the tips of her fingers began to

tingle unpleasantly. There was something about this book she didn't like. She tried to throw it to the floor but her hands were stuck fast. It was as if ice was slowly travelling up her arms. With a sickening certainty she knew she was holding the diary of one of the evil spirits, and it was somehow reaching out through the words to ensnare her for a second time.

★ ★ ★

Adam watched Miss Bennet stalk off and waited for one of the others to call her back, but no one did; and before he could do so himself she was gone. 'Miss Darcy, I do not think Miss Bennet should be wandering around the corridors on her own at the moment.'

As the girl scrambled to her feet, her brother held up his hand. 'No, Georgiana, King is quite correct. I shall go myself and find her. We should not have laughed at her; she is too young to take that in her stride without embarrassment.' He turned to his wife, who was looking anxious, but made no attempt to join him. 'Lizzy, I shall not be long, and in my absence could I suggest that together you try and come up with something that might work in this difficult situation?'

'I should like to accompany you,' Adam said. 'I believe that knowledge of this vast establishment will hold me in good stead.'

Mr Darcy's lips thinned and he looked every inch the aristocratic owner of the biggest estate in Derbyshire. Then he nodded. 'Very well, King. She cannot have gone far. We should have no difficulty discovering her.'

After a fruitless twenty minutes, Miss Bennet was still missing. 'The temperature has dropped in the past hour,' said Mr Darcy. 'I believe this corridor to be below freezing.' He pointed at the window. 'Well I'll be damned! There are icicles forming inside — I cannot remember that ever happening before.'

'It's unnatural. I believe that somehow what lives in the east wing has managed to migrate to this part of the house.' His fists clenched and an icy dread squeezed his heart. 'I can think of only one reason this might be happening, Darcy: they have found access through Miss Bennet. She is in extreme danger. We must find her immediately.'

He stood, unable to decide what to do next. He was an ex-soldier, used to taking charge and making life-or-death decisions. His breathing calmed and he was once more in control. Mr Darcy was watching him, waiting for him to dictate their next move.

Adam made his decision. 'If we follow the

icy chill that is pervading these corridors I am certain we shall find Miss Bennet. She must have taken refuge in one of the little-used chambers in this part of the house.' He breathed in deeply whilst slowly rotating clockwise. 'This way; it is definitely colder in this direction.' Not waiting for Mr Darcy to follow, he removed the large brass cross from his pocket and held it in front of him, praying that the power of God would offer him, and the girl in the devil's clutches, some protection.

The inside of his nose was freezing. He saw frost forming on the door on the right. He skidded to a halt and charged through shoulder first.

12

Kitty was reciting the Lord's Prayer over and over again in the hope that this might slow down the inexorable progress of whatever it was. She would not sit here and be devoured by evil. Somehow she would fight back and gain her freedom.

She jumped from the chair and shook her hands frantically, but the book did not budge. The fire. If the diary were pushed into the flames she would surely be released. That she might well be seriously hurt in the process seemed of little consequence — better burned than frozen solid.

The power of the book was attempting to drag her to the far side of the room but she fought back. Inch by inch she edged towards the fireplace with her arms unwillingly outstretched. The ghosts were almost wrenching them from her shoulders.

The closer she got to the heat the harder it was to move. Whatever was controlling her understood what she was trying to do and was equally determined to prevent it. The pain was unbearable. With a final heave she attempted to fling herself backwards, but the evil force was too strong and instead she tumbled forwards to land face first on the carpet. Winded, she gasped for breath, knowing that every second she lay there brought her certain death closer. She was finding it more difficult to concentrate — but still managed to send up a fervent prayer for deliverance.

The door crashed open and both Mr King and Mr Darcy were at her side. From somewhere she found the strength to whisper, 'It is the book — take it from me, I beg you, before it kills me.'

'God's teeth!' exclaimed Mr Darcy. 'The damn thing is glued to her fingers. How in God's name are we going to release her? Her hands and forearms are already as cold as ice — if we do not set her free immediately the ice will reach her heart.' Darcy was trying to tear the book from her hands with no success.

'Let me try. My cross is more powerful than any devil's book.' Mr King slammed the cross onto the book cover and for a moment Kitty thought he had failed. Then the hideous thing dropped to the floor. Immediately Mr King snatched it up and hurled it into the flames.

Mr Darcy put his arms around her and, just as the diary exploded in a shower of red-hot pieces, pulled her clear of danger.

The room went black, the candles and flames extinguished instantly. For a dreadful moment Kitty thought she had been transported into the east wing and was trapped as she had been before. Then the heavy, warm weight of Mr Darcy pressing her into the boards reassured her that wherever she was, she wasn't alone.

'Are you hurt, Kitty?' he asked urgently. 'There was some sort of explosion.'

'I am well, thank you. Why is it so dark? Should there not be light coming in from the window?'

Before he could answer, a stream of impolite invective poured from Mr King. She had never heard such dreadful language and hoped never to do so again. This was accompanied by the strong smell of burning.

An unexpected bubble of mirth escaped her. 'Mr King, are you on fire?'

He stopped swearing and laughed. 'I do beg your pardon, Miss Bennet. Barrack-room manners. I am indeed a trifle singed, but otherwise only my dignity is damaged. It's damned dark in here, Darcy.'

'Indeed it is. How very observant of you both.' His snort of laughter made Kitty feel a little less terrified. He rolled away from her and in one smooth movement regained his feet and pulled her up to join him. 'Are you able to stand up, King?'

'I shall be on my feet immediately. I must remove my jacket, for it is still smouldering. I am puzzled that we cannot see each other.'

Kitty heard him stand and then remove his jacket, but the blackness remained impenetrable. All desire to laugh evaporated. 'I think we are in the east wing. It was as black as this, but when there I could hear nothing. Please, can we go somewhere I can be warm again?'

'Of course, sweetheart,' said Mr Darcy. 'You will soon be safe.' He removed his own jacket and draped it around her shoulders. 'This should help until we are back in the main part of the house.'

There was a thump and Kitty almost lost her balance as Mr King arrived beside her. 'Here, let me get past; I shall lead the way. Miss Bennet, hold on to my shirt. Darcy, stand behind her and put your arms on my shoulders. That way I believe we will all have the protection of my cross.'

They did as he suggested; the feeling of dread lessened once Kitty was parcelled between the two gentlemen. She pressed her cheek into Mr King's waistcoat and almost choked from the stench of burnt material. There was no time to ponder on this worry as he spoke firmly in the black obscurity.

'If we are still, as I pray we are within the chamber in which we found you, then the door must be a few feet in front of me. Unnatural forces are at work here, which is why the door closed behind us. I intend to walk forward holding the cross out. Stay in close contact; we are less vulnerable as a unit.'

'Get on with it, man,' Mr Darcy urged. 'There is something moving behind us. We need to get out of here.'

Kitty's knees almost gave way beneath her at his words. She could hear the hideous shuffling too. They were not alone in this room. Something was looking for them in the darkness.

'Hold tight, and whatever you do don't let go. Your lives might depend on it.' Mr King lurched forward and Kitty hung on desperately. Mr Darcy's arms supported her as they moved rapidly towards the exit. Mr King's outstretched arms crashed into the closed door and Kitty was cannoned backwards. Fortunately Mr Darcy retained his grip and they all remained on their feet.

'The door won't open,' said Mr King.

The shuffling, scraping sounds were closer. The room was colder. The air was being sucked from Kitty's lungs and the smell of gunpowder was overwhelming.

'I demand that you release us in the name of the Father, Son, and God Almighty,' Mr King roared.

Suddenly light flooded over them, the door opened, and they tumbled head first into the passageway. Mr Darcy was on his feet first and slammed the door behind them. Now that they were in his own domain, he took charge.

'Quickly — we must barricade this door; make sure nobody attempts to enter and whatever is in there cannot get out.'

The two men dragged two wooden settles from an adjoining room and stacked them, one on top of the other, against the door. Kitty leant forlornly against the wall, watching them in their feverish activity. This was not how things were supposed to be. Her new life at Pemberley should have been filled with gaiety and laughter, family and affection — but instead she was in a living nightmare.

She wanted to go back to Longbourn, to safety; to hear Mama complaining and see Papa skulking off to the library to read his books on astronomy and science. She closed her eyes and pressed her fists into her mouth trying to hold back her sobs, but tears dripped unheeded down her cheeks.

Then she was enveloped in a strong, warm embrace. She didn't have to look up; she knew immediately this was Mr King. 'Miss Bennet — Kitty — don't cry. You have been so brave. Just hold on a little longer and all will be well. Hush, now; I cannot bear to see you so distressed.' He rocked her like a child, and stroked her back whilst murmuring reassurance and comfort.

'Bring her to my apartment, King. We cannot hang about here; it is not safe.'

'Up you come, sweetheart. Put your arm around my neck and I shall carry you.'

She did as Mr King bid, too exhausted and dispirited to argue that she was quite capable of walking. She snuggled into his embrace and her eyes closed. She was warm, protected, and so very, very tired.

* * *

Adam followed Mr Darcy through the rabbit warren of smaller corridors until they re-emerged into the central passageway he recognised. 'Kitty is asleep. I hope this second experience will not prove too much for her nerves.'

'I shall take better care of her in future. I must admit I was not altogether in favour of her moving here; she had not endeared herself to me on our previous meetings. However, within a few hours of her arrival I had revised my opinion. She is like a sister to me now, and I will protect her with my life as I would any other member of my family.' He stopped in front of a pair of handsome double doors and pushed them open. A footman belatedly appeared at their side.

'Send word at once to the drawing room that we shall be joining them soon. Have coffee and refreshments sent there as well.'

The chamber was substantial and expensively furnished, Adam noted, if a trifle old-fashioned. They were greeted by Mr Darcy's valet, who kept a commendably straight face. 'Kindly direct me to Mrs Darcy's room. Miss Bennett is in need of attention,' Adam said.

'If you care to follow me, sir, she will be well looked after.'

Darcy spoke from behind him. 'When you have left Kitty, come through to my room. We are much of a size and I shall find you a fresh shirt and jacket. Will you require the services of the physician?'

'I think not; the book did not penetrate more than my jacket. I shall be with you directly.' Adam placed the sleeping girl on what was a bed that was never used. Mrs Darcy obviously occupied Mr Darcy's chamber full-time. He decided at that moment that when he eventually married, it would be to a girl like Elizabeth Darcy: someone who could share his life in every aspect and not just be the mother of his children and the chatelaine of his house.

As he turned to leave, Kitty stirred. 'Please, Mr King, I beg you — do not leave me to find my way alone to the drawing room.'

'I should not dream of abandoning you to the empty corridors. Darcy and I are going to change and will remain in this apartment until you are ready to leave, however long that might be.'

She sat up and managed to summon a wan smile. 'I am feeling a lot better and no longer wish to sleep. When I am tidy I will join you.'

'Do not hurry on our account, Kitty. We are content to wait. We have sent word to the drawing room that you are safely restored to us, so they will not be waiting anxiously anymore.'

He left her in the hands of two maids, one of whom must be Mrs Darcy's dresser. No doubt they would find the girl something suitable to wear — she was about the same size as her sister. He knocked on the communicating door and was bid to enter.

This chamber was the larger of the two, dominated by a massive tester bed, but still leaving room for several groups of furniture. Mr Darcy shouted to him from an adjoining room, presumably the washroom.

'In here, King — there is sufficient hot water for both of us. My valet is sorting you out some fresh garments. How is Kitty doing?'

'She is awake and getting changed.' He joined his host in a commodious bathing room and stripped off the remnants of his ruined shirt, neckcloth and waistcoat. 'I fear she will not walk about this house without an escort in future. And I cannot say that I blame her after what she has experienced.'

'I have been thinking about that these past few minutes and believe this house is no longer safe. I have no other option but to close it down and move elsewhere until the east wing is demolished and the remains of the structure scattered many miles from here.'

'If you do that, Darcy, then you must give your staff a reason for the evacuation, find accommodation for all of them, and then suffer the gossip that will inevitably follow such an action.' He scrubbed his face and forearms, but needed assistance to do his back. He was about to ask Mr Darcy, when his companion swore.

'God's teeth, King, your back needs urgent attention. Does it not hurt like the very devil?'

'I wasn't aware of it until I removed the remnants of my shirt, but now it is decidedly sore. I have no wish to send for the doctor and explain how I came by these injuries. Would your man be prepared to clean me up?'

After several painful minutes Dawson declared him free of burnt material, had liberally spread Mr King's back with a noxious ointment, and declared him fit to dress. Mr Darcy had left him to it.

'Allow me to assist you into your shirt, sir. I have found a voluminous one that will cause you no discomfort.'

In order to tuck the tails of his shirt between his legs he would have to lower his breeches, and hesitated for a moment to do this in front of a stranger. Then shrugged and did what was necessary, glad that his buttocks had not been damaged in the assault from the exploding book.

Dawson helped him put on a green silk waistcoat and then carefully slid a dark green jacket across his injured back. His own man, Hobson, never offered to tie his neckcloth for him, but he did not object when Darcy's man deftly folded his and arranged it.

'There, Mr King, as good as new. You are broader in the shoulders than Mr Darcy, but this jacket was ill-made and he has never worn it. Is there anything else I can do for you, sir?'

Adam examined himself in the glass and was more than satisfied with his appearance. 'Thank you; I much appreciate your assistance.'

★ ★ ★

Kitty sat on the edge of the bed whilst a selection of gowns were held up for her inspection. The third one — a long-sleeved, high-necked dress in a heavy green cambric — would be ideal. The lace around the cuffs and hem relieved the plainness. 'That one will be perfect, thank you,' she said to Annie. 'Thankfully my chemise and petticoat are undamaged by my fall, so I do not need to change those. However, I would be grateful for hot water so that I may wash my face and hands.'

Despite her wish to hurry, so she would not keep the gentlemen waiting any longer than necessary, everything seemed to take an age to complete. Finally she was ready, her hair freshly dressed with dark green ribbons threaded through it, her face and hands free of smuts; and Lizzy's gown had been dropped over her head.

'You look a picture, miss, if you don't mind

my saying so. Green brings out the colour in your eyes.'

'It is a very pretty gown; thank you so much for helping me.' The servants had not asked how she came to be in such a state and she had offered no explanation.

She hurried into the pretty sitting room, but found it to be empty. The sound of male voices came from a half-open door on the far wall — they were in there waiting for her. She moved towards it, not sure if she should knock or just walk in. While she had been busy with her toilette she had been able to push what had happened to the back of her mind; but now that she was about to rejoin Mr Darcy and Mr King and be obliged to go out into the corridor again, her fear flooded back.

She could not dither about out here: Georgiana, Lizzy, Jane and Mr Bingley must be beside themselves with worry at this long delay. She raised her hand to knock on the door, but instead of a polite tap her fist came down hard and the door smashed back against the wall.

The two gentlemen stared at her in shock and she wished the floor would open and swallow her up. Heat travelled from her toes to the crown of her head and she was struck dumb by embarrassment.

Then Mr King was at her side. 'Kitty, are you quite well? You startled us by your dramatic entrance and I feared something else had frightened you.'

She hung her head and mumbled an apology. 'I did not mean to. I'm sorry I have kept you waiting; I am ready now.'

'You look charming in that gown, Kitty,' said Mr Darcy, 'and you have not kept us waiting; King has only just arrived.' He walked towards her, his expression serious, and held out his hand. She had no option but to place one of hers in it. He drew her closer to him. 'I want you to know, sweetheart, that I think of you as my little sister and will not let anything do you harm. In future I wish you to call me Fitzwilliam.'

Her mouth fell open. It took several seconds to recover her voice. 'I could not do that — Mama would go to bed for a week with her nerves if she was to hear of it.'

He laughed and dropped an affectionate kiss on the top of her head. 'Then it is fortunate, Kitty, that she remains in Longbourn.'

He kept his arm around her shoulders whilst he and Mr King entertained her with light-hearted chatter, and before she realised it they were walking through the library and almost at their destination.

'If I have your permission, Darcy, might I too dispense with formality and call her Kitty?' asked Mr King. 'After what we have shared together, I believe we have earned the right to call each other by our given names.'

'Excellent. It will be far easier if we are on familiar terms.' He raised an eyebrow and Mr King — no, he must be Adam in future — chuckled.

'Have no fear; I have no intention of addressing you as anything but Darcy.'

'That is a relief, for I do not believe my toplofty standing could survive such a thing.'

They entered the drawing room in a remarkably good humour, considering what had taken place, and were greeted by shrieks of excitement and joy as if they had been gone for weeks and not an hour or so.

13

'At last!' exclaimed Lizzy as she ran and threw herself into Darcy's arms. (Calling him Fitzwilliam even in her head was going to be nigh on impossible, Kitty thought.) 'We have been waiting this age for you to come. I am not sure if the coffee will be hot enough; I shall send for fresh immediately.'

'We apologise for keeping you waiting, my love. You will understand when we explain the whole to you.' He returned her embrace in full measure. At that moment Kitty decided that if she ever got married, it would be to a gentleman who would love her as wholeheartedly as Fitzwilliam loved Lizzy.

Georgiana kissed her on both cheeks. 'You are wearing one of Lizzy's gowns; it suits you admirably. But I am curious to know why you are obliged to do so.'

'Your brother will explain everything; but if you will forgive me, I wish to sit by the fire and have something hot to drink.' Kitty surveyed the spread laid out on a large octagonal table. 'I shall also have piece of plum cake, and scones and strawberry conserve.'

She settled on a small sofa and her friend joined her. She glanced up to see Mr King — no, he was to be Adam now — smiling in her direction. She beckoned him over. 'After all the excitement I find myself quite ravenous. Would you like me to butter a scone or cut you a piece of cake . . . Adam?'

The shocked gasp at her breach of etiquette coming from beside her made her want to giggle. He grinned and winked. Even more shocking! 'I should love both, Kitty, if you would be so kind. Shall I pour us both a cup of coffee?'

Whilst they were occupied with cake and coffee, the others joined them around the fire. There was almost a party atmosphere as they chatted brightly and munched the delicious cake and scones and drank the bitter aromatic brew Kitty had come to love. Then everything changed.

'If you have all finished eating, we have much to discuss,' Mr Darcy said, putting down his cup.

Each in turn did as he had, and then sat quietly waiting for him to speak. He gave a brief but detailed description of what had taken place. Hearing it so boldly put sent tremors up Kitty's spine, despite being so closely situated to the substantial fire. When Mr Darcy had completed the terrifying account, he sat back and waited for their reaction. Adam was the first to respond.

'I have a suggestion to make before you start packing to remove from here. I should like to walk around the house and see for myself if the evil has gone. I am of the opinion that they can only reach us if we come into contact with an object that once belonged to one of them, or get too close to a communicating door.' He paused and looked around to see if his words were being received well or rejected.

'Whatever you say, King, both Lizzy and the girls have come into contact with them in the gallery several yards from the door,' said Mr Darcy.

'Would it not be possible to close the gallery and great stairs? We could all use the oak staircase in future,' Georgiana said, 'rather than move away just before the festivities start.'

'I was about to suggest that you girls move downstairs, but after this morning's episode I am not sure that would be any safer.' Lizzy looked at Mr Darcy for confirmation. 'I would much prefer to remain here, Fitzwilliam, if you and Adam decide that it is safe to do so.'

'We could move into the west wing with Jane and Mr Bingley, couldn't we?' suggested Georgiana.

'Excellent idea,' said Mr. Darcy. 'In fact it would make more sense for Lizzy and me to take an apartment there as well. In fact, I believe there are sufficient chambers to accommodate our guests if we decide to proceed with the Christmas arrangements.' He frowned and ran his hands through his hair, making it stand on end. 'However, until I am satisfied that whatever lurks in the east wing is not going to be a danger to us, I shall not make a decision about closing Pemberley.'

Adam stood up. 'I am going to patrol the corridors. Unfortunately I do not know this vast establishment and will need a guide if I am not to become lost.'

Kitty found herself on her feet beside him with no clear recollection of having made that decision. 'I shall come with you. If I can walk about safely I think everybody else will be able to as well. I believe that for some reason they are drawn to me.'

'Out of the question, my girl. You have endured more than enough today. I will not have you putting yourself in any further danger. I shall come with you, King — '

Lizzy interrupted him. 'I think that Kitty is right, dearest. She will be perfectly safe if both of you are beside her. Let her come; that way I shall be sanguine about remaining under this roof.'

The gentlemen exchanged glances and then both nodded. Mr Bingley made no move to join them. Was he not brave enough to face whatever spirits haunted this house? Jane was looking peaky; was it possible she too was in an interesting condition? Kitty decided she would make discreet enquiries later on.

'You shall not go on your own — I shall come too.' Georgiana rushed to her side and put her arm through Kitty's in a proprietorial manner as if daring anyone to detach her.

'Very well, you shall both come with us,' declared Mr Darcy. 'Do you have a crucifix you could put on before we leave? The one that Adam has seems to be an excellent barrier.'

'I believe I have one in my reticule,' Georgiana said and ran over to snatch up her bag and rummage in it. She held up the delicate cross and gold chain triumphantly. Mr Darcy helped her put it on.

Immediately Jane began to fumble at her neck. 'Here, Kitty, I am wearing one. You take mine; you need it more than I do at the moment.' Mr Bingley removed it for her and brought it over, still warm from her neck.

Adam reached out and took it, then gestured for Kitty to turn so he could fasten it securely. 'There, I believe you will be safer now. You must stay close together and let

186

Darcy and me walk on either side. Is that quite clear?'

Kitty thought it strange Adam was issuing orders when Mr Darcy was standing right beside him. She supposed that being an ex-soldier and a man of God gave him precedence in this matter. The thought of her formidable brother-in-law taking second place was a novel one; she was quite certain that before he had married Lizzy this would never have occurred.

The room was subdued as they set off, Jane and Mr Bingley sitting close together holding hands in front of the fire, pale-faced and anxious. It seemed inappropriate to bid them farewell, so Kitty contented herself with a smile and a nod of her head.

Once outside and the door closed, they waited for Adam to decide where they should go first. 'I would like to walk around the guest wing, Darcy, as this is where you will be living if you decide to remain here.'

'Although we tend to refer to the oak staircase in derogatory terms, it is a magnificently carved set of stairs and of equal importance historically as the others. It will be no hardship using those for the foreseeable future.'

Georgiana's fingers were digging painfully into Kitty's arm. Kitty wished her friend had not decided to accompany them, as she had been terrified in the gallery. 'Your sister should not come with us; we would do better with just the three of us.' This sounded rather abrupt, but she had no wish to say she thought Georgiana too weak-spirited to cope with what might happen.

Instantly her arm was released. 'If you are sure you can manage by yourselves, I should much prefer to stay behind with Jane and Bingley.' With an apologetic smile, Georgiana rushed back into the drawing room.

'That was well done of you, Kitty,' said Mr Darcy. 'King and I are in a better position to protect you now.'

She wasn't sure how they would proceed, in single file or side by side. Adam made the decision for her by taking her hand and placing it through his arm. She stepped closer, wanting to feel the security of his warmth through her gown. Mr Darcy took the lead and they fell into step behind him.

The route down the central flagstone passageway was straightforward and mercifully free of the icy chill associated with the evil spirits. They passed several footmen about their duties but they ignored them. What they thought of this strange parade Kitty had no idea, but no doubt it would be the subject of gossip in the evening when they had finished work.

By the time they reached the second staircase that led directly to the west wing, Kitty was rather breathless but was certain this side of the house was free of ghosts. 'Have we walked through all the passageways we would be using if we moved here?' Kitty asked when Mr Darcy finally paused.

He nodded and pointed to a staircase that must lead to a third floor. 'There are still the smaller chambers, which would be used by the older progeny of our guests, to examine; then we will have done. Am I right in assuming that so far you have found nothing untoward?'

'If there was anything unpleasant I would have felt a strange coldness in my fingers, and I have not done so. I was wondering, do the servants sleep anywhere near the east wing?'

'No, the men sleep downstairs and the girls in the attics in this wing. Fortunately they will not have come in contact with that side of the house at all — apart from when they clean the chambers that adjoin.'

After a brief inspection of the smaller but more than adequate guest rooms on the upper floor, Kitty was convinced this half of the house was quite safe. As they were making their way back to the drawing room something occurred to her. 'Have you thought of what you are going to say to your staff to explain why we are abandoning our chambers? Also, there will need to be an underlying reason given to your guests.'

Mr Darcy smiled. 'I have some ideas, but thought we could discuss them when we rejoin the others. Lizzy might well have some pertinent suggestions.'

★ ★ ★

That was indeed the case, as Kitty's sister had been discussing this very subject in their absence. Once they were all ensconced around the fire, Lizzy told them what she had in mind.

'Mr Bingley suggested the closure of this part of the house could be put down to an infestation of some sort.' She looked at Mr Darcy and he nodded.

'My sisters and I were once invited to visit a grand house in Herefordshire,' said Mr Bingley, 'and when we arrived the place was in turmoil. Insects that destroy the fabric of the building had been discovered and half the house was abandoned until they could be dealt with.'

'Were you still able to stay there, Bingley?' Adam asked.

'Although not as grand as Pemberley, the

place was substantial and the family and house guests used the rooms that were free of infestation. If I recall correctly, we had a very jolly time.'

'If we use the same ploy, Fitzwilliam, I believe we can continue to live here without alarming the staff or cancelling our arrangements,' Lizzy said. 'Even if we close the music room and the reception room holding the great staircase, we will still have more than enough space to entertain a hundred guests.'

He looked thoughtful and didn't answer for a moment. 'Kitty, could I prevail upon you to do one more thing? I want to see how far the *infestation* has spread. I believe that only our apartment, being adjacent to the east wing, is at any risk. If I am proved correct, then you and Georgiana can remain where you are, and so can Jane and Mr Bingley.'

Adam looked unconvinced but made no adverse comment. 'I am prepared to come with you, but can we do it immediately, before it gets fully dark?'

'The sconces will have been lit by now, Kitty dearest,' Lizzy said. 'However, I wonder why no servant has complained of seeing apparitions or experiencing unpleasantness when they have been in this part of the house.'

'That is a question I cannot answer, Mrs

Darcy, but I sincerely believe anyone venturing there is at risk, although for some reason we are more vulnerable than your staff.'

Adam was on his feet and held out his hand. Kitty took it without hesitation; his calloused palm and strong grip were becoming pleasantly familiar. Strangely none of the assembled company looked at all shocked or put out by this. A warm glow suffused her cheeks as she considered what might be the reason for this acceptance of such a breach of etiquette.

She glanced at him and his eyes held hers for a moment. Her heart skipped a beat and she could not prevent a smile from curving her lips.

* * *

Adam caught his breath. He had known Kitty for less than a week and had quite inexplicably fallen irrevocably in love with her. He had never thought to meet the young lady of his dreams in such a bizarre fashion. Neither had he expected to give his heart so suddenly to a girl who must be almost ten years his junior.

Her smile was radiant. She was without doubt the most beautiful woman he had ever set eyes on. He was not easily bedazzled by such things, being more interested in what went on inside a person than in their outer appearance. Kitty had proved herself braver than many soldiers he had fought with, kind and considerate and with a lively wit. When this wretched business was over he would speak to Mr Darcy and ask his permission to pay court to his ward.

A surge of happiness and confidence flooded through him. He knew now why God had sent him to Bakewell: not only to fight the demons that had taken root in Pemberley, but also to meet the girl who would become his wife. He sent up a heartfelt prayer of thanks. His life was not to be a lonely one, clattering around in a large house on his own; but he was to have a loving partner to share in his mission and, God willing, the blessing of children to make their family complete.

Buoyed up by this amazing revelation, his hands tightened on hers and to his joy she returned the pressure. 'If you are quite sure you are ready for this, Kitty, let us get on with it. There is no need for anyone else to accompany us this time; we are now familiar with the layout of the house.'

His host's lips thinned. Mr Darcy did not like being given orders in his own house, and

Adam didn't blame him. Before the well-deserved set-down could be given, Adam raised his hand in a gesture of surrender. 'That was unpardonably rude of me. I hope you will forgive me, Darcy. Less than six months ago I was still an officer and am still over-fond of giving orders. No excuse, I know, but I hope to do better in future.'

Disaster was averted. 'I am a proud man and find it difficult to take second place. However, in *this* matter I believe you must be the leader. You have a connection to a higher power and I must stand aside because of that.'

Adam understood his message. He could take the lead in fighting the evil, but when this matter was finished he would resume his place if he wished to remain within the Darcy family circle. 'If you have no objection, sir, Kitty and I will make an excursion to the music room, great stairs and gallery. I shall keep her safe; no harm shall come to her whilst she is under my protection.'

Her hand was trembling as he tucked it through his arm. He gave her a conspiratorial wink and was rewarded with a stifled giggle. He guided her to the far side of the room where the door that connected to the music room was situated. 'Are you ready, Kitty? No one will think the worse of you if you change your mind.'

'I can do anything if you are beside me. Darcy is right to say you have a strength that none of us possess — but I am not certain if it is coming from within you or because you are a man of the cloth.'

Although the drawing room was less than half the size of the music room it must still measure more than ten yards from side to side. This meant the group by the fire could no longer hear them.

'Kitty, my dear, there is something most important I must say to you before we venture forth.' She looked expectantly at him, her beautiful eyes widening as if she guessed his intention.

'Please, Adam, we must not think of ourselves at this time. We must concentrate on keeping everyone safe and finding a way to defeat the spirits. As far as I am concerned, containing them is not enough; we must find a way to send them to hell where they belong.'

'You are right, my love, to stop me. But be very sure when everything is settled I shall be speaking to Darcy and your sister. Are you ready to go through the door?'

14

Lizzy watched her sister and Mr King talk earnestly by the door and then walk through. 'Fitzwilliam, have you noticed how close Kitty and Mr King have become over the past few days? I am not entirely sure of her feelings, but he is definitely besotted with her. What do you think? Am I imagining things because of my condition?'

He glanced across to see that his sister was occupied with Jane and Mr Bingley before answering quietly. 'I agree with you, darling, and applaud his choice. She would make him an ideal wife, and to have her living permanently so close to us would be ideal.'

'Good heavens! Have you too fallen under her spell? Being closest to Lydia in age, Kitty became influenced by my youngest sister's wild behaviour. However, I believe her to be more like me in character than either Jane or Mary, and I am very fond of her too.'

The third time she glanced at the door he took her hands in his. 'They will come to no harm. I have every confidence in King. Let us talk about something else; it will take your mind off what might be going on next door.'

He raised his voice and called to the other three. 'Come and join us over here; we wish to make plans for the soirée that will be taking place in two days' time.'

After a lively discussion the evening had been planned down to the last minute. When their guests arrived there would be champagne served in the great hall, dinner would be *à la français* with four courses and several removes, then afterwards there would be dancing, and cards for those who did not dance.

Satisfied that her first Pemberley party would be a success, Lizzy now asked them to put their minds to what entertainment should be provided for the six families who would be joining them at the end of next week.

'There will be three young gentlemen and two young ladies around the same age as you and Kitty, Georgiana, and I was hoping you would get together and put on a Christmas pantomime or play. This could be performed the afternoon of Christmas Eve, which always seems to drag a little.'

'I should like that above anything. We have never done anything of that sort before. It would be great fun to enact a fairytale — perhaps Cinderella would be a good choice.'

'I was thinking of inviting King to stay with

us for the twelve days,' said Mr Darcy. 'He has only to take three services during that time, and whatever the weather I am sure he can get to and fro without difficulty. I think he might enjoy being in the congregation in our chapel instead of leading the prayers himself.'

'I would feel more comfortable knowing he was living here,' Jane said. She smiled sweetly at Bingley and then continued shyly, 'I too am in an interesting condition, Lizzy. Our babies will be born next summer. I sincerely hope Charles and I have found ourselves a suitable property by then.'

'Ingram has been looking for the past two weeks and should have a list of properties for you to view in the New Year,' said Mr Darcy. 'There are several substantial estates that would be suitable and all are within ten miles of here.'

A further half-hour went by, and still there was no sign of Kitty or Mr King.

★   ★   ★

Kitty and Adam stood arm in arm looking down the length of the music room. Since the pianoforte, harp and all the other musical instruments had been moved into the great hall, the room looked strangely empty. Mind you, as it was more than thirty yards in length and twenty in breadth, this was hardly surprising.

'Do you feel anything odd, Kitty? This chamber feels no different from next door to me.'

She released her hold on his arm and stepped away to stand in the centre of the polished boards. At this end there were no expensive carpets and she felt vulnerable and alone, but if she were to remain at his side she was certain his presence would be protecting her. This was the only way to ascertain how far the spectres had managed to spread.

'I think that despite this room sharing a wall with the east wing, the lack of a communicating door has kept it free from harm. Shall we go into the chamber next door where the great stairs are and see how we feel? I don't remember if there is a connecting door on that floor, do you?'

'The only time I used them was when I came to help you. I was in too much of a hurry to notice.' He walked to her side and retrieved her hand, this time putting his arm around her waist. This was a dreadful breach of etiquette; Mama would have a conniption fit if she were ever to hear about it.

Instead of complaining, she smiled up at him and saw his eyes darken. For a delicious moment she thought he might be going to kiss her; however, he merely smiled and that had to be enough for now.

'Let us get this over with as quickly as we can,' she said. 'I don't like being away from the others, even though I know you will take care of me.'

'We will walk slowly to the centre of the room. As soon as you feel anything, we will retreat. I am not letting you stand by yourself, and I have no wish to ascend the stairs either.'

The double doors that led to the stairway were firmly shut but he managed to open them without releasing her. Once they were through he pulled them closed. Kitty's heart was hammering so hard she was surprised he did not hear it. Her stomach lurched unpleasantly and she wished she had not eaten so much cake.

Slowly they walked the short distance from the door to the stairs. So far nothing untoward had occurred.

'Let me stand on the stairs by myself, Adam. You can stay close by.' Reluctantly he removed his arm and she took two steps on her own.

'I do feel something, but it is not the same as before. I can't quite describe it, but it is as if something or someone is calling to me. I'm in no danger today.'

Before he could restrain her she picked up her skirts and ran to the gallery. As soon as she stepped onto the expanse of polished boards a swirl of grey and black mist enshrouded her. She had made a grave error — she should have stayed with Adam. She tried to retrace her steps but was being dragged inexorably towards the communicating door behind the curtain.

Somehow she managed to look over her shoulder but could no longer see the head of the staircase or hear Adam calling to her. She was surrounded by these beings from the underworld; they were going to take her and there was nothing she could do about it.

She waited for the cold to spread from her fingertips, for the air to be slowly sucked from her lungs, but she remained relatively warm and her breathing was as normal. Her panic subsided. For some inexplicable reason the demons were not intending to kill her.

Slowly her hands unclenched and her heart returned to its normal place behind her bodice. She dared to open her eyes, and to her astonishment the clouds of vapour were forming into a recognisable shape. The figure of a man emerged from the mist, a man dressed in the clothes of long ago. He had dark hair and was quite recognisably a Darcy ancestor.

Was he going to speak to her? Should she curtsy to a ghost? Strangely she was less afraid of this apparition than she had been of the suffocating darkness and odd shuffling noises.

He bowed low and his golden frock coat flapped around him almost as if he were real. 'I bid you good morrow, mistress. Henry Darcy at your service. I wish to speak to you most urgently.'

Kitty wasn't sure if she had actually heard his words being spoken or if the sound was only in her head. 'I am Miss Catherine Bennet. You almost killed me the other day, so why should I wish to speak to you now?'

'I beg your pardon for that error, Miss Bennet. At that time we did not know you would be of assistance to us.'

'I don't understand; how can I be of use to you? Surely you should be contacting a Darcy.' The shape shimmered and an icy shiver gripped her. The apparition was not pleased. She spoke again, hoping to placate him. 'Are you seeking justice for your untimely deaths? I am not sure how this could be achieved, but I am willing to do what I can to put matters right.'

The cold retreated and the ghost regained its human form. 'In order for us to depart this world we must have retribution. Someone must pay. A descendant of the man who orchestrated our murder must also die unnaturally.'

'That is what I thought must happen. If I give you my word I will do everything in my power to help you, will you agree to leave the family alone?'

Again the spectre wavered, its edges becoming indistinct, its shape more wispy than before. 'You have until Christmas Eve. After that we shall wreak our own revenge and take the lives of all who remain within these walls.'

His image faded, leaving her alone in front of the curtain that concealed the burnt panelling and communicating door. Before she could make sense of what had transpired, she was swept into a fierce embrace.

'My God, what happened to you? I was held fast, could not move my feet an inch, and saw you surrounded by those demons. Are you unhurt?'

'Adam, you will not believe what I saw.' She pushed herself free and ran around the space. 'He has kept his word; the gallery is safe. We do not have to barricade anything or change our plans; Pemberley is safe until the night before Christmas.'

They returned using the main staircase and dashed to the drawing room, bursting in so eagerly that the occupants were scared half to death. Kitty, breathless with excitement, told them the whole; and when she had finished her extraordinary story they were all struck silent.

Eventually Mr Darcy shook his head. 'If you had told me all this two weeks ago I would have thought you fit for an asylum, my dear. But now I am just horrified by your story.'

Kitty's excitement evaporated. 'But surely what happened is a good thing? All we have to do is — ' Then the enormity of Henry Darcy's demands finally sank in. She collapsed on a chair and buried her head in her hands.

'I see you have realised the invidious position we are now in,' Mr Darcy continued, his tone bleak. 'I'm afraid that we must cancel our Christmas guests, Lizzy. We cannot risk being here on the day before Christmas. We cannot fulfil his demand, as we cannot commit murder in order to satisfy these devils. That will make us no better than the villagers who caused this catastrophe.'

Kitty had spun from elation to despair in the space of a few minutes. Mr Darcy was quite right. In anguish she cried out, 'My promise to help was foolish, like most of the things I have done in the past year. I have made matters worse by my interference, and now we shall all have to move away.' Her shoulders slumped and tears trickled through her fingers.

Unexpectedly, a soft white handkerchief was pushed into her hand. 'Please, little one, do not cry,' said Adam. 'None of this is of your making, and nobody is blaming you.' He stroked her shoulder and gradually she controlled her tears, blew her nose and mopped her eyes, and sat up expecting to see everyone looking at her with disapproval. Instead she saw the exact opposite.

'Good girl,' said Mr Darcy. 'King is quite right: you have been incredibly brave, and have brought us ten days of safety. You must not distress yourself further.' He was smiling at her with genuine affection, and despite her fear she felt a flicker of happiness that by some miracle she had become part of this powerful gentleman's inner circle. Whatever happened over the next two weeks, she would not be sent packing back to Longbourn in disgrace.

Georgiana looked so miserable that Kitty forgot her own distress and hurried over to join her friend on the daybed. 'Everything will work out in the end, dearest, even if your brother has to demolish the east wing next year before we can return. I am now absolutely certain we are in no danger and can walk around this wonderful house without fear of being molested by evil spirits.'

'I wish I were as brave as you, Kitty, but I believe I could endure whatever might happen if I had you to keep me company.' Then her expression changed and she lowered her voice to whisper conspiratorially in her ear. 'Mr King has taken you to his heart. Do you feel the same way about him?'

Kitty glanced across at Adam, who was deep in conversation with Lizzy and Mr Darcy, so she could watch him unobserved. He was quite the most attractive man she had ever seen. He had no need of extra padding to broaden his shoulders, and was, in her opinion, even more handsome than Mr Darcy. But far more importantly, he was kind, intelligent and resourceful. She had her answer.

'Yes, he is everything a young lady could wish for in a partner. We have not spoken of our feelings, but when this business is done I believe he will be speaking to your brother. He is, I suppose, my guardian.'

Lizzy beckoned to them. 'Girls, join us over here and we will tell you what we have decided.' Once they were settled she continued. 'We are going to have our small party as planned, but letters will be sent out to our

Christmas guests that we can no longer have them here.'

She exchanged smiles with Adam, and Kitty guessed what was coming next. 'Are we to move to the rectory?' Her interruption was unpardonable. 'I beg your pardon — I should not have spoken out of turn.'

'No need to apologise, Kitty dearest. You are quite right in your assumption. Adam has kindly offered to house us all for the foreseeable future. He has more than a dozen bedrooms, as well as his own apartment on the ground floor. Our guests will be invited to join us there instead.'

This was indeed the best possible news. They could stay together as a family, enjoy the festivities as planned, and Pemberley could be scoured of the restless spirits in their absence.

'What about the staff, Lizzy?' Kitty asked. 'We cannot leave them to the mercy of those devils. Even though they need not go anywhere near the east wing, I believe the ghosts to be strong enough to escape and terrorise the entire household.'

'Fitzwilliam has decided that those we do not bring with us can move to the Dower House. It has a dozen or so chambers upstairs — sufficient for them to live comfortably until it is safe to return.'

Kitty was satisfied with this response. 'Have you come up with a suitable explanation for your neighbours and staff for the sudden vacation of Pemberley?' she asked.

'We are still of the opinion that Bingley's suggestion of an infestation by some sort of insect should be enough,' said Mr Darcy. 'We will put the house under holland covers and let it be known the restoration work will not be started until next year.' He appeared remarkably sanguine for a man whose ancestral home was about to be abandoned because of something as outlandish as an invasion of ghosts.

The handsome mantel clock struck five o'clock and Kitty prepared to leave for her apartment to change for dinner. Lizzy held up her hand to prevent her. 'After all the excitement this afternoon the gentlemen have had no time to play billiards, and we ladies have not had time for a pleasant chat. Therefore we are to dispense with both formality and dinner today. Do not look so surprised, Kitty my love; the customs here are not so set in stone they cannot be adjusted occasionally. As we all ate heartily not long ago, I have asked Cook to serve supper at nine o'clock, and so we have no necessity to change this evening.'

The gentlemen sauntered off to play

billiards, promising to return within an hour or two and join the ladies in the drawing room. Georgiana suggested she and Kitty go into the great hall and spend the time at the piano practising their duets.

* * *

Lizzy watched the girls leave and sighed. Immediately Jane came to join her. 'What is wrong, my love?' she asked. 'I know that my pregnancy is making me unnaturally fatigued, as well as having made me lose my appetite somewhat.'

'I wish that were all I had to worry about. Fitzwilliam has blithely announced we are to remove our household to the rectory at the end of the week and has also announced we will be taking some staff with us and sending the rest to idle their time away in the Dower House. However, what he has not done is set anything in motion. That, it would appear, is to be left for me to organise.'

'As you know, there is nothing I like more than writing lists, so we shall do it together. Send for Reynolds and the steward, Ingram; let them get started.'

'Calling Mr King by his given name, so soon after making his acquaintance, makes me feel a little uncomfortable, but Fitzwilliam insists that he is part of the family now. He is to make an offer for Kitty once this wretched business is over. How can that be? It took me months to realise that I loved Fitzwilliam, and yet these two appear to have made up their minds after less than a sennight.'

'I think it very romantic, Lizzy, and we could not have found a better partner for our dearest Kitty. They will have ample opportunity to get to know each other better once we are residing under his roof. Now, shall we call in your housekeeper and get started?'

'Not today. Let us enjoy this evening and try and forget we are being driven from this wonderful place by evil spirits.'

15

The billiard room was at the far end of the central part of the house. Something occurred to Adam as they were walking towards it. 'Darcy, if you are to tell your servants the house is being closed down because of an infestation of some sort, then would they not expect an expert to have visited and made this suggestion?'

'Devil take it! My wits are wandering. I should have thought of that for myself. I am afraid billiards will have to wait for another day. We must spend the next two hours marching up and down examining non-existent insect damage and generally making a fuss about nothing.' He gestured towards the great hall. 'We might as well start in there.' He grinned, making him look far more approachable. 'Remember, a lot of sighing and scratching of heads is called for.'

They wandered through the house making a great to-do about examining the panelling, shaking their heads and looking despondent, collecting together and discussing deep and meaningful matters in low and sombre voices. Adam was hard put not to laugh, but really it was no laughing matter.

Eventually they made their way back to the drawing room. If Adam had not known the truth, he would have truly believed Mr Darcy had just discovered his house was falling down about his ears. If he ever lost his fortune he could make his living on the boards.

The ladies were gathered together like a group of colourful butterflies, chatting and laughing as if they were not living next to a group of dangerous ghosts with murder on their minds. Mr Darcy closed the door behind them and immediately turned. 'I had never thought of myself as a play-actor, but I must admit I thoroughly enjoyed stalking around my house muttering gloom and doom. Word that something is seriously amiss will already be circulating below stairs.'

'Will your steward not ask why you have not called in a surveyor to confirm your findings?' Adam asked.

'Good God, he values his employment more highly than that. He will take my instructions without question.'

This was the autocratic gentleman Adam had been told to expect, but these past few days Mr Darcy had shown himself not to be a proud, toplofty gentleman at all, but a man he was coming to like very well. Adam smiled at Kitty, who had glanced through her eyelashes at him and then turned a becoming shade of pink. He thought himself a straightforward sort of man, not given to artifice of any sort; but exchanging secret smiles and whispered conversations with this delightful girl over the next few weeks was something he was actually looking forward to. Mr Darcy was not the only one who had changed.

When the ladies learned of what they had been doing the past two hours they were impressed. Lizzy became quite agitated. 'Thank goodness I did not send for Ingram or Reynolds as I had intended to, Fitzwilliam. Now they will be expecting a summons from both of us, and that will make matters so much easier. I do so hate to become involved in falsehoods, but in this case the truth cannot be shared with anyone else.'

Adam draped himself against the fireplace so he was facing Kitty. 'I'm not sure if I explained that my house is only partially furnished. My uncle, although he lived there for many years, never used the major part of the building. Perhaps tomorrow, Darcy, you could all come over and see for yourselves what you think you will need for your stay. You will also have to bring a dozen or more indoor servants if we are to open up the whole of the building. Better not to bring your butler and housekeeper, but I have accommodation for as many as you wish to bring.'

The remainder of the evening was spent pleasantly discussing how the move might be managed with the least difficulty. Both Mr Bingley and Mr Darcy were quite adamant that, as their wives were in a delicate condition, they should not do any more than was absolutely necessary. Therefore Georgiana and Kitty were to accompany Mr Darcy the next day to make the necessary lists.

After a delicious supper, the time had come for Adam to depart, but he was strangely reluctant to leave this happy family group. He had had no opportunity to further his objectives with Kitty, but the more he saw of her the more certain he was that there was no other young lady in Christendom he could love so well.

As he was driven home he had time to consider the implications of Henry Darcy's threat. It was all very well the family and staff abandoning Pemberley, but nobody had taken into account the fact that the workmen who would be demolishing the east wing would be in grave danger. Adam was sure Mr Darcy would realise he could not ask anyone to go into the place after Christmas Eve unless there was somehow a way to fulfil the ghost's demand for vengeance. The situation was impossible. He could see no way out of it.

The pleasure of the evening was replaced by a feeling of despondency, which even prayer did nothing to alleviate. The situation was insoluble. Pemberley was doomed. Unless there was a miracle, the family could never return, and the house would be left to decay. They would be unable to return and collect family treasures, so Adam must speak to Mr Darcy when he came tomorrow morning. Things could be stored in the two huge barns that were only partially filled with animal fodder. Mr Darcy already had a list of empty properties in the vicinity drawn up for Bingley and his wife; he would have to move into one of these himself, or leave the area entirely.

Adam spoke briefly to both his butler and housekeeper before retiring in order that they could get the covers removed from what furniture there was in the unused rooms. He had also asked them to make a list of what they thought was needed both upstairs and downstairs, and also to decide how many extra staff they would require when the house was fully occupied.

When he climbed into bed, after communing with the Almighty, he was feeling slightly more positive about future events. However bleak things might be for Pemberley, it was only a building. The Darcy family would continue to thrive wherever they lived.

★ ★ ★

The next morning Georgiana scrambled out of bed and ran to the window. 'I knew it! I can always tell when it has snowed in the night. Come and look, Kitty — everywhere looks so beautiful under its white blanket.'

If there was one thing Kitty did not like, it was snow. The horrid cold white stuff not only froze one's fingers; it crept into one's boots as well. She pushed herself up onto the pillows but did not vacate the warm nest the bed had become.

'I am not happy to hear the weather has deteriorated. Removing the contents of Pemberley, plus staff and ourselves, to Bakewell is going to be decidedly unpleasant in the snow.'

Her friend scampered back to bed just as two chambermaids arrived with their morning chocolate and sweet rolls. After the trays had been placed across their laps, the maids dithered a few feet from the bed as if they wished to say something.

Georgiana took pity on them. 'What is wrong, girls? Have you something you wish to ask us?'

They both bobbed in a curtsy and then the more daring of the two spoke up. 'It's like this, Miss Darcy. We've been hearing ever so many things downstairs. Is the house falling down about our ears?'

'It is not quite as bad as that, Ellie, but Mr Darcy has discovered the very fabric of Pemberley is at risk from an infestation of some sort. No doubt Reynolds will explain it all to you later today. You must not worry; everybody's employment is secure, even if they do not accompany us to the rectory whilst the remedial work is organised in the New Year.'

The maids looked relieved and, without further conversation, took themselves away, no doubt to tell everybody in the servants' hall what they had discovered.

'Is the snow deep, Georgiana? Indeed, is it still coming down?'

'There is about an inch on the windowsill, no more than that, and the sun is out and the sky is without a single cloud. I believe it more likely to freeze than snow again today.'

After they were dressed in their promenade gowns and were waiting until the time came to descend for breakfast, they discussed the forthcoming social event. 'You will like the Gordon family, Kitty. They have a raft of young children — indeed their nursery is already overflowing. I cannot understand why anyone would wish to have so many children. When I get married I intend to have only three. What about you?'

Kitty flushed scarlet. Obviously her friend did not know what took place in the marriage bed, which she supposed was only right and proper for girls of their age. However, Lydia had not been reticent in passing on the details when she had come to stay at Longbourn for the last time. Kitty had been so shocked by this revelation — and if she were honest, quite revolted — that she had not found the courage to ask Jane to confirm what she had been told. Should she tell Georgiana how babies were conceived, or leave it to Lizzy to pass this information on in due course?

'I believe babies are the result of sharing the marriage bed,' she said. 'Unless a husband and wife sleep apart, a baby every year is the inevitable result.' There, she had said as much as she was prepared to.

Georgiana laughed gaily. 'In which case, I shall remain in my own chamber unless I wish to have a baby. Now, do you have pencil and paper? We must make lists for Lizzy and

Jane when we are at the rectory. I think I might have a notebook in my escritoire and shall fetch it immediately.'

When they arrived in the breakfast room Lizzy and Jane were absent, but Mr Darcy and Mr Bingley were there. 'I do hope we are not late,' said Kitty.

Mr Darcy raised a hand but neither gentleman stood up from their laden plates. 'Not at all, Kitty. We have only just arrived. As Lizzy and Jane are not accompanying us, they will not join us this morning. I expect you noticed that it snowed overnight.'

Kitty was finding his friendly chit-chat quite refreshing. She had always thought Mr Darcy taciturn, proud and distant; and adjusting to his new persona, along with everything else that had changed in her life so suddenly, was proving a challenge.

Georgiana answered whilst piling her plate with a miscellany of tasty items. 'Kitty does not take to snow, Fitzwilliam. I could not entice her to the window to admire it.' She sighed theatrically. 'I suppose that means you will not wish to go outside and build a snowman with me either.'

'If the snow has not gone tomorrow morning I promise I will come out with you, however much I dislike it,' said Kitty. 'Fresh air is good for one, and I have not been out for more than two walks since I arrived.'

Whilst she was munching through her breakfast the gentlemen continued their conversation. Mr Bingley waved his fork in the air. 'When will the letters for your house guests be ready? They must be sent as soon as possible to be sure they do not get held up in the inclement weather.'

'My secretary has the matter in hand. I am more concerned with the logistics of being obliged to transfer the contents of Pemberley to the rectory in a blizzard. Ingram is rounding up as many outside men as he can to help. Lizzy is concerned that the removal will take several days and we shall not have sufficient time to prepare for our guests.'

Kitty swallowed her mouthful, and could not keep back her comment however much she tried. 'The rectory is Adam's house — surely the preparations will be done by him? We shall be his guests, will we not?'

They stared at her and she wished the words unsaid. Then they both nodded. 'You are quite right, Kitty my dear,' said Mr Darcy, 'but King said that he is handing over the house to us; that he will consider himself our guest and not the other way round.'

His response was perplexing. The rectory belonged to the incumbent; would not the parishioners be outraged if their rector was displaced in his own home? Seeing Kitty's puzzlement, Mr Darcy laughed.

'I do not expect King to be obliged to foot the bills for so many of us. This way he will not be out of pocket; and Lizzy, Georgiana and you can be as extravagant as you like in the preparations for the Christmas festivities.'

'I was so looking forward to spending my first Christmas here, but as long as I am with you all I shall be content wherever I am.'

Mr Darcy finished his meal and stood up. 'The carriage will be outside in half an hour, girls. Make sure you are ready, as I do not wish to keep the horses standing in this weather.'

On the journey over, Kitty was entranced by the views of snow-covered fields and naked trees which were now clothed in a sparkling white blanket. The lane from Pemberley to Bakewell was quite smooth, and even with a few inches of snow on the ground the carriage made good progress and they arrived unscathed.

Both Kitty and Georgiana were wearing their warmest clothes and stout boots, as Adam had warned them that he only heated some of the rooms, and the remainder of the building would be perishing. He opened the front door himself and welcomed them in as if they were old friends.

'Where do you wish to start, ladies? I am to show Darcy the barns in which he can store his surplus furniture.'

'I see you have drawn the same conclusions as I,' Mr Darcy replied, his face grim.

There was no opportunity to ask to what they were referring as they were ushered inside and handed over to the housekeeper. Although this house was not a fraction of the size of Pemberley, it was far bigger than Longbourn. 'Georgiana, the rectory reminds me of Netherfield, where Jane and Bingley live at the moment,' said Kitty. 'Although the rooms are somewhat shabby, once your furniture is installed and they have been given a good clean, it will look quite smart.'

Her friend was enjoying writing her lists and making note of everything that would be needed to make them comfortable. However, Kitty was becoming bored with examining chambers and exclaiming over cobwebs, and decided to return to the reception rooms in the hope she might meet Adam. He would tell her what he and Mr Darcy had been talking about earlier.

'I shall leave you to continue your tour, Georgiana. I am going downstairs to look at the ball room.' She received no more than a vague hand wave, so knew she would not be missed. It was a pleasure to wander around this elegant house, and she was looking forward to living somewhere she would not be in constant fear.

She had been in the drawing room, and must suppose that the main reception area would be accessed from that. She walked in to find the room already occupied. Adam greeted her warmly. 'I was about to come and look for you, Kitty. I want to talk to you.'

'Where have Darcy and Bingley vanished to?'

'They are outside talking to my steward about storage and so on. Whatever is placed in the barns must be carefully covered or it will become home to vermin, and be of no use when he wishes to recover it. Darcy will have to get wooden cases and boxes made for the valuable items.'

'Why did Mr Darcy look so fierce? Is there something going on that I'm not aware of?'

When he explained she was deeply shocked. There was no need for him to say any more. She understood immediately that the Darcy family would have to find themselves another home. Pemberley would be uninhabitable after Christmas Eve. Her heart skipped a beat as she realised she did not include herself in these future plans — she was beginning to consider becoming Adam's wife a real possibility and that the rectory would be her home sometime in the future.

'Why would the ghost banish his own family from Pemberley?' mused Kitty. 'I cannot see why he would wish to drive them out, as this will not further his wish for revenge.'

'I cannot answer that question. It is one that has been puzzling me too.'

They sat together on a comfortable sofa, he at one end she at the other, with a respectable distance between them. 'There is something else that remains a mystery to me, Adam. Although there has been some sort of activity from these beings whenever a Darcy baby was on the way, why is it only now that they are able to manifest themselves and are taking such an evil interest in the family?'

He sat forward, his expression earnest. 'I believe I might have an answer to that, Kitty. I think that you are the catalyst; for some strange reason your arrival has given them a conduit into our world.'

Shocked rigid, she jumped to her feet. 'How can that be? Surely I would have been approached by other spirits before now if that were the case? I can honestly say I have never, until I arrived here, seen a ghost — or indeed, even believed that they truly existed.'

16

Kitty sank back on to the sofa in despair. This catastrophe was all her fault. As long as she was living at Pemberley she was putting her dearest Lizzy, Georgiana and Mr Darcy at risk.

'Then I shall not return there. If I am gone, then the horrible things will remain where they were. I shall go back to Longbourn where I belong, and hope that one day they can forgive me for destroying their lives.'

Adam slid along until he was next to her. Gently he raised her chin with a finger. 'Sweetheart, this is not your fault. It is no more your fault than being born with blue eyes or black hair. For some reason you have been given this ability to communicate with beings from another world, and you must consider it God-given, not a curse.'

Her eyes filled and she blinked, but was unable to stop unwanted tears from trickling down her cheeks. Then Adam picked her up and she was sitting on his lap, being cradled in his arms. 'Hush, darling. You mustn't cry. I truly believe that somehow this situation will resolve itself. I shall not let you return to

Longbourn. You belong here, with me.'

They were breaking all the rules — even young ladies who were betrothed were not allowed to sit on the laps of their future husbands — but a strange lethargy held Kitty where she was. She relaxed into Adam's arms, and her misery and fear were replaced by a strange warmth that raced around her body. Was she going down with a fever?

She placed a hand on his chest. His heart was pounding. Was she doing this to him? She tilted her head and stared into his face. His eyes had darkened, and there was a strange flush across his cheekbones. Then she was unceremoniously tipped back onto the sofa and he was standing with his back to her, looking out of the window.

Her wanton behaviour had grievously offended him, for why else would he reject her like this? She gulped back a sob, scrambled to her feet and ran from the room, her heart breaking. She was no better than Lydia after all, and no fit friend for someone as innocent and gentle as Georgiana.

She raced to the front door, which was standing ajar, tore down the steps and continued her mad dash down the drive. It was barely three miles to Pemberley; she could walk that in an hour with no difficulty. When she returned she would find assistance and demand that she be allowed to return home immediately. One disaster after another followed her, and she would be better living quietly with Mary and her parents. There she would do no one any harm, or cause any other gentleman to think of her so badly.

★　★　★

Adam remained with his back firmly to Kitty, appalled that he had taken such advantage of an innocent girl. His love for her had caused him to behave as no gentleman should. What must she think of him? He was a man of God; his behaviour should be beyond reproach at all times. He came to a decision. He would apologise to her, declare his feelings, and ask her to become his wife at the earliest possible opportunity.

He turned to find the sofa empty. He was about to rush after her, but then thought better of it. He had shocked her by his actions; it would be better to let her return to Georgiana and recover her composure. He would go and find Mr Darcy and explain what had taken place. As he marched towards the barns, Adam considered the very real possibility that when Mr Darcy heard of his reprehensible behaviour he would knock him to the floor. This would be no more than he deserved, and he would not retaliate in any way.

He was beginning to think he was not cut out to be the vicar of any parish, let alone one as parochial as this. He owned the rectory and the lands around it; perhaps it would be best to renounce his ministry and let somebody more suited to the profession take over.

He must have been out of his mind to consider he could be a man of God. All his adult life he had been a soldier. His decision to leave the army had been prompted not by a genuine calling, but by his revulsion at the wanton destruction of property and life that he had become part of. The strength of his commitment to Christianity did not waver — he would always be a believer in the power of God — but his nature was too volatile and violent to make a good priest.

Speaking to Mr Darcy could wait; his letter to the bishop could not. He turned back to the house and crunched through the snow; with every step he became more certain that his decision was the right one. He owned a respectable house in the village with several acres of land around it: that would do splendidly for the new incumbent. He would appoint his curate, who was an able young man and more than ready to take over the responsibilities of his own parish.

Adam did not regret for one minute his decision to sell his commission, but neither did he regret coming to Derbyshire. If he had not done either thing, he would not have met Kitty and been able to help fight the spirits that had invaded Pemberley.

Once secure in the privacy of his study, he wrote two letters: one to the bishop renouncing his orders; the other to his older brother with the same news, though in this one he added that he was about to get married. Richard would be relieved that he had come to his senses, as he had never thought Adam cut out for a religious life.

His missives were sanded, folded, dressed and sealed with a blob of wax before he left the sanctuary of his study. Immediately he came face to face with Georgiana and her brother.

'Is Kitty with you, King? My sister has not seen her for an hour or more, and your housekeeper has no knowledge of her whereabouts either.'

For a moment he was unable to respond. His behaviour had driven her out into the snow — she had run away. 'This is an unmitigated disaster, and it is entirely my doing. Kitty came to see me and we . . . we . . . I believe I frightened her, Darcy, and she could not bear to remain under the same roof as me.'

The girl shrank back from him in horror; Mr Darcy's expression darkened and his fist clenched. Adam braced himself for a well-deserved blow, but it never arrived.

'Do you love my sister-in-law, King? Are your intentions honourable?'

Fury engulfed Adam at the suggestion he might be toying with Kitty's affections. 'Devil take it, Darcy, how dare you suggest I would do anything to harm her? I am going to marry her as soon as I can.' He waved the two letters under his nose. 'The only reason I did not come and speak to you immediately is because I was writing these. From today I am no longer the rector of Bakewell, but Adam King, a gentleman of means.'

He had expected the dramatic announcement that he had renounced his calling to be received with horror, but Mr Darcy surprised him. 'Good decision, King. You are the least likely vicar I have ever met. I'm sure the good Lord has other plans for you. Now, how long is it since you saw Kitty?'

'No more than half an hour. She cannot have got very far. I shall ride after her; perhaps you could follow in your carriage?'

He didn't wait to put on his riding coat, but raced around to the stables, and in less than five minutes he was astride his stallion and galloping down the drive.

★ ★ ★

Kitty, after marching briskly for thirty minutes along the road, had not revised her opinion of the nasty white snow. The hems of her thick cloak and gown were caked with the wretched stuff, and already it was creeping into her boots and making her feet very uncomfortable and cold. For some time she had been walking along the boundary of Pemberley, but now she could see a farm gate leading into the estate. If she cut across the park she would save herself a considerable distance.

She scrambled over the gate, through the coppice, and was then able to see her destination clearly across the acres of white coated grass. The lake was opaque, the surface frozen, but the vista was quite beautiful. Fortunately the rest of her journey would be downhill, and going this way would mean she would be out of reach of anyone who might seek to pursue her in a carriage.

She was barely halfway across when she sincerely regretted her impulsive decision. Away from the shelter of the high hedges that ran along the lane, the bitter wind whistled across the open space, and she could no longer feel her extremities. She had the hood of her cloak pulled down over her ears, her muffler tied around her face, and gloves upon her fingers, but she was still chilled to the bone.

Then as if from nowhere a horse appeared at her side and, without a by your leave, the rider reached down and plucked her from the ground by the scruff of her neck. Next she was draped face down across the pommel, and a far from gentle slap upon her derrière settled her in place.

'What were you thinking of, you little idiot? You could have frozen to death out here.'

They were already cantering, and Kitty was being trounced around too much to answer Adam. She would never forgive him for this indignity; she was not a pig being taken to market and should be treated with more respect.

Thankfully they were at their destination in a few minutes and she was tipped unceremoniously to the ground, where she fell painfully onto her knees. Her stomach was roiling and her head spinning after the unpleasant ride.

'Up you come. We need to go inside.' He grabbed her under her arms and lifted her to her feet. 'Can you walk, or do you wish me to carry you?'

She had finally recovered her breath. 'I have no wish for you to do anything further for me, sir. You have done quite enough for one day. There is no need for you to come in. I bid you good day.' She tossed her head and stalked off, hoping he would take the hint and go back to the rectory and leave her in peace. Instead he strode beside her, looking none too pleased at her dismissal. 'I told you, Mr King, that I wish you to leave. We have nothing further to say to each other.'

In answer he snatched her hand and put it through his arm, then clamped his own across it so she could not wriggle free. 'You are mistaken, Miss Bennet. Our conversation has yet to begin. However, I have no intention of bandying words with you out here.'

She was whisked through a door opened by an ever-vigilant footman, and bundled down the central passageway and into the library. He slammed the door behind them and then she was taken willy-nilly to a position by the roaring fire.

'Remove your cloak; you will be warmer without it.'

This was the outside of enough. She was not going to be ordered about like one of his soldiers, not in her own home. 'How dare you drag me in here like this? You have no rights over my person and I refuse to be dictated to by someone of your ilk. Neither do I intend to stand here dripping when I could go to my room and change into something warm and dry.' Her intention had been to stalk away with her nose in the air, but before she could do so he stepped in front of her, blocking her passage.

'Please, I have handled this appallingly. It is too long since I've dealt with a gently bred young lady, and my manners are distinctly lacking. Kitty — Miss Bennet — will you please sit down for a moment? There is something I wish to say to you most urgently.'

Unless she wished to make an unpleasant scene, she had no choice but to do as he said. He was behaving quite strangely, not at all like the dreadful Mr Collins or any other vicar that she had ever encountered. With bad grace she perched on the edge of an upright wooden chair, ignoring the more comfortable seats that were available.

The room was dominated by floor-to-ceiling shelves packed with leatherbound books on every subject under the sun. This was where Georgiana had found the diary that had started this catastrophic series of events. Kitty shivered. Had her friend not said she had returned the book to one of the shelves? She glanced around nervously, not wishing to be in the same room as anything that might incur the wrath of the ghosts.

'What is it? Are you unwell, my love? I am a brute to order you about like this, but I upset you dreadfully and caused you to run away and I wish to put matters right.'

Now he had her full attention and she forgot about what might be lurking on the shelves. 'Very well, sir, I am listening.'

He snatched up a similar chair and swung it round so that he could straddle it and rested his hands across the back. 'I should not have embraced you; such things are not permitted even when a couple is engaged. I know that I distressed you so much by my disgraceful behaviour that you ran away.'

Her eyes widened. Had he run mad? 'I was not upset about that. I could have protested at any time, but I chose not to. I thought that you turned your back on me because my wanton behaviour had given you a disgust of me.'

He shook his head and tentatively reached out to cover her hands. 'This is a catalogue of misunderstandings and I blame myself. I turned my back to give you time to recover your composure and then intended to apologise.'

His smile made her toes curl in her boots; he slowly pushed himself upright and spun the chair away with one hand. Then he dropped to one knee. 'Darling Kitty, I have fallen irrevocably in love with you. Will you do me the inestimable honour of becoming my wife at the earliest possible opportunity?'

She didn't hesitate. 'I will marry you, but I'm not sure about your suggestion that we do it at the earliest possible opportunity. We have only known each other a very short while and, although we are certain of our feelings, I think it would be sensible to get to know each other a little better before we tie the knot.'

With a shout of triumph he kicked the chair aside and pounced on her. She was crushed against his chest and she instinctively tipped her head so she could receive her very first kiss. It was over far too soon, but left her lips tingling delightfully. He gently returned her to her feet and pointed to the sofa closest to the fire.

'There are other things I must tell you. I hope you will not be disappointed by my news.' When he had completed his announcement she was, on reflection, more relieved than disappointed.

'Actually, I do not think I would make a suitable wife for a vicar. I shall be far more comfortable being married to an ordinary gentleman.'

He chuckled and ruffled her hair. 'Ordinary? And here I was thinking I was a splendid fellow.'

'Adam, I really must change my clothes, for I am wet through to my undergarments.' She giggled, but did not apologise for her unseemly comment. 'However, before I do so there are several things we need to discuss.' When she had told him her fears for Pemberley, he agreed with her that the future did indeed look bleak for the Darcy family.

'They must store everything of value in my barns; then, when they find themselves a new home, they can have their familiar belongings around them once more. As long as they are all well I don't think it matters where they live. And, in response to your earlier comment about when we shall have our nuptials, we will have ample opportunity to get to know each other whilst you are living at the rectory.' He grinned, making him look almost boyish, as the hard planes of his face softened for a moment. 'In fact, as my home is no longer the rectory, we must come up with a suitable name for it together.'

'Good heavens, Adam, your jacket is steaming. You are as damp as I am. When Mr Darcy returns you must borrow another from him.'

'I have yet to return the first garments; I can hardly raid his wardrobe again so soon. I shall stand in front of the fire until you return, sweetheart. No doubt I shall have ample opportunity to dry out before you reappear.'

'I'll wager that I am back within a quarter of an hour.'

'And what shall be my prize when you fail?'

She tilted her head to one side and placed a finger on her lips in a parody of her sister Lydia. 'I shall reward you with a kiss, sir. But what will you give me when I win?'

His eyes burned into hers. 'Your prize will be the same as mine. Now, go and change before you catch a head cold.'

Kitty hurried up to the apartment and was glad Annie was there to help her, as she was feeling strangely tired. The long walk, and the excitement of becoming betrothed to the most wonderful man in the whole of England, must be proving too much for her delicate constitution. She eyed the comfortable bed with longing, but was determined not to lose her wager and be back in the library within the agreed time.

She scarcely noticed what her abigail put on her. Clothes were no longer important to her, as she knew her beloved did not care what gown she wore. Adam would love her if she appeared dressed in a sack. Once she was warm and dry her fatigue lessened, and she ran back through the house eager to join him in the library.

17

The sound of voices approaching the library jerked Adam from his doze in front of the fire. He had hung his jacket over the back of the chair and placed it next to the flames, but there was no time to put it on before Mr Darcy and Mr Bingley arrived.

Adam had not let the ladies know he was there, or the circumstances that led up to his arrival, but both the butler and housekeeper were aware Kitty was safe. At least his jacket was dry enough to put on, so he could make himself respectable before he joined the others in the drawing room, and he had it in one hand when Mr Darcy walked in.

'I have brought your riding coat, King, so you will be able to return in more comfort. Is Kitty well? Have you resolved matters between you?' He stepped across and took the jacket from him. 'Here, allow me to assist you.'

He had just managed to restore his appearance when his beloved burst in triumphantly. At first she did not see her brother-in-law as he was hidden by the open door. 'There, Adam, I am on time and I have come to claim my forfeit.'

She did not allow him time to warn her they were not alone, but ran straight into his arms. He could not resist enfolding her, but had the sense not to do more than kiss her on top of her head. Darcy cleared his throat noisily and she all but jumped from his arms.

'I can see that congratulations and good wishes are called for, Kitty. I shall write at once to your father and tell him I have given my permission for you to become engaged to King. I take it you do not wish to marry until next spring?'

'We are intending to be wed as soon as my parents and Mary can be with us.' Kitty's happy smile almost unmanned him.

Mr Darcy looked from one to the other of them and then nodded. 'Although it took Lizzy and me a considerable time to discover our true feelings, I sincerely believe you have arrived at the same point already. Hopefully Lizzy and I will have decided where we wish to live, and Bingley and Jane have purchased a suitable property, by then.'

'I am going to tell my sisters my good news.' Kitty looked at him askance and grinned. 'I think that neckcloth is beyond redemption, Adam, but I'm sure Mr Darcy can supply another if you ask politely.' She squeezed his hand, smiled at Mr Darcy, and hurried from the room. He hoped she never lost her *joie de vivre*; he adored the way she ran from place to place with such enthusiasm.

'Are you sure you do not mind giving me another item of your clothing, Darcy? I doubt that anyone here will complain if my cravat is a trifle rumpled.'

'I take it you have not looked into the glass? When Kitty said it was beyond redemption she was speaking no more than the truth. Do you know, King, in all the time I have been friends with Bingley I have never had recourse to give him anything from my wardrobe; and yet here I am, within the space of two days, heading that way once more.' He chuckled and his smile was friendly. 'I do not have a close circle of friends; I have always found it difficult to interact with those I do not know well. Yet once again you have confounded me.'

'Are you saying that you consider me as a friend?' Adam laughed out loud, the noise echoing down the wide flagstone passageway. 'I suppose you have no choice if I'm to marry one of your sisters.'

They were now in Mr Darcy's dressing room and his valet, with a commendably straight face, handed Adam a freshly starched and folded strip of linen. He faced the mirror and deftly tied it in a simple knot. 'There, I will pass muster. I'm hoping Kitty will also have told the ladies the news, as I do not wish to go through that explanation a third time.'

'It has taken an unconscionably long time to return you to sartorial elegance, my friend, so I am sure all the news will be safely transferred to the ladies.'

Adam was about to slap Mr Darcy on the back but restrained himself in time. They might be friends now, but Mr Darcy would never be a man who encouraged physical intimacies. Then Adam realised he was quite wrong in that assessment. He had seen Mr Darcy embrace his sister and put his arm around Kitty.

The moment had passed when such a gesture would be acceptable, but next time it occurred he would not hesitate. Adam was a demonstrative man, and during his years as a soldier he had frequently embraced fallen comrades, hugged those men who had lost a close friend, and was all the better for the physical contact.

In the excitement of his engagement, and the announcement that he was leaving the church, there was little time to dwell on the darker side of things. He could hardly invite himself to dine a second night, as he was coming to the party the next day and he was to spend the night, so reluctantly he took his leave at dusk.

Kitty wanted to escort him to the front door, but he refused. He didn't want her wandering about on her own, even if the house was supposed to be safe. Why should they trust a ghost? They were not bound by things that kept this human world in place.

They stood outside the drawing room to say their farewells. 'I have no betrothal ring for you, sweetheart, but I shall send for a family heirloom. My mother left a box of jewellery to be handed to my future wife; no doubt there will be something suitable in there.'

She stretched up on tiptoe, sliding her arms around his neck, and all but asked him to kiss her. How could he resist, even though he knew his future in-laws were listening on the other side of the door? He kissed her gently, loving the feel of her soft lips beneath his, and blessed the day when she had tumbled into his life.

'I must go, Kitty darling. I shall see you tomorrow evening. Shall we announce our betrothal at the party, or do you wish to wait until your parents can be here to share in the celebrations?'

'Tell everybody. The more people who know, the better. Then you cannot renege on your promise and leave me in the lurch when you realise what a bad bargain you have struck.'

'You are a baggage, my love, and I wish I could spend longer taking you to task. Go back inside; it is perishing in the corridors despite the sconces burning on the walls.'

★ ★ ★

Lizzy watched her sister leave to bid Adam goodbye and sighed. Immediately Fitzwilliam turned to her anxiously. 'Are you feeling unwell, darling? Has all the excitement been too much for you in your delicate condition?'

'I am perfectly well, thank you. My sigh was of happiness that Kitty has found the perfect match. Despite all the unpleasantness, all is not gloom and despondency. Jane and I are increasing, Georgiana has found a dear friend in Kitty, and I believe that you and Mr Bingley have found a good friend in Adam.'

He nodded. 'You are quite right in your surmise, my dear. We have a lot to be thankful for. Tomorrow we must make a list of what we are taking into the rectory — or whatever it is to be called now — and another of what is to be stored in King's barns until we find a new home.'

He sounded so sad at the thought of abandoning his ancestral home that her eyes filled in sympathy. 'We will come back here one day, my love, I am sure of it. The good Lord will provide a solution. Has not he been keeping us safe until now?'

He managed a weak smile. 'You are right. I must be strong for all of us. We have our first party to look forward to as well.'

He did not need to say this was likely to be the last party at Pemberley for a very long time. He continued in a stronger tone, sounding much more like himself. 'The day after the party, the workmen are coming in to pack everything. My steward has arranged for every diligence and bullock cart to be here. It is going to take a prodigious amount of vehicles to transport our belongings to Bakewell. Have you instructed your maids to start packing your clothes and personal items?'

'They are already filling trunks. I think the majority of the staff are living in fear that the building will collapse around their ears at any moment. Have you not noticed them glancing surreptitiously at the ceiling at every opportunity?'

'I have indeed and do not like to deceive them, but better this explanation than the truth. I think it might be wise to remove ourselves from the chaos the workmen will produce. I thought that we could go in search of somewhere else to live and Bingley and Jane could come with us.'

'That is an excellent idea, Fitzwilliam. We cannot take the girls with us in the carriage, as it will be too much of a crush, but I do not like to leave them alone here at the moment.'

'Georgiana and Kitty can supervise the arrangement of the furniture at the rectory. They will be safe there.' He glanced at the mantel clock. 'Are we to change for dinner tonight?'

'No, we are comfortable as we are. I shall go and tell the others not to bother.' In her opinion the least time spent by anyone upstairs the better. She had no faith in the promise of a dead man.

★ ★ ★

When the time came to retire Kitty had no wish to use the main staircase, even though Jane and Mr Bingley were happy to do so, and Georgiana was happy to follow her suggestion.

'I thought this ghost had made a vow to remain away from us until after Christmas Eve,' said Georgiana. 'Do you not trust him?'

They were now halfway up the oak staircase, and the closer they got to the upper floor the more nervous Kitty became. 'Trust a spectre who is bent on murder and mayhem? I should think not. I know we decided that no one is any danger at the moment, but I have a premonition that something dreadful is going to take place before we leave here.'

Her friend moved closer and slipped Kitty's hand into hers. 'Do you feel there is someone wicked on this side of the house?'

'It is not the same as before — nothing definite, but a vague notion something is not quite right up here.' She swallowed the lump in her throat. There was no need to involve Georgiana in her insubstantial fears. 'Anyway, tomorrow night there will be a party and Adam is staying overnight. When he is here I shall feel much safer.'

Without conscious thought they both increased their pace, and were almost running by the time they reached their sitting-room door. Kitty rushed in first and was delighted to see a substantial fire burning merrily in the grate and a supper tray already waiting for them. They had dined early and she had been unable to do justice to the meal. 'Shall we get into our night things before we eat, Georgiana, and then we can dismiss the girls? They have been working hard to get our garments packed for the move on Friday and deserve to have an evening free.'

'Hardly an evening, dearest, but at least

they will finish at eight o'clock instead of eleven.'

Once warmly dressed in nightgowns and robes, they settled in front of the fire with mugs of chocolate and slices of cake. Although this drink was more commonly served first thing, Cook was aware how much both Kitty and Georgiana loved the expensive brew.

Kitty sipped appreciatively and bit into the cake. 'I have only been here a short time and already it feels like home. I cannot imagine what you must be feeling at the thought of abandoning this wonderful place, which has been your residence since birth.'

'I do love Pemberley, but surprisingly enough have spent more time elsewhere than here. Fitzwilliam spends a lot of time abroad, you know; I have no notion what he does there, especially when things are so dangerous in France at the moment.'

'I had no idea he was so well travelled. I suppose Lizzy would have accompanied him in future, but now she is with child she will be obliged to remain at home — wherever that will be. If you were not here, where did you go?'

'We have family and friends all over the country and, until last year, I had a governess, and she accompanied me everywhere. We have a magnificent house in Grosvenor Square, and I stay there sometimes and attend concerts and plays and informal family gatherings.' She paused and shifted in her seat. 'I expect you are aware of what transpired between George Wickham and myself.'

Kitty slopped her chocolate into her lap. 'No, I know nothing about it. Do not feel obliged to enlighten me unless you wish to.'

'You have met him and know that he is a very attractive man. When I was fifteen years of age, still in the schoolroom, I was staying in Brighton with my governess, and Wickham arrived unannounced and pretended he was in love with me. God knows what would have happened if Fitzwilliam had not arrived unexpectedly and sent him packing. My governess was dismissed, as she had been in league with Wickham. They hoped to entice me away and thus ruin my reputation. They would then have forced Fitzwilliam to pay a vast sum of money in order to keep their silence.'

'How absolutely dreadful for you. I think even Lizzy was flattered by Wickham's attention when he first appeared at Meryton. However, your story does explain why your brother so dislikes him. Poor Lydia, to have married such a scoundrel.'

'You are not shocked by my sorry story?

The experience made me wary of being in company just in case my disgrace became common knowledge.'

'Fiddlesticks to that! You did nothing wrong, my love. He was the villain of the piece and you the innocent. Anyway, as you did not actually run away with him, you have nothing to be ashamed of.' The brown stain in her lap had been ignored during this tale. 'I had better take this off and put it in some water or it will be quite ruined.'

'Do not go right away, Kitty. I do so enjoy sharing supper with you. When you marry Adam I shall be lonely again, and I am not looking forward to it.'

'Good heavens, I shall not be getting married before next spring, so we have several months to spend together. You have your season to look forward to as well; and although I will probably be Mrs King by then, I intend to come to London with you as I promised.'

Georgiana was delighted with this information and did not suggest that quite possibly Kitty would be increasing and unable to attend any parties in town, although this thought did occur to Kitty. Both her sisters were expecting and they had only got married last August. She would make a point of talking to Lizzy about this subject; now she was engaged to be married, she wanted to know if there was a way to avoid a yearly pregnancy. Normally one's mama would explain the intimate details which Lydia had already imparted, but fortunately Mama was safely in Longbourn, so Kitty would speak to her sister instead.

It took another hour or two for Georgiana to describe in detail the guests who were coming to the party tomorrow evening. No doubt the news of Kitty's betrothal and Adam's decision would be the talk of the evening. As long as the conversation did not turn too often to the imminent abandonment of Pemberley, Georgiana would be content. She had no wish to become embroiled in a complicated falsehood and was certain she would inadvertently reveal the real reason for their removal.

There had been three bathing rooms installed: one in the master suite, one adjacent to Georgiana's apartment, and the third in the guest wing. When Kitty had been shown this wonder of the modern age, she had been suitably impressed. Although the hot water must still be carried from the basement, the dirty disappeared as if by a miracle through a small aperture in the base of the bath tub. Her friend had been uncertain where the water went, but Kitty was fairly sure it must gurgle down the drainpipe and be channelled outside into the garden.

Tomorrow was to be her first use of this chamber. In all her life whenever she had bathed she had been obliged to sit with her knees under her chin in a hip-bath in front of her bedchamber fire, her modesty maintained and the draughts excluded by a lacquered screen. Being able to stretch full-length whilst immersed in lemon-scented water was a treat she was looking forward to.

As she settled down beside Georgiana, the curtains at the far side of the room appeared to move, the flames in the fire flickered, and she was almost certain she heard a hideous shuffling on the other side of the door.

18

The next morning Kitty was woken by Georgiana, who was already dressed. 'Come along, lazybones! We have so much to do today. Neither Fitzwilliam nor Mr Bingley will wish your sisters to do everything for the party tonight.'

Kitty yawned and stretched. 'I thought that was why one kept a retinue of servants, Georgiana, so that they could do everything whilst one sat with one's embroidery drinking a dish of tea.' She waved a languid hand and her friend snatched a pillow and threw it at her.

By the time she was dressed and on her way downstairs, Kitty had forgotten her night fears and quite happily used the main staircase. Although the hour was early, the house was abuzz with industrious footmen and parlourmaids. The great hall was being transformed into the ballroom: gilt chairs and small hexagonal tables were being arranged along the window side of the magnificent room. The pianoforte and harp were in the far corner on the left of the fireplace — this was obviously where the musicians would stand.

'Are we to use the music room tonight?' Kitty asked. 'As the guests come in through the vestibule in which the great staircase stands, they are already walking on dangerous ground.' She had spoken without thought and regretted her insensitive words immediately when she saw her friend's reaction.

'I wish you had not reminded me, Kitty. I was trying to forget and enjoy today.' She glanced around anxiously, as if expecting to see a ghostly shape drifting through the open doorway.

'Forgive me; I should not have said that. There is no need for concern unless we are still in residence on the twenty-fourth.'

'I shall forget you mentioned it. And in answer to your question, the music room is being set up for cards and conversation. We shall have dinner, of course, in the grand dining room. I cannot tell you how much I am looking forward to this event. Apart from a few house guests occasionally, we rarely entertain.'

'Pemberley is made for parties and balls. Is there not an annual summer fête held in the grounds for the villagers?'

They were joined by Lizzy and Darcy as they crossed the wide central corridor. 'No, Kitty, there has never been such an event held in my lifetime,' said Mr Darcy. 'However, once we are safely back again, I shall ask Lizzy and you to instigate it.' He looked remarkably relaxed for a man about to lose his ancestral home.

If he could dissemble, (for he must be as worried as Kitty), then so must she. Until they moved she would not mention the reason for the removal again. For some unfathomable reason she appeared to be more sensitive to these unnatural goings-on; but that was her problem, and she was not going to burden her family with her apprehensions.

'As long as it does not snow again today our guests should be able to come. Have we invited anybody else to overnight with us?' Georgiana asked eagerly.

'Adam you know about, but I expect one or two others might decide to stay,' Lizzy answered. 'I have asked Reynolds to prepare several chambers for that eventuality. You will be delighted to know, girls, that I spent my time yesterday writing lists of what needs to be done — both for tonight and for our move next week.'

Kitty and Georgiana exchanged smiles. Lizzy was famous for her lists, and they usually involved a lot of work for anyone unfortunate to be given a copy.

'We are both ready to do whatever is required, Lizzy,' said Kitty. 'Neither you nor Jane need rush about the place. Georgiana and I can take care of everything.'

Over a substantial breakfast, lists were exchanged. Georgiana and Kitty were first tasked to discover sufficient playing cards, counters, pencils and paper for those who had no wish to dance after dinner. They were also to find boxes of dominoes, chess sets, boards and spillikins. Lizzy wanted there to be a selection of entertainment for her guests.

'Mr King will be here this afternoon. I need to show him what is to go into store and what we shall need in the house. I believe you girls are going to label things to make it easier for Mr King and the labourers?'

'We have a list of everything for inside,' said Georgiana. 'Then the articles that are not labelled will be taken to the barns. We thought to tie wool to them. What do you think, Fitzwilliam?'

'I think it an excellent idea, Georgiana. I doubt that you will get everything done today, but as long as the carpenters can start the day after tomorrow, there will be ample time for you to finish the job.' Then Lizzy caught his eye and he frowned. 'Devil take it! I had forgotten — we are to go out to look at properties then, and you and Kitty are to return to the rectory with King and oversee the arrival of the furniture.'

'If Adam remains with us for an extra night, Mr Darcy, we shall be perfectly safe,' said Kitty. 'After all, we will be surrounded by your staff and nothing untoward could possibly happen.'

'Very well, but remember we shall not be back until dark, as we have several places to go, and two of them are a considerable distance from here.'

'I was thinking, Fitzwilliam,' Lizzy said. 'If the girls use different coloured wools, they could indicate into which room each item is to go.' She beckoned to Kitty and Georgiana. 'We must go through your list and allocate a colour to each item. This will remove the necessity for you to be at the rectory at all. Mr King's housekeeper and butler are efficient and can supervise the dispersal.'

Kitty feigned enthusiasm, as everybody else appeared to consider the idea an excellent one. She had a growing sense of foreboding, believed that the unwanted intruders had no intention of keeping to their vow, and were in fact planning something catastrophic. If she voiced her concerns the party would probably be cancelled, and she had no wish to ruin what might be the last happy day the Darcy family spent at Pemberley.

Soon she and her friend set off with a basket of multicoloured wools and Lizzy's extremely long list. It had been decided they would take on the task of finding the cards and other games for themselves. 'Shall we start in the music room, Georgiana? There is far less furniture in there and we can watch the preparations for tonight.'

'I agree. We should start there and then move into the vestibule, and from there to the great hall. We should be able to do those rooms this morning, and then we can take a break and continue with the drawing room and library.'

'What about all the other smaller rooms? They don't appear on Lizzy's list.'

'One must suppose that your sister is prepared to let whatever is in those chambers remain there. Do you think we should enquire before we start?'

'No, we have wasted enough time already. We can ask when we stop for refreshments at midday. I wonder what time Adam will arrive. If we can persuade him to help us, we will finish this task in no time.'

Georgiana giggled and gave her a knowing look. 'No doubt you will wish me to work elsewhere so that you can spend time alone together.'

'Absolutely not. We stay together at all

times.' Her sharp retort drove the happy smile from Georgiana's face. 'I am sorry, I did not mean to snap. After my horrible experiences I can't help but be nervous, and would much prefer to have both of you at my side when we are working.' Her friend was mollified by this fabrication and her sunny nature was restored. She would not let her out of her sight; this house was no longer a place one should walk alone.

The music room was bustling with chambermaids polishing and dusting and footmen running back and forth with items of furniture. 'Oh dear! We have not thought this through, Kitty. We can hardly tie bits of wool to anything in the chambers that will be in use tonight. We shall have to start upstairs instead and leave these until tomorrow.'

'It is hard to credit we were so silly. In fact, we can only do the rooms that we use; we cannot venture into the guest wing either.' Georgiana sighed heavily. 'This means that everything will be in chaos unless we can get everything done before the guests depart in the morning. The workmen will not know what to take from down here. They can hardly move furniture from the bedrooms until after we depart.'

'Do not look so downhearted, dearest. We shall finish upstairs in no time, and can then do the library and all the other rooms on that side of the house. I am sure that Adam will not care one way or the other if the furniture is festooned with coloured wool.'

Going upstairs meant walking through the gallery, and Kitty had no desire to do so, but she could not voice her fears. She must be brave and pretend there was no danger for her up there. They negotiated their way around the busy servants and walked the length of the huge room and through the double doors into the vestibule.

Here was also a hive of activity as huge vases of hothouse flowers were being placed on pedestals around the entrance hall. 'Which one of the chambers upstairs is to be designated as a retiring room for the ladies?' asked Kitty.

'I believe I heard Lizzy and Jane discussing this very matter. Four of the anterooms downstairs are to be used, which will be ample as there will only be thirty of us tonight.' Georgiana stopped to admire the flowers. 'I hope we can still keep the hothouses going even when we are not living here. It would be such a shame if everything within them were allowed to wither. Do you think it will be safe for our people to work outside?'

'I should imagine so,' Kitty replied brightly,

hoping the tremor in her voice would pass unnoticed. The closer they got to the staircase, the greater her sense of dread. 'I am relieved there is nothing to do in the gallery, as I have no wish to linger there.'

She grabbed her friend's hand, finding comfort in the contact, and together they hurried up the stairs and on to the expanse of polished parquet flooring. Even though she was thirty feet or more from the velvet curtain which covered the communicating door, Kitty knew instinctively the ghosts were not keeping to their word. The feeling she had was not the same as before — it was less menacing and more vague — but without a doubt there was something supernatural going on. She paused in her headlong dash for a moment and closed her eyes to try and identify what she was experiencing. She could not prevent her shocked gasp.

Without waiting for Georgiana she bolted for the safety of their apartment, scattering the balls of wool from her basket as she fled. Her friend arrived seconds later, looking equally terrified.

'What did you see? Are they back? Should we cancel the party?'

Kitty shook her head but was unable to speak until she had recovered her equilibrium. 'I am so sorry to scare you like that.

The ghosts are behind the door. There is no need to cancel anything.' She hesitated, not sure if she should say what she'd seen in her head. 'I overreacted. I don't think I shall ever feel comfortable in the gallery.' She looked down at her half-empty basket. 'Oh dear, I shall have to go back and collect what I dropped. Why don't you start in here? I shall not be more than a minute or two.' Her feet seemed glued to the floor but somehow she forced herself to walk across the carpet as if she was not shaking from head to foot. Was it her imagination, or did the door knob seem colder than usual? She closed her eyes and prayed for strength and protection, then stepped out into the corridor. She remained leaning against the wall for a few moments, allowing herself to become accustomed to the atmosphere.

Then her feet began to move of their own volition and, however much she tried to remain stationary, she was inexorably moved down the passageway towards the gallery. Although her feet were no longer under her control, her hands still obeyed her commands. She reached under the bodice of her gown and pulled out the gold crucifix.

As soon as her hands closed around this she regained control of her body and flung herself sideways into the nearest room, slamming the door behind her. This was Mr Darcy's bedchamber, somewhere she had never thought to enter. On the other side of the wall was the east wing; the master suite, with its multitude of dressing rooms, bathing room, servants' pantries and so on, took up the entire length of the connecting wall.

She was no safer here than she was in the corridor. She had been foolish to come in. Nobody would think to look for her in here. Her knees gave way beneath her and slowly she slid down the wall until she was huddled on the floor. There was no way she could prevent what was going to happen — even her cross was no protection from the evil that was stalking her.

★ ★ ★

Adam rose early, determined to arrive at Pemberley that morning and not wait until the afternoon. He intended to drive himself as that way he would save his team two unnecessary journeys along the snow-caked lanes. His valet had already packed his valise, so he was ready to leave as soon as he had broken his fast.

His housekeeper and butler were primed and ready for action. They would be able to organise the cleaning preparation of all the chambers in the house far more quickly if he was not in residence. He was eagerly anticipating the arrival of his guests because his darling girl would soon be living under his roof, but also because he hated rattling around by himself in a house meant for a large family.

He was certain that by the time the first diligence arrived everything would be ready to receive the furniture and trunks. He had directed half a dozen outside men to clear the barns and make them weatherproof. With the addition of dust sheets, holland covers and tarpaulins, whatever was stored inside should remain pristine until it was needed again.

He didn't think his early arrival would be a problem. He already felt like part of the close-knit family. After giving his staff their final instructions, he strode out to his waiting carriage and clambered onto the box. Today he had asked for the most robust of his cattle to be harnessed as, from his experience, a heavy grey sky meant further snow was imminent. He had no intention of risking his finest horses in such inclement weather.

He hoped the snow would hold off until tomorrow and allow this party to take place. It would be better for the Darcy family to leave their home on a happy note, and not be obliged to slink away. He had yet to come up with a suitable name for his abode, and he thought he would ask Kitty to decide as, after all, it would be her marital home very shortly.

The horses that had been selected for this excursion were ideal. They had thick coats and sturdy legs, and were a trifle slow but well able to cope with whatever weather might be in store for them. He had not discussed with Mr Darcy what was to become of the well-stocked Pemberley stables. The grooms and coachmen lived in separate accommodation outside, and he could see no reason why they shouldn't remain there and take care of their charges. It would be a simple matter to send for a carriage when one was needed, and Mr Darcy would only need to have his riding horses on hand.

Adam guided his carriage expertly into the cobbled coachyard and was unsurprised when two stableboys and a groom appeared immediately. He grabbed his valise and headed for the side door he had used on a previous occasion. This time there was no footman waiting to fling it back, but it was unlocked and he walked straight in.

He was no more than a few yards along the passageway when a piercing scream made the hair on the back of his neck stand to attention. He flung his bag to one side and raced towards the sound, shoving his way through the milling group of terrified servants. He tore across the great hall and had just reached the vestibule when Mr Darcy and Mr Bingley erupted from the music room.

'Quickly, it's one of the girls — I don't know which one,' Adam said. 'I thought this place to be safe. I shall never forgive myself if anything has happened to them.' Mr Darcy shoved past him and took the marble stairs two at a time. Adam was close behind him, Mr Bingley bringing up the rear.

As they reached the halfway point, a second scream ripped the air apart. Adam recognised the voice; it was not Kitty. His chest constricted in fear, and he was forced to grab onto the banister to steady himself. Then he was in the gallery, and Georgiana flew from the direction of the bedrooms, her hair awry and her face contorted with terror.

The distraught girl flung herself into Adam's arms, but he was unable to decipher what she was babbling. Then he understood that Kitty had gone into the passageway outside their apartment and had vanished.

'Go with Bingley; he will take you to Lizzy and Jane. Darcy and I will find Kitty. You must not worry; everything will be well.' He all but shoved the unfortunate girl towards Mr Bingley, his mind already focused on how to find his beloved. They were at the head of the stairs and he was aware there was something drifting about the gallery. He couldn't see the things that Kitty did, but his skin crawled and he knew they were not alone up here.

'I don't think she has been taken into the east wing as she was last time,' he said. 'She is somewhere up here. They are looking for her, but I don't think they have found her yet.' Adam held his cross in front of him and moved softly down the corridor.

'God's teeth! This time I can feel it too. We will have to cancel the party and leave here immediately.'

Adam was about to agree when he realised there was something odd occurring. 'Wait a minute. These spirits are not malevolent. I am certain they do not wish to harm us, but only to communicate. That is why they were looking for Kitty, as she has the ability to speak to them directly.' He put the crucifix back in his pocket. It would not be needed this morning. 'Kitty, Kitty darling, where are you?' There was no answer. 'We must look in all the rooms on this side of the passageway, as those are the ones that share a wall with the east wing.'

Darcy nodded. 'I shall start here. You take the next door.'

Adam continued to call periodically as he rushed in and out of the rooms. He was aware he was being followed by spectres but felt no danger. Then he put his hand on a doorknob and recoiled. Mr Darcy was beside him.

'That is my bedchamber. What is wrong?'

'The door handle is icy cold. Kitty is in there, and so are the malevolent spirits.'

★ ★ ★

'Can you hear me, sweetheart? Bang on the wall if you cannot shout, and let us know you are in there.'

That was Adam's voice, Kitty realised. He had come to save her. 'I am here, but I dare not move. Something tried to drag me towards the gallery, so I hid from it. I do not think it's safe for me outside this room.'

'I can't get in to you, Kitty. The door is jammed. Darcy is making his way to you through one of the dressing rooms. Stay where you are until he arrives. I shall remain and talk to you.'

Just knowing he was only a few inches away from her gave her the courage to raise her head and risk a glance at the far wall. It was as if she could glimpse something in the corner of her eye, but couldn't quite work out what it was. A shapeless, nameless something, but strangely this time she felt no fear.

A surge of energy pushed her to her feet. Whatever had been pursuing her was not in here; a more benign spirit lurked across the chamber. Emboldened by her discovery, she stepped forward, deciding to try speaking to them. 'What do you want with me? You have broken your promise. You vowed to remain in the east wing until Christmas Eve.'

Adam rattled the door. 'Try and open it from your side, Kitty. The handle is no longer possessed. Perhaps you locked it without thinking when you hid in there. Is Darcy with you already?'

She ignored him. She could not speak to spirits and humans at the same time. This time the amorphous shape did not materialise into a human form, but a voice spoke to her in her head.

'*We wish you no harm. We believe you have been sent to save us. We have been trapped here for over a hundred and fifty years and wish to move on. We have been waiting for the one who would be able to communicate with us — and you are she.*'

She could not repress a shiver. Hearing words in her mind was even more unsettling than speaking directly to a ghost as she had before. 'What can I do? Henry Darcy said the only thing that could release you was justice for your murder.'

'He does not speak for us. We are the three who were with him that dreadful night. We should have known better than to accept his invitation. We were not friends of his, but young men who thought it would be a lark to attend one of these notorious house parties. We had no idea that he planned to abduct local girls for his pleasure. We did not deserve to die that night; for our families to be forever tainted by association with such an evil man.'

'We had no idea that some of the victims were not part of his coterie.'

'That night two evil men came face to face. Darcy showed no repentance and laughed at Josiah Bainbridge. It was Bainbridge who killed us all. He was like a man possessed, and we were struck down before we could resist. The others were guilty of not stepping in to prevent the massacre, nothing else.'

'Surely one man could not have murdered all of you? Why did nobody fight back?'

'When they burst in we were all three sheets to the wind. Darcy and his two cronies, all as bad as each other, had taken the village girls to another room whilst we disported ourselves with the ladies of the night who had accompanied him from

London. *We were not violent — merely boys seeking adventure, sowing our wild oats. We were slaughtered before the villagers could intervene. Bainbridge continued his killing spree and disposed of the others.'*

Someone was hammering on a door at the far side of the room. The noise was so great that Kitty managed to hear it over the voice of her ghostly visitor. Fitzwilliam (she would never be able to call him Mr Darcy again without thinking of that dreadful night) was attempting to enter. Then she realised Adam was also banging and shouting. 'I am well; do not worry. I am talking to quite different ghosts and am at no risk by so doing. I am certain I will be released presently.'

'Thank God!' exclaimed Adam. 'I have been beside myself since you went quiet ten minutes ago. If you are certain you are in no immediate danger, I shall desist from my racket and leave you to continue your conversation.'

She turned her mind inwards and was relieved to find the extra occupant was still there. 'I apologise for the interruption. Would you be so kind as to give me your names? It might be possible for me to exonerate your memories. If I did so, would that let you leave?'

'I fear not. We are trapped by Henry Darcy

271

and his brothers. Until he is satisfied, we cannot depart. I wished to warn you that unless a Bainbridge dies by the hand of a Darcy, we are forever doomed to keep company with that devil and not join our families in the light.'

Suddenly the door to Kitty's right flew open and Adam erupted into the room. Simultaneously, Fitzwilliam appeared through a door in the panelling on the far side of the chamber. Whoever had been talking to Kitty had released his hold, and she was free to go.

'My darling, you are shaking. Let me hold you.' Kitty threw herself into Adam's arms but could not control her tears. She could never tell anyone how the curse could be lifted; she must bear the burden of this knowledge alone. Her brother-in-law, having finally been allowed in, strode across to join them.

'Take her downstairs, King. We are not safe here.'

Kitty was too fatigued to argue when Adam picked her up and carried her down the main stairs and into the drawing room, where her family was anxiously gathered. An hour had passed before the room was calm again and she was ready to give them an edited version of what had transpired.

When she had completed her tale, they

were suitably shocked. 'Fitzwilliam,' Lizzy said, 'would it be possible to discover the names of those poor young men and remove the stain from their characters?'

He frowned. 'I doubt it, but I suppose King could check the parish registers to see if the names were entered there, or where they were buried.'

'I must find the wool that I dropped so that Georgiana and I can get started,' Kitty told the gathering as she stood up.

'I have decided that things will be done differently,' said Mr Darcy. 'I shall give Lizzy's lists and the wool to Reynolds, and she can get the staff to tag the furniture.' He had all their attention now. 'I have postponed the move until the weekend, as I have faith in what Kitty has told us and believe we are safe for another ten days.'

'The day after our party we shall spend together quietly,' said Lizzy. 'The following day, are we not to go in search of somewhere else to live?'

'We are indeed, my love, and I am hoping that King will agree to remain here until our move. I have no wish to leave the girls on their own, especially as there will be several villagers working inside. Ingram has arranged for carpenters to make up crates to store our paintings and other valuables. I have said they can do this in the gallery, as we no longer wish to use it ourselves.'

'We are not to help in any way with the move?' Georgiana said sadly.

'I thought perhaps Adam would be kind enough to escort you to Lambton when Jane, Mr Bingley, Fitzwilliam and I are out looking at suitable properties,' said Lizzy.

'I should be delighted to. We shall have refreshments at the local hostelry, which is famous — so I'm told — for its table.'

The matter settled satisfactorily for all concerned, the men retreated to play billiards, and Lizzy and Jane settled in to discuss how they were to set up their nurseries. Georgiana and Kitty were left to their own devices.

'We have yet to build a snowman, Kitty. Shall we do so now? The sun is out and there is plenty of snow in the park we can use.'

'I should enjoy getting some fresh air, but I am not convinced that building a snowman will be particularly enjoyable.'

'You will love it once we have started. We must find lumps of coal for the buttons and eyes, and a hat and muffler in which to dress it. I must do something, Kitty dearest, or I shall go mad with waiting for tonight.'

The spot Georgiana selected was on the west side of the house, as far from the ghosts as they could be. Two footmen followed carrying the necessary equipment, a selection of old scarves and hats, and a basket with assorted vegetables of the pointed variety and a dozen small lumps of coal. They did not volunteer to remain to help with the building and Kitty did not blame them. There was a bitter wind blowing across the park and already she regretted agreeing to this escapade.

'This is perfect, Kitty,' her friend called cheerfully. 'The snow has been blown into a lovely white pile against the wall. We have to make a huge snowball first for the trunk and then a smaller one for the head.'

It would be mean to remain unenthusiastic in the face of Georgiana's obvious delight. Together they worked until there was a ball of snow sufficiently large to begin rolling it. To her surprise Kitty was no longer cold, and in fact was quite enjoying the experience, despite the fact she had fallen face first on more than one occasion.

'How big does the body have to be?' she asked Georgiana. 'Is this not large enough? The ball is certainly getting almost too heavy to move.' She had on her oldest, warmest clothes, stout boots, an ancient bonnet, and two pairs of mittens. She looked like a vagrant and Georgiana did not look any better.

A familiar voice, speaking from somewhere behind her, caused Kitty to stumble to her knees. 'Remain where you are, ladies. We gentlemen are coming out to help you.' The billiard room overlooked the place where they were, and Adam was leaning on the windowsill.

'By the time you get on your outdoor garments, Adam, we shall have finished,' Kitty replied somewhat tersely.

He laughed, and to her astonishment swung his legs over the windowsill and dropped to the ground without bothering to claim his greatcoat, warm muffler or gloves. He shouted back over his shoulder as he brushed himself down. 'Tally ho, gentlemen! Do not stand dawdling in the warm. Join us out here and let us get this snowman finished.'

Mr Darcy appeared at the window and looked with considerable disfavour at Adam, who was already knee-high deep in snow. 'I think not, King. Bingley and I will continue our game.' He grinned as he began to lower the window. 'We shall, of course, applaud your efforts when you are finished.'

With Adam's help the job was soon completed, and only the finishing touches were needed. Georgiana selected a battered cap and scarf and put them on the snowman.

'There — once he has turnips for eyes, a carrot for his nose and twigs for his mouth, he will look quite splendid. Adam, perhaps you would like to finish him for us?'

He laughed, knowing the offer was made because neither of them wished to get any dirtier than they already were. 'Whilst I am doing this, why don't you fetch something suitable for his arms?'

Kitty surveyed the huge expanse of empty parkland. 'That is all very well for you to say, sir, but I cannot see a tree within half a mile of here. Where do you intend that we find these branches, might I ask?'

'I am not suggesting that you trudge across to the woodland, my love, but walk a few yards around the building and ask one of the outside men who are working in one of the outbuildings. There is a team of carpenters from the village based there preparing the timber for the packing cases.'

'I shall come with you, Kitty,' Georgiana offered. 'I am familiar with the buildings and you might get lost. This might take some time,' she added, addressing Adam, 'so do not feel obliged to wait for our return. You look like a snowman yourself; you will no doubt wish to find something dry to wear before we congregate for refreshments in half an hour.'

Adam waved casually and returned to his

task. Once they were out of his earshot Kitty grabbed her friend's arm. 'I have so enjoyed this past hour or so. Thank you so much for insisting that I came.' She giggled. 'Having Adam with us made it even more fun. I cannot understand what possessed him to climb out of the window in order to join us. If I had known he was watching from the billiard room I would have been more careful not to fall face first into the snow so often.'

'He is quite besotted with you. It is just like a story in a book. He is your handsome prince sent by a higher power to rescue you from evil.'

This light-hearted remark jerked Kitty back to the horrors that lurked indoors; she had been able to forget the ghosts whilst she was enjoying herself in the snow. Her sudden silence went unnoticed as they turned the corner. This was the first time she had ventured to this side of Pemberley, where the laundry, the ice house and various other outbuildings were situated.

'I can hear the sound of hammering coming from across the yard — that must be where the carpenters are working,' Georgiana said. 'I must say I was shocked that Fitzwilliam is going to allow these men to work inside. In the past he was a stickler and would not dream of having any work done whilst we were in residence.'

'I suppose everything is different now, not just because he has married Lizzy, but because he has had to come to terms with the fact Pemberley is haunted. A month ago, if anyone had told me I could speak to spirits, I would have thought them fit for the lunatic asylum.'

'We all believe in God, so believing in the supernatural is not so very different, is it?'

'You are right, Georgiana. I suppose that is why it is called 'the Christian faith'. Believing in something for which you have no actual proof is an act of faith.'

They had now reached the barn where the carpenters were, and the foreman of the gang spotted them at once. He put down his tools, smiled, touched his forelock, and hurried over. 'Miss Darcy, I reckon I know what you want. One of the lads says as you have been making a right decent snowman.'

'Jed, you have guessed our reason for appearing here and interrupting you. We would like something to use as arms — do you have any off cuts that would do?'

'Tommy, you ain't busy — you bring them bits for Miss Darcy and take them round.'

A smiling urchin appeared with an assortment of pieces of wood tucked under his arm, obviously not bothered by being given an errand that involved being outside in the snow. Kitty drew her friend to one side. 'Would you mind if we asked the boy to put in the arms for us? I am frozen to the marrow and would dearly like to go in and change before we eat.' That she was also in urgent need of the commode was not something she thought it delicate to mention.

'Of course. I too am quite exhausted after our exertions.' She turned to the boy waiting patiently just outside the barn. 'Miss Bennet and I are going in, Tommy, so you can finish off the snowman for us.'

The child nodded and trotted off, leaving them free to return to the warmth and comfort of inside. As they were stamping snow from their boots in the passageway, Georgiana mentioned the carpenter who had been so pleasant and helpful.

'Jed Bainbridge is well liked by all of us. He and his men do all the repairs and renewals here.'

20

Somehow Kitty completed the long walk across the cobbled yard and into the house without her legs giving way beneath her. Everything became clear to her now — the ghost had deliberately terrified the family so that they would have to call in villagers to help them retreat from the danger. But how could he have known a descendant of Josiah Bainbridge would be working in the gallery?

She shivered and Georgiana patted her arm affectionately. 'I should not have kept you out so long, dearest friend. I keep forgetting you are not so robust as I. We shall go upstairs immediately and change into something warm and dry. Do you wish to retire to bed?'

Kitty's teeth were chattering so hard it was all but impossible to answer. 'I shall be fine once I am warm.'

They dashed through the house and up the oak staircase and were in the comfort of their own apartment in no time. There, with a cheerful fire crackling and four maids fluttering about, Kitty was able to push her terror aside. She could not tell anyone what she knew. It would be too much for them to bear if she informed them that in order for the curse to be lifted, Fitzwilliam must kill Jed Bainbridge.

She scarcely noticed what her abigail had chosen for her; being fashionably dressed was the least of her concerns right now. Her gown was in a pretty shade of russet, the material of heavy damask, and the spencer a golden shade with a matching collar and cuffs.

'I don't remember having this gown made up,' said Kitty to her friend. 'Either I am becoming forgetful or you have lent me one of yours.'

'I have so many in my closet I shall never wear them all. We are of similar build and colouring and I am determined to share everything with you, for I shall lose you to Adam when you are married next year.'

'You shall do no such thing. You are my bosom bow, and I shall see you as often as I can. I am certain that you will be living in the vicinity even if you're not here any longer.'

There was only one way her friend could remain in this house, and that was too dreadful to contemplate. Georgiana embraced her and, arm in arm, they hurried back through the chilly corridors to join the rest of the party in the small drawing room. The main chamber was being prepared for the party tonight.

Lizzy looked up with a smile of welcome. 'There you are at last, girls. We are famished but did not wish to start on the delicious repast set out in the breakfast parlour before you arrived.' Her smile slipped as she stared at her sister. 'Kitty, you are very pale. I do hope that you did not become chilled outside.'

'I did, but it was worth it. Have you all admired our snowman?' When they shook their heads she put her hands on her hips and glared at them. 'How very remiss of you! After all the effort Georgiana, Adam and I put in, the very least you could do is look out of the window.'

Adam led the way to the windows, which also overlooked the park. The boy had not only put in wooden arms, he had also added feet. 'He looks wonderful!' exclaimed Lizzy. 'I cannot believe the three of you made such an enormous snowman on your own. I declare he must be taller than you, Fitzwilliam.'

Their work was much-admired, and then they all made their way to the breakfast parlour to eat. The gentlemen usually did without a midday meal as they were often about estate business, or hunting, or some such masculine pursuit. Kitty was glad all three were there today, and was even able to drink half a bowl of soup and nibble at a small piece of venison pie.

Afterwards they retired to the warmth of the small drawing room once more, and Georgiana went to join Jane and Lizzy, but Kitty could not endure an afternoon of trivial chatter. The burden of her knowledge weighed her down and she wandered to the window to stare morosely out at the bleak vista. To the others it would seem she was admiring her handiwork.

'Sweetheart, what is wrong?' asked Adam. 'You have not been yourself since you came in. Has something occurred to upset you?' He stood behind her and kept his arms at his sides, but Kitty could feel his warmth through the material of her gown.

'I cannot tell you — I cannot tell anyone!' With a muffled sob, she picked up her skirts and fled. She had gone no more than a few yards when Adam was beside her, and this time he gathered her close and she rested her cheek against his waistcoat, trying hard not to cry.

'Come, Kitty darling. We cannot talk here; we shall freeze. We can go into the library. I have been there already today, and the fires are lit and the room is cosy and warm. I shall not let you go until you tell me what is upsetting you. I am to be your husband; it is my right and pleasure to take care of you, and

I shall not be gainsaid in this matter.' Keeping his arm around her waist, he escorted her quickly across the central corridor and into the library. They could hear servants working next door in the drawing room, but the doors were closed and they were quite private.

'We shall sit together on the sofa by the fire,' he said. 'I care not that being alone with you is a breach of etiquette. We have endured too much together already to be bothered by such niceties.'

Once they were comfortably settled, he took her hands and stared earnestly into her face. Before she could stop herself, she had blurted out the whole and he was as shocked as she to learn Henry Darcy's true intent.

'What are we going to do, Adam? Somehow we must think of a way to prevent Jed from working in the house; and if we cannot do that, we have to keep Fitzwilliam away from the gallery.'

'The latter will not be hard to achieve, sweetheart. Darcy has no need to go upstairs, as he and Lizzy still have their accommodation downstairs. However, I believe it to be far more important to keep the carpenter outside. Remember, you were told that in order to achieve revenge a Bainbridge must meet his end at the hand of a Darcy — and three of the ghosts are Darcys. I think it far

285

more likely they will attack the poor young man if we do not keep him safe.'

'I suppose you could be correct, but the young man who spoke to me said that the Darcy ghosts must keep their word and cannot come through into our world until after Christmas Eve.' The weight on her shoulders lifted. 'All we have to do is make sure Jed has completed his task before then and all will be well. After that day this house will be left empty — possibly for ever.' She was herself again and jumped to her feet. 'I do hope there is something left on the sideboard in the breakfast parlour, as my appetite has returned. As we are not to dine until seven o'clock tonight, I am likely to fade away from hunger if I do not have something now.'

He was looking at her in a most peculiar way. His eyes were burning into her, and an unexpected warmth gathered in her nether regions. She stepped forward and linked her arms around his neck, tilting her face and inviting him to kiss her. His arms tightened and his mouth covered hers, transporting her to a place she had not known existed.

Then she was free. 'We must not be alone together, sweetheart. I cannot resist kissing you and I have no right to do so until we are wed.'

She skipped away from him, her heart pounding and her cheeks rosy. 'Then we must be wed as soon as possible, for I have no intention of avoiding you.'

Unfortunately the remains of their meal had been removed. Kitty surveyed the empty sideboard with dismay and her stomach rumbled. With a sigh of disappointment, she walked back to the small drawing room to find Adam already there and deep in conversation with Fitzwilliam and Mr Bingley. They all looked so serious that she was certain Adam must be passing on her information. She shrugged and wandered across disconsolately to sit with her sisters.

'Do not look so sad, Kitty,' said Lizzy. 'I have sent for a tray. I am not surprised you were unable to eat earlier and I'm glad that your stomach has now settled. I cannot imagine what they are discussing with such long faces; surely there cannot be further bad news?'

There was no need for Kitty to answer, as a footman appeared with a delicious selection of food; and by the time she was finished the gentlemen had gone. The remainder of the afternoon passed pleasantly, and they all retired to their respective apartments to begin the long process of preparing for the evening's event.

'Your evening gown is divine, Georgiana,' said
Kitty. 'I have never seen anything so fine as
the Vandyked lace and rouleau bound with
strings of pearls. I had not thought I could
like a white dress so well, but yours is quite
beautiful.' She reached out and touched the
elaborate arrangement of shining brown plaits
that encircled her friend's head. 'I love the
matching silk roses and ribbons threaded
through this.'

Not to be outdone in giving fulsome praise,
Georgiana responded. 'I think the pink silk
petticoat of your gown is quite charming with
the silver sarcenet overskirt. The silver and
pink bugle beading around the hem and
neckline are quite perfect. We shall be the
belles of the ball, shall we not?' She picked up
her wrap and slipped her wrist through the
loop that would hold her train aloft and keep
it from under her feet.

'Indeed we shall, if we both manage not to
trip over our demi-trains. I have yet to see
Adam in his evening rig; I wonder if he will
wear breeches and stockings or the new
fashion of trousers and evening slippers.'

Georgiana had lent her a soft pink paisley
shawl, as the corridors and passageways in
this vast establishment were always chilly. The

sound of lively conversation and the clink of glasses greeted them as they stepped into the rear vestibule.

'Oh dear, I believe we are tardy,' observed Georgiana. 'It sounds as if our guests are here already.'

Kitty glided after her friend towards the great hall. As soon as she crossed the central flagstone passageway she was aware that tonight this grand house had come alive. Everywhere she looked there were vases of flowers; footmen, resplendent in burgundy livery and half-wigs, were dashing back and forth with trays upon which were sparkling crystal glasses.

Georgiana waited for Kitty just before they reached the open double doors. 'We shall make our entry together, dearest, and we will turn every gentleman's head and make all the young ladies envious.'

This remark made Kitty smile, and together they walked in. It seemed to her that the conversation stopped and every person in the great hall turned to stare at them. This too had been transformed for the evening: one end was now the ballroom, and a dais had been made upon which a trio of musicians was assembled; the other end, where Kitty stood, now served as a gathering place before dinner was announced.

Then Lizzy and Fitzwilliam strolled over to greet them. 'You both look quite enchanting,' he said with a smile. 'Kitty, I wish to introduce you to my neighbours. Do not look so worried, my dear; they will all be charming and respectful.' To her astonishment he winked at her and whispered in her ear, 'They would not dare be otherwise. After all I am Fitzwilliam Darcy, and Pemberley is the greatest house in Derbyshire.'

Emboldened by his light-hearted chatter, she smiled up at him. 'La, sir, this is surely the greatest house in the world.'

He was still chuckling when he introduced her to dozens of extremely elegant ladies and gentlemen, all of whom greeted her with enthusiasm. However, one face merged into another and by the time they were done she had forgotten every name. The one person she wished to see was conspicuously absent.

Fitzwilliam returned her to Lizzy. She could see that Georgiana was surrounded by a bevy of attractive young men and apparently enjoying the attention. 'Lizzy, where is Adam? Should he not be here with me so we can be introduced as a betrothed couple? I have no wish to dance with anyone else tonight.'

'A friend of his from the army, a major I believe, has arrived unexpectedly for a visit and Adam has taken him up to his chamber. Fitzwilliam has invited him to join us and also to spend the night. I have not met him myself as yet, but no doubt they will be here momentarily.'

'How exciting! I do hope the major is wearing his regimentals — a splash of red amongst the black will add colour to the evening.' Her sister raised an enquiring eyebrow. 'Do not look so worried; I am not returning to my bad habits, but merely making a comment that having every gentleman present wearing black is a trifle funereal, don't you think?'

'I had not thought of it; Fitzwilliam looks so handsome in his evening clothes that I do not notice the sartorial elegance of any other gentleman. The ladies are so colourful tonight that the black is a foil for them. I expect you have observed there are far more than the twenty guests we thought we had invited. When we sent out the invitations we did not realise that everyone would have so many Christmas house guests with them.'

Kitty gazed around the assembled company and lost count after fifty. There appeared to be as many young people as old, and all were enjoying the hospitality of Pemberley. She turned to her sister with alarm. 'If we have double the number of guests, how will you accommodate the extra? There must be pandemonium in the kitchen.'

'Extra leaves have been placed in the dining room table, so that is no problem at all. Reynolds spoke to me earlier and said Cook had prepared sufficient courses to serve double this number. As we are to leave here at the end of the week, she is using up what will not keep.'

'I am afraid that while I have been introduced to everyone, I can remember none of them. Quickly, Lizzy, give me the names of the young ladies and gentlemen surrounding Georgiana.'

'I fear I do not know them all. Since I have been in an interesting condition my memory is like a sieve and retains nothing. However, the well-set-up, fair-haired gentleman is the eldest son of Sir Matthew Rawlings; they have an estate the other side of Bakewell. I know little of the family, but they are well thought of and Fitzwilliam seems to like Sir Matthew. I have no idea who the two blonde young ladies in white muslin are, but they could be cousins of young Rawlings, or perhaps his siblings. The dark-haired young man is the grandson of another wealthy landowner, but I have no notion of his name. Look, here comes Adam and his friend.'

Kitty followed her glance, but she had eyes

for no one but her beloved. As far as she was concerned he had no equal; there was not a gentleman present, Fitzwilliam included, who could put him in the shade. His dark hair, cut fashionably short, curled endearingly on his forehead, and the strong column of his neck was framed by his snow-white neckcloth. His grey silk waistcoat fitted snugly across his broad chest, and his shoulders were encased in a superbly cut black evening coat. His evening trousers made his legs look even longer.

He headed straight towards Kitty, ignoring the admiring glances he was receiving from all the women in the great hall. He bowed to Lizzy but held his hand out to Kitty, drawing her slightly away from her sister.

'You look *ravisante*, my love, and I apologise most abjectly for my tardiness. Blame it upon my friend.' He gestured to the man standing politely behind him. 'Let me introduce you to Major Jonathan Brown-stone, who will be my groomsman when we are wed in the New Year.'

The major bowed and only then did she look at him more closely. He was a tad taller than Adam, but was not so wide in the shoulders. However, it was his hair that you noticed first. It was the colour of autumn leaves, a mix of red and gold, and his startling green eyes made him an attractive gentleman indeed. That he was also wearing the dark blue of a Hussar only added to his appeal.

She curtsied. 'I am delighted to meet you, Major. I am glad that Adam will have you at his side.'

'Miss Bennet, you are even more beautiful than King's description. I'm not surprised you stole his heart so quickly.' He turned to bow again to Lizzy. 'Mrs Darcy, I must thank you for your kind invitation to join you tonight. I am honoured to be included in such a prestigious occasion.'

By the time Adam had introduced his friend, and been introduced in turn, it was time to go in to dinner. Everyone proceeded in a fairly orderly manner. Kitty was on Adam's arm and by some quirk of fortune, Georgiana was being escorted by the major.

Once in the enormous dining room the guests found their way to the nearest seat. The footmen were kept busy until everyone was in their place. The only seats reserved were those for Lizzy and Fitzwilliam at the head of the table.

Kitty had never been at such a formal occasion and was worried she would feel out of place, but with her beloved at her side she would be comfortable anywhere. Mr Rawlings was seated a few places from her and he looked most displeased; in fact he looked decidedly put out. He was glaring down the table at the major, who was seated beside Georgiana; both seemed very happy at this arrangement.

Was this how the wind blew? Did Mr Rawlings have designs on Georgiana?

21

'I am going to go now, Fitzwilliam,' said Lizzy. 'I hope you and the gentlemen do not linger too long over the port.'

'I think some of the young gentlemen have already consumed far too much alcohol. I am tempted to forego the port and follow you immediately,' he said with a wry smile and a nod towards the noisy group at the far end of the table.

'Once they are dancing they will be out of mischief. It is impossible to drink and dance at the same time.'

Lizzy caught the eye of several of the guests and prepared to stand, and all the ladies followed her example. She was bowed through the doors and into the spacious corridor. 'The retiring rooms are to your left if any of you wish to visit them.'

Jane drifted up beside her. 'I am so full, Lizzy, that I cannot contemplate the thought of dancing. That was the most delicious dinner. Your cook is to be congratulated on being able to prepare so fine a meal for almost double the number she was expecting.'

'I hope that Adam's domestic arrangements are up to catering for all of us, having not had more than one gentleman in residence before.'

'We were only there for two nights, but I was impressed with the efficiency of the housekeeping. I am sure we will be comfortable there, if not as luxurious as here. Did you notice that Georgiana seemed very taken with Adam's major? I am afraid the sight of her flirting with an officer, however innocent, sends a chill through my body.'

'She is a sensible girl; she will not do anything she shouldn't. Also, I am quite sure any friend of Adam's will be reliable.'

In less than half an hour the company had reassembled in the great hall, and the orchestra was ready to open proceedings. Those who wished to find a more sedentary occupation for the evening made their way into the music room, which was set out for cards and conversation. Kitty thought there would be around fifteen couples left to dance.

There was to be a country dance first. Already the gentlemen were leading out the ladies and forming in two long rows, men on the one side and the ladies on the other. Kitty was standing next to Georgiana. She was partnered by Adam, and Georgiana by the major. Fitzwilliam approached Lizzy and held out his hand.

'I think we should take our places at the head of the line, my love. It will be expected of us.'

'I am delighted to do so, but have no wish to spend the entire evening prancing about; I shall leave that to the unattached. After all, I believe the only reason gentlemen dance is so that they might flirt with the young ladies.'

'How right you are, my love. However, tonight I shall dance with you, and then with Jane, Kitty and Georgiana. After that I shall retreat to the music room and play cards or indulge in insipid conversation.'

When the final strains of the music faded, Lizzy was relieved and more than ready to drift to the edge of the ballroom and chat to the matrons perched on the gilt chairs that bordered the wall. These ladies were keeping their beady eyes on their daughters to make sure that nothing improper took place on the dance floor.

An elegant lady in cherry red, with a startling turban decorated with ostrich plumes, patted the empty chair beside her. 'What a splendid soirée, Mrs Darcy. I have never had the pleasure of visiting Pemberley before and do so hope you will continue to entertain on a regular basis.'

Lizzy had no idea who the speaker was but felt it would be uncivil to ask if she had been introduced to her earlier that evening. Hopefully the name would come to her as the conversation progressed. She smiled brightly and nodded at the twirling couples. Darcy was doing the pretty with Jane, and both were enjoying the experience.

'Unfortunately, madam, we have a problem with an infestation in the fabric of the house and therefore are being forced to abandon Pemberley until the remedial work can be done,' Lizzy replied. 'However, I am sure that once we are safely returned there will be further entertainment here.'

Her companion nodded sagely. 'I had heard some such rumour. Who is the soldier in the blue regimentals? He appears to be popular with the young ladies.'

'That is Major Brownstone. He and Mr King served together in India, I believe. Which of these young people are your offspring?'

'My son, Peter, is partnered with Miss Darcy at present. They are quite well acquainted, you know; they have met at several functions in the neighbourhood since she came out last year.'

Now Lizzy knew to whom she was talking. 'Lady Rawlings, please excuse me; I have yet to speak to all my other guests. Thank you for coming tonight, and I do hope you find your accommodation comfortable.' This family was one of the three that were staying overnight.

'Most luxurious, Mrs Darcy. We are delighted to be here.'

By the time she had chatted to all the guests who were not otherwise engaged, Lizzy was fatigued, and the thought of spending a further three hours being sociable did not appeal to her. She rather thought that pregnancy did not suit her, as it appeared to be sapping her energy and making her unnaturally tired.

Jane was dancing again, this time with the major, and looked quite radiant. She was glad that her dearest sister was not suffering as she was. Darcy was now promenading with Kitty and they appeared to be having an animated conversation.

She found herself a quiet corner and sank gratefully into a chair. Was it the malaise that hung over the house that was making her feel so unwell? Was this why all Darcy wives moved away so swiftly? She should not indulge in such morbid thoughts; tonight was a happy occasion. Pemberley was being seen at its best this evening, and it was possibly the very last time guests would be enjoying themselves under this roof.

As dinner had been served so late, there would only be tea and cake brought in at eleven o'clock. Those who were driving home that evening would not wish to stay after midnight. Had Lizzy remembered everything? She had no wish for anyone to consider her an inferior chatelaine of this great house. Her eyes filled and she blinked furiously, not wishing anyone to see she was upset. She was a veritable watering pot lately and put this down to her condition as well.

Already there was a noticeable rounding of her stomach; if she did not know better, she would think she was more forward in her pregnancy than three months. Her sister was still as slim as a reed, perhaps a little fuller in the bosom, and Lizzy was fairly sure that Jane's baby was due the same month as hers.

The dance finished, Kitty glided across the room to join Adam, and Georgiana hurried towards Fitzwilliam; they conversed for a few moments and then his expression changed. He appeared to grow several inches and his lips thinned. He glanced around the vast room and then strode towards Adam. Something was wrong, but Lizzy just did not have the energy to walk over and enquire. She would leave the gentlemen to deal with whatever was making Fitzwilliam look so fierce.

★ ★ ★

'Fitzwilliam is heading this way, Adam, and he does not look at all happy,' Kitty said, and she could not prevent her fingers tightening on his arm.

'We shall go and meet him at the far end of the hall where we shall not be overheard.'

As they threaded their way there, Fitzwilliam changed direction also. He nodded towards Major Brownstone, who was presently surrounded by an eager bunch of young ladies. 'Sweetheart, I think he wishes Jonathan to join us,' said Adam. 'Georgiana is also making her way across. Go ahead; I shall be with you directly.' He squeezed her hand reassuringly and then shouldered his way towards his friend.

Her heart was thumping uncomfortably, her hands were clammy, and she wished she had not eaten quite so much at dinner.

'Kitty, I cannot tell you how relieved I am that you have come as well,' said Georgiana. 'There has been an unpleasant incident in the small drawing room, and we must go and comfort Miss Denning whilst Darcy, Adam and the major deal with the perpetrators.

Miss Denning has no wish to involve her parents or anyone else.'

As they hurried through the brightly lit passageways, Kitty was so relieved the ghosts were not involved that she did not fully consider the implications of what she had been told. Then she understood. 'Tell me, how bad is this incident? Has Miss Denning been . . . been molested? Is her reputation ruined?'

'Good heavens! It is not as bad as that. One of the young men, Mr Rawlings, pretended that her sister was in need of her and thus led her away from the party. When Miss Denning discovered she had been brought under false pretences, she attempted to leave, and the three of them frightened her dreadfully.'

This rather oblique explanation did nothing to reassure Kitty. She took Georgiana's arm and forced her to halt. 'Do not prevaricate; tell me exactly what took place. In what way was she frightened?'

'I am not sure exactly; she was too distressed to explain. However, apart from the tears she did not appear to have been physically harmed, as neither her hair nor her gown was in any way disturbed.'

'That is a relief. How did you discover that something had taken place on the other side of the house?'

They now resumed their brisk walk. 'I was on my way to the retiring room when I saw the three gentlemen emerge from the drawing room laughing and being quite vulgar. I was curious as to what they had been doing in there and went to investigate and found Miss Denning.'

They were about to enter when Kitty heard pounding feet behind them. Adam, Fitzwilliam and the major arrived looking grim and determined. She would not wish to be in those young gentlemen's shoes at the moment.

'Which way did they go, Georgiana?' her brother asked. 'I know exactly who they are from your description.'

'They headed for the dining room. Do you not wish to wait for us to discover exactly what took place before you search for them?'

He shook his head. 'No, the fact that they accosted Miss Denning is more than enough. I will not countenance such behaviour under my roof.'

Kitty had moved closer to Adam and whispered to him. 'What are you going to do? Do not be too harsh; there has been enough violence in this place already.'

He grinned. 'We will break no bones, I promise you, sweetheart. However, I can assure you that they will think twice about playing such a prank again.'

There was no time for further conversation, as Fitzwilliam took off and Adam and the major were obliged to follow. Georgiana beckoned Kitty into the small drawing room and together they hurried over to the still-sobbing girl huddled on a sofa by the fire.

It took several minutes to establish exactly what had taken place. Miss Denning gulped and sniffed and was eventually able to give them the details. 'Mr Thorogood told me that Emily, my sister, was feeling unwell and wished me to come to her aid. I did not think twice about following him; he has always seemed an amiable gentleman.' She dabbed her eyes and blew her nose for the third time. 'When I got here I realised at once that I had been tricked. The other two — they are cousins of his whom I had not met before — were hiding behind the door.'

'Did they do anything inappropriate, apart from being in here alone with you?'

'No, they did not touch me in any way, Miss Bennet. However, they walked round me discussing my appearance as if I were a horse at Tattersalls. I have never been so humiliated in my life.'

Miss Denning was above average height, with pretty features, an abundance of soft brown hair and sparkling green eyes. However her figure could best be described as statuesque, and she did not fit the accepted idea of feminine beauty. Petite, blonde young ladies were in vogue at present.

'How absolutely beastly — but I can promise you no word of this will ever become public,' said Georgiana. 'My brother and his friends are dealing with the matter now and I can assure you, Miss Denning, when they have finished you will receive three grovelling apologies.'

Miss Denning shot to her feet. 'I have no wish to have speak to them again. I am quite recovered, thank you, Miss Darcy, and wish to return to the dance. Mama will become anxious if I am missing for much longer.'

'You cannot return with your eyes so red,' said Kitty. 'Come with us to my sister's apartment, where you can wash your face before going back.' She led the way to the rear of the building, and Miss Denning was so impressed by the frescoes and other paintings that she had quite forgotten her distressing experience by the time they arrived at Lizzy's chambers. Within a quarter of an hour they were on their way back, and Kitty decided she had made another friend.

Miss Denning had been delighted with everything she saw and would have lingered admiring the artefacts if they had not persuaded her to hurry. 'We shall tell anyone who might enquire that we were showing you around the house,' said Kitty. 'I am sure that your family and friends are well aware of your interest in art.'

'Miss Bennet, Miss Darcy, thank you so much for coming to my aid. I believe I can honestly say my unpleasant experience was worth it, as I would not have seen the wonderful paintings otherwise.'

They entered the noisy ballroom in good spirits, and Kitty was certain nobody could detect there had been anything untoward taking place. Where was Lizzy? She had not seen her for a while, and she thought it best to explain what had happened and where Fitzwilliam and the others were at present.

★ ★ ★

'Hold hard, Darcy. We cannot go into this without a plan,' Adam said when he caught up. 'What exactly had you in mind as a punishment for these three miscreants?'

'I was not intending to take a horsewhip to them, if that was what you thought. They are little more than boys who have drunk too much and thought it would be a lark to upset the young lady. The three of us should be enough to terrify them without resorting to fisticuffs.'

'A tongue-lashing should suffice, then toss them out into the snow,' suggested the major. 'By the time they find their way back in, they should be sober and suitably chastened, don't you think?' Jonathan was well used to disciplining soldiers and had only resorted to flogging if there was no other option.

'I think it might add to their discomfort if we hemmed them in and then removed our jackets,' said Adam. 'We are a formidable trio, all of us over two yards high and with an impressive width of shoulder too.' He was enjoying this escapade; it reminded him of the good times in the service of His Majesty, when comrades-in-arms acted together.

They could hear the chink of glasses, inebriated laughter, and slurred conversation quite clearly as they approached the grand dining room. Mr Darcy smiled and waved Adam forward. It would appear that he and Jonathan were to take centre stage in this play. They paused outside and then, at his signal, flung the doors back. They smashed against the wall, causing the three villains to leap to their feet. What followed was more farce than drama. When faced by three huge, furious opponents the bravado of the young men collapsed.

Adam found it difficult to keep his scowl in place. Jonathan stepped forward and gave the perpetrators a dressing-down they would never forget. There was no need to remove their jackets; all that was necessary was a bit of flexing of muscles and the young men were reduced to blubbering apologies.

Mr Darcy took over. 'You will remove yourselves from my house immediately. If I hear you are still within these walls, we will return and give you the thrashing you well deserve.'

Without a murmur of dissent, they shuffled in the direction in which they were pointed; and when Darcy opened the door, they stepped out into the icy darkness like sheep to the slaughter. He slammed and bolted the door behind them. 'Well, gentlemen, that was fun. Let us hope they do not freeze to death out there before they realise they can find warmth and shelter in any one of the barns or coach houses.'

Adam collapsed against the wall, shaking with laughter. It was several minutes before they had recovered sufficiently from their merriment to make their way back to the great hall. Mr Darcy had said he would speak to Mr Thorogood and explain what had taken place. Not the details — just that his son and his nephews had been ejected for drunkenness but would come to no harm outside.

'I need to speak to you about something far more dangerous, Jonathan, but it can wait until tomorrow,' said Mr Darcy. 'I cannot tell you, my friend, how pleased I am to have you here. I think your military expertise might well be needed in the next few days.'

22

When Kitty awoke the next morning, Georgiana was still asleep on the far side of the vast bed. The fire flickered in the darkness and the tick of the overmantel clock seemed loud. The hour was too early to rise, but she was wide awake and had no wish to remain in bed.

Carefully she slipped out from between the covers, pushed her feet into waiting slippers, and shrugged on her warm robe. There was no need to light a candle, as she could see perfectly well by the firelight. She had enjoyed last night, and so had the rest of the guests. She smiled to herself. That was, apart from the unfortunate young men who had been turned out into the cold for upsetting Miss Denning.

Fortunately Sir Nigel Thorogood had thought their punishment appropriate, and had left his son and nephews to languish outside for a full two hours before sending a footman to find them. They had been discovered shivering in the stable and on their return had behaved impeccably, but steered a very wide berth around Fitzwilliam, Adam and Major Brownstone.

Kitty wandered into the sitting room and stirred the fire with the poker, then added some logs and half a scuttle of coal. Satisfied she would soon be warm enough, she searched the bookshelf for something to occupy her time until the morning chocolate was fetched or Georgiana woke up.

There was nothing of interest remaining on the shelves, as they had been packed away ready for the move. The Pemberley books were being left in the library; removing them from the shelves would require cataloguing and there was no time to do that. Perhaps she would venture downstairs — the back way of course — and find something to read from the shelves in there.

On glancing at the pretty ormolu clock, she discovered the time to be a little after half past five. Good heavens, she had only been asleep for a few hours. She doubted even a staff as efficient as those at Pemberley would be up and about so early, and the house would be in disarray.

The door behind her opened and her friend walked in, rubbing her eyes. 'Shall I ring for our chocolate? I know it is early, but I heard you out here and thought we could do with something to keep us going until we break our fast at half past ten.'

'I have no wish to wake anyone up. Why don't we get dressed and go down to the kitchens and make it for ourselves?'

'That is a wonderful idea. I have never visited the kitchens before, and once we move away I might never have the opportunity to do so again. I am sure there is something in our wardrobes that is both warm and serviceable and does not require the assistance of either Ellie or Annie.'

Once they were ready they took a candlestick each and set off through the sleeping house, down the oak staircase, and then headed for the bowels of the building. Kitty was impressed by the spaciousness of the servants' quarters, in which there were too many rooms to count. With an indoor staff of almost one hundred souls it was hardly surprising there was so much accommodation.

'The kitchen is just along this corridor,' said Georgiana. 'Although I have never been there, I can remember my governess explaining where it was.'

'We could have found it by using our noses. I can smell the dough for today's bread. I expect a kitchen maid will be along shortly to put it in the bread oven, so we had better not be too long; I have no wish to be found where we should not be.'

The kitchen was immaculate, with no sign of there having been food prepared for over fifty people last night. They discovered a substantial pantry with cool slate shelves upon which stood jugs of fresh milk. Of the chocolate needed to make their drink there was no sign. They decided to settle for hot milk with cinnamon and sugar instead. Kitty also found a plum cake and cut two generous slices to take up with them.

'I don't think we shall need more than one tray, Georgiana. One of us can carry that and the other the candles. I wonder how the chambermaids manage — I suppose that they must take a companion to open the doors for them.'

They had just regained their own apartment when Kitty distinctly heard steps outside. The tray wobbled and the jug of milk slopped. Hastily she placed it on a convenient table. 'There is somebody in the passageway. It does not sound like Mr Bingley or Jane; I think they are workmen's boots we can hear.'

'Why should they be wandering about outside our rooms at this time of the morning? Do you dare to investigate?'

Kitty shook her head vehemently. 'Absolutely not! I am going to enjoy my drink and cake and wait for daylight. Then I shall be happy to take a look, but I have no intention of going out there in the dark when we have no idea to whom the footsteps belong.'

'Well it cannot be a ghost, as they are all gentlemen and do not wear work boots.' She pursed her lips and frowned. 'Actually, I'm not sure if ghosts have footsteps. You are the resident expert on these matters, Kitty dearest, so must tell me how things are.'

The conversation was so ridiculous that they both laughed. 'I have heard shuffling and dragging noises,' said Kitty. 'But now that you mention it, nothing else at all. I hear their voices in my head, I feel an intense cold when they are near me, and they have the power to transport a human from place to place. But I cannot remember ever hearing their foot-steps. You are quite right — it is an overenthusiastic workman out there and nothing more sinister.'

The matter settled satisfactorily, she poured out a cup of milk for each of them and they munched through the plum cake with pleasure. When every crumb had gone and every drop was drunk, dawn had arrived and there was sufficient light coming in from the huge windows at the far end of the corridor to allow them to venture out without their candles.

The wall sconces had long since burnt out,

but no doubt an industrious footman would be sent round to replace the candles before they were needed again. Kitty remained where she was for a moment, breathing in the atmosphere, trying to decide if there were any unwelcome visitors in the vicinity. 'I am certain we are perfectly safe to go and investigate the hammering even though it is taking place on the gallery. I cannot imagine what possessed this carpenter to begin work so early in the day and risk waking everybody up.'

'I expect they have so many cases and chests to construct that they will not get the task completed in time for our move if they do not work from dawn to dusk. Look ahead, Kitty — our path is quite blocked by a huge structure made of bits of sawn timber.' She pointed to where the passageway opened up into the gallery, and Kitty could see it would be almost impossible to venture past without there being a danger the stack would collapse. 'They must have been working all night to bring in so much wood. For I am certain it was not here yesterday. I am not sure Fitzwilliam was correct in allowing the carpenters to work inside. It is quite unprecedented.'

'Lizzy explained that the cases and boxes being made to store our valuables must be bone-dry inside, or the paintings and sculptures will be ruined, so I suppose it makes sense to have the men inside. After all, we have no wish to traverse the gallery anymore.' They had now reached the timber waiting to be turned into packing cases. 'There must be at least two workmen up here. One can hardly hear oneself speak above the noise they are making. Do you wish to go any further, or shall we return to our apartment?'

'We have come far enough,' Georgiana said. 'I have no wish to get in the way of such industry. Fortunately Jane and Mr Bingley will be too far away to be disturbed by the racket.'

They were about to turn back when a sudden shout, as if someone had injured themselves, made them pause. Without a second thought they both raced towards the sound. Georgiana rushed forward and, in her hurry to get past the obstruction, became entangled with the end of a piece of wood and fell forwards. The stack toppled sideways, burying her beneath it. The timber cascaded like a row of dominoes, and suddenly the air was rent by the hideous sound of splintering wood and the despairing cries of those sent head first down the marble staircase, followed by dozens of cases and chests.

With a horrified scream, Kitty leapt forward and began to tear at the loose planks. 'Georgiana, Georgiana, can you hear me? Oh please God, do not let her be harmed.'

The noise from the accident had roused Mr Bingley, and he arrived at her side in his nightshirt. 'Stand aside, let me do it. I shall get to her more quickly. You must rouse King and Brownstone. This is the most horrendous catastrophe, and it will require more than myself to rescue those buried beneath the debris.'

'Please hurry; she might be gravely injured under there.' Kitty scrambled to her feet and ran through the house to the west wing to be faced by two rows of closed bedchamber doors, with no idea in which Adam and the major were sleeping. Should she start at one end and work her way down, or stand in the passageway and shout?

She would knock on a door and pray that whoever answered might know in which room Adam was sleeping. The doors were in pairs, one larger than the other, and the smaller one was the entrance to the bedchamber. It would be a shocking breach of etiquette to bang on a gentleman's bedroom door, but she cared not a jot for that.

She knocked sharply on the first door in the row and immediately she heard someone approaching. The door opened and Adam was standing there in his unmentionables and nothing else. 'There has been a terrible accident and Georgiana is buried under a pile of timber in the gallery — you and the major must come at once. Mr Bingley is already there.'

'Fetch Darcy. We will be with you directly.' He slammed the door. For a few seconds she was immobile, not sure if it was the shock of seeing him half-naked, or his abruptness, that had given her palpitations. Then common sense reasserted itself and she picked up her skirts and raced along the passageway, down the oak staircase, and was about to run to wake Mr Darcy when she spied the dinner gong.

She grabbed the beater and hammered on it a dozen times, hoping this would wake the staff. When she skidded to a halt outside Lizzy and Mr Darcy's bedchamber she was breathless, but found the energy to bang on the door.

This was flung open by Mr Darcy, who was bootless but at least had his shirt on. She gabbled out her message and was about to run back to help with the rescue when he reached out and grabbed her arm. 'No, my dear, you must stay here with Lizzy. Leave matters to us. I heard the gong and was already getting dressed. I shall send my valet for the doctor.'

She hesitated, not sure in which direction to go, for she could hardly walk into his bedchamber. He pulled her inside and pushed her gently towards the communicating door. 'Wait in the sitting room. Lizzy will be with you soon.'

★ ★ ★

Adam and Jonathan were ready in minutes — soldiers were well used to turning out to fight at a moment's notice. Neither of them bothered to put on their jackets; shirtsleeves were the order of the day.

'This is a damnable business, Jonathan,' said Adam. 'It has to be connected to the unpleasantness I told you about last night. I pray Georgiana is not seriously hurt.' He pounded through the house and saw Mr Bingley on his knees, and in his nightshirt, frantically throwing pieces of wood in all directions.

'Bingley, we shall take over. Get dressed; you will injure yourself if you continue as you are.'

'I shall not go until we have got her out. She has made no sound. I fear she has been crushed.'

Adam nodded to his friend, and together they took Mr Bingley's elbows and lifted him aside. 'Get dressed, Bingley. That's an order.'

This time the man nodded. Few were brave enough to disobey when Adam gave an instruction. 'We must lift these large planks first; there is little point in pulling out the smaller ones.'

They worked methodically without the need for conversation. Adam sent up a fervent prayer to God that the girl was safe beneath this pile of wood and her silence was not as ominous as he feared. Mr Darcy joined them and did not waste time asking for an explanation; just waited to be told how he could help.

Soon the larger pieces were stacked to one side and a surge of joy flooded through Adam. Somehow the timber had fallen diagonally, leaving the girl cocooned in a small, safe space. 'Look, Darcy — we have found her. We will reach her in a moment.'

'Georgiana, sweetheart, are you hurt?' Mr Darcy spoke softly to the still shape, but received no response. 'Give me a light, King. We need to see if she is injured before we attempt to move her.'

'I think she is merely stunned, Darcy. I can see no blood and her limbs are not twisted. You continue to talk to her whilst we clear a larger space so you can pull her out safely.'

Why was the girl so still? Adam had a bad feeling — he had seen soldiers with not a mark on them stone dead after such an accident as this. Five minutes passed before sufficient room had been made for Mr Darcy to crawl in to his sister.

Only then did Adam become aware he could hear shouting from somewhere on the other side of the pile of broken cases and chests. From the way the voices echoed, these men must be at the bottom of the staircase. He was at a loss to understand why there was so much timber piled in the gallery, but now was not the time to ponder about trivialities.

He crouched down beside Jonathan. 'Darcy, how is she? Do you need our assistance to bring her out?'

'I have her. She is breathing evenly and I can see no obvious injuries. I am coming now.'

The remaining timber creaked ominously as Mr Darcy began to inch backwards with his precious burden. Adam and Jonathan braced themselves against the wood. When Darcy emerged, Jonathan reached down and lifted the unconscious girl from the floor, which allowed her brother to regain his feet.

The passageway was now filled with anxious watchers. Word had spread amongst the other guests, and the gentlemen were fully dressed and ready to assist in any way they could.

'She has a good colour, Darcy,' said the major. 'I'm certain she has come to no serious harm.'

'Thank you, Brownstone. I shall take her to her apartment.'

He strode away with the girl in his arms, leaving Adam to speak to the assembled guests. 'I fear there may be workmen trapped as well. There are men on the other side of the obstruction looking for survivors. We must continue to clear the gallery.'

No one argued. Soon Adam and Jonathan had organised a team and they were working methodically towards the head of the stairs. Once the loose timber had been removed, it was easier to move forward.

'We are almost there,' said Adam. 'I can see the balustrade. Our work will be completed soon.'

His willing assistants had been stacking as they went, and Adam could now see how this disaster had occurred. The carpenters had brought in the cut timber from the barn and arranged it by length against the wall. The containers for the paintings and other valuables were being constructed in the open space of the gallery. Those that had been completed had been left at the head of the stairs, to be taken wherever they were needed. When Georgiana had fallen into the loose timber, this had caused one thing to fall against another, and whoever had been standing in the way must have been swept down the marble staircase and buried under the finished articles. There was no one on the gallery, but he could hear someone moaning under the debris on the staircase.

He raised his voice and shouted down to those attempting to reach the injured men from the other direction. 'How many are trapped under this?'

'Three, sir — the gaffer and two from the village,' someone called back. 'I don't reckon we can reach them from our side.'

They renewed their efforts and eventually discovered the first of the buried workmen. Adam didn't need to examine the man to know he was beyond human aid. The cadaver's head was resting at an unnatural angle; his neck had been broken by the fall.

In silence they extracted him, and he was passed back along the line and then placed reverently on the boards. Adam did not hold out much hope for the other two, but they must continue to search. Then he quite distinctly heard another groan. 'Quickly, one of them is alive at least. Make sure we don't send the whole lot crashing down the staircase, as they are precariously balanced against the wall and banister.'

He and Jonathan took the lead, carefully removing each item and handing it back to those waiting behind them. It was damned difficult trying to keep one's balance, and he feared if they did not reach these men soon it would be too late.

There was something going on above him but he did not turn to discover what the fuss was about. Then word came down from the gallery that the doctor had arrived. He had examined Georgiana and she was now wide awake; she had suffered only superficial bruising in her fall.

Knowing the girl was unhurt gave Adam renewed vigour. His hands were cut and full of splinters; if he had known what he was going to be involved in, he would have put on his riding gloves. Too late to repine — he was in no worse a state than his friend, and no doubt there were other gentlemen with similar injuries, but they were all determined to complete the rescue.

'We have them! There are two, and both appear badly hurt,' he called back, hoping the doctor could hear him.

To his surprise, the older of the two opened his eyes and managed to smile. 'I ain't too good; not much you can do for me I reckon. Get Ned out first; he's got more chance than me.'

Adam knelt beside him and could see at once the poor devil was crushed beneath two chests; it was a wonder he was still able to speak. He remained where he was whilst Jonathan and the others carefully removed the other injured man. As soon as the weight was lifted from the man he crouched beside, he would die.

'I am the vicar. Would you like me to pray with you? What is your name?'

'Jed Bainbridge, and a few prayers wouldn't do me no harm.'

23

Kitty could not remain downstairs a moment longer. 'Now Jane has joined you, Lizzy, I am going to my apartment. They will take Georgiana there and I wish to make sure everything is ready for her. I promise someone will come down to bring you news as soon as there is any.'

'I should never have allowed Bainbridge to bring his work inside.'

'None of this is your fault, dearest Lizzy,' Jane said as she patted her sister's hands. 'Pemberley is cursed, and the sooner we have all departed the safer I shall feel.'

'It is I who have caused your world to be ripped apart so rudely,' said Kitty. 'Until I arrived to be the conduit for these beings, nothing untoward had taken place here. My name should be Cassandra, as I am the harbinger of bad luck and disaster.' She knew she should have remained at Longbourn, where she belonged; then none of this would have happened.

'That is fustian, my love, and well you know it,' said Lizzy. 'These apparitions have been haunting the place for generations, and it is my pregnancy that stirred them into action. The fact that they can communicate through you is a good thing. Without your intervention we would not have thought to move away so soon, and think what danger we would all have been in then.'

'It doesn't really matter anymore, Lizzy, what has caused this nightmare to erupt around us. I'm going now, but I shall be back directly to tell you when Georgiana is safe.'

The house was in chaos: footmen running back and forth without their livery on, no sign of breakfast being set out in the breakfast parlour, and there were several guests wandering around looking bewildered. Kitty stopped to direct them to the small drawing room. 'My sisters are in there. Please go and wait with them until this matter has been rectified.'

As she emerged into the passageway in which her apartment was situated, she could see at the far end there were a dozen or more gentlemen in shirtsleeves working feverishly to rescue Georgiana. Kitty would only be in the way if she went up there, so she went into her sitting room and rang the bell for attention.

Ellie burst in wringing her hands, her face tear-streaked. 'Lawks a mussy, miss, what a dreadful thing to happen. We thought as you wouldn't wish to be sharing when Miss Darcy is unwell, so we have taken the liberty of moving you back to the suite you occupied the first night you were here.'

'Thank you. I had come to suggest that very thing myself. Fortunately there won't be too much to transfer, as the majority of my garments have already been packed away in trunks and are waiting for our removal in three days' time.'

She wandered back and forth from her own rooms to those of Georgiana, unsure what she could do to help. Dr Bevan went past clutching his black bag, and she was glad he had arrived so promptly. A further interminable time went past, and then Mr Darcy came down the passageway carrying her friend.

'How is she? I have been beside myself with worry.'

He smiled warmly at her. 'She is unscathed, and will be wide awake and telling you her story very shortly. The doctor has already examined her, so do not look so worried, little one.'

She followed him into the bedchamber and was about to offer her assistance to disrobe her friend when he took her arm and gently guided her away. 'Let her maid take care of her. You must tell me how this accident occurred.'

When she had finished explaining he nodded. 'I shall go and tell Lizzy and Jane that Georgiana is perfectly well, just a little shocked by her experience. Are you coming with me or remaining up here?'

'I shall stay here so that I might talk to her when she is feeling more the thing.' She pointed to his disarray with a smile. 'There are guests with Lizzy and Jane, Fitzwilliam; I think it might be wise if you put on your jacket and neckcloth before you join them.'

He grinned and for a moment looked quite different. 'Thank you for reminding me, sweetheart. I shall do exactly that. I shall also ask for breakfast to be served downstairs, for those working in the gallery will be hungry after their exertions.'

When Kitty looked into the bedroom Georgiana was sleeping, and she had no wish to disturb her. Perhaps it would not hurt to see what was happening in the gallery. As she stepped into the passageway the gentlemen who had been assisting with the rescue were approaching, and she hastily stepped back out of sight.

Now it would be in order for her to go, as only Adam and his friend remained. She remembered the cry of pain they had heard, the sound that had precipitated this disaster, and prayed that whoever it was had been found and was not too badly injured.

She was obliged to pick her way through the broken packing cases and freshly sawn timber until she reached a clearer space. There were two shrouded shapes laid out on the floor and she shuddered. Then she saw that the doctor, Adam and the major were halfway down the flight of stairs attending to a third injured man. Then all three stood up and bowed their heads. There was now another corpse to join the two already there. Her eyes filled and her throat thickened. She should not be here; this was not a suitable place for a young lady.

She was about to turn away when Adam looked over his shoulder. He said something quietly to his companions and then bounded up the stairs towards her. 'This is an unimaginable tragedy — that three good men should have died in such circumstances is unbelievable.' He gestured towards the wooden remains. 'I don't understand how Georgiana could have caused this disaster. The place where she fell is a considerable distance from here — how could these cases and planks of wood have moved so far and so fast?'

Kitty shivered as an icy draft enveloped her. 'She might have started the wood moving, but I believe supernatural forces must have been involved.' She looked nervously over her shoulder. 'Something is happening. I can feel the ghosts are very close.'

He moved closer to her and put his arm around her shoulders. 'I feel it too. We must get away from here.' He raised his voice and shouted at the doctor and the major. 'Leave him; we are in dreadful danger. We must leave the gallery at once.'

Both gentlemen scrambled to their feet and shot up the stairs. They were a few yards away when the air was sucked from Kitty's lungs; but even with Adam's support, her knees buckled and she sank to the floor. The air around them became thick and heavy, and each breath Kitty took was more difficult than the last. Through the grey swirling mist she saw the curtain covering the fire-damaged panelling on the far side of the gallery tear from the wall. Then the communicating door flew from its hinges and she was surrounded by screaming ghosts. At first she could discern one from the other, and then they merged into a single entity.

This hurtled down the marble staircase and towards the beautiful mullioned windows. Kitty's world went black for a second as they blotted out the light. Then with a hideous crack, the glass and frames exploded outwards in a shower of broken shards, and the howling, swirling black shapes disappeared into the park.

From a distance she was aware that Adam was beside her. 'Sweetheart, are you unhurt? Can you stand on your own, or shall I carry you to your apartment?'

Slowly her head cleared and her lungs began to work normally again. She nodded and held out her hands. 'Did you see that? They've gone. I don't understand why this should be so after so long, but Pemberley is no longer haunted.'

He gently helped her to her feet. 'The curse was lifted because poor Bainbridge died. When Georgiana fell into the timber she indirectly caused the accident that killed him — therefore a Bainbridge died violently at the hands of a Darcy and the ghosts were satisfied.'

'Thank God we did not tell anyone how the curse could be lifted. Georgiana would be destroyed by such knowledge. Do you think we shall still have to vacate these premises?'

He gently turned her towards the ruined windows through which the howling gale was blowing. 'The entire front of the house is damaged; it will take weeks to replace all the glass that has been destroyed. God knows what explanation Darcy will give for this. I have never heard of an infestation of any sort that was able to cause an explosion.'

As they reached the junction of the passageways, Mr Darcy and Mr Bingley arrived at a run. 'What the hell was that? Was anybody hurt when the windows blew out?' Darcy's face was chalk-white and his usually immaculate hair was standing on end.

'The windows went out, not in, so there was no danger to anyone inside the house,' said Adam. 'Your ghosts departed when Jed Bainbridge died. Pemberley is your own again.' He patted Fitzwilliam on the shoulder.

'At the risk of stating the obvious, my friend, it is damnably cold with the windows gone,' said Mr Bingley. 'Adam, is there any chance we can move in today?' He smiled hopefully.

'I think that it is imperative to spend Christmas elsewhere,' said Mr Darcy. 'There have been three tragic deaths today, and I have no wish to upset Lizzy in her delicate condition. What about it, King — will you take us today?'

'As there is no need to put any furniture, paintings or other artefacts in store, I can see no problem with that,' Adam said. 'As your stay will only be for a few weeks, I am sure my staff can look after you and your Christmas guests for so short a time.'

The door behind them opened and Georgiana rushed out. Fortunately she had taken the time to dress. 'I heard the most dreadful bang and could not stay in my bed a moment longer.'

Kitty rushed over and embraced her. 'The ghosts have gone, but unfortunately their departure took the windows out. We are going to move immediately to the rectory. We had better make sure we have what we need for the night, because I do not suppose our trunks will arrive until tomorrow.'

★ ★ ★

Eventually the overnight guests departed, and Kitty was certain that news of the extraordinary events that had taken place would be all over Derbyshire by night-time. Lizzy and Jane were horrified by the tragic events, but equally delighted to hear that there were no longer ghosts at Pemberley. Fortunately nobody questioned Kitty's explanation that it had just required the violent death of a Bainbridge to satisfy the ghosts.

Mr Darcy had told the staff at Pemberley tale that explosive vapours caused by the insect infestation had caused the damage, and they appeared to accept this. After all, any other explanation would be too fantastical.

They were to take only their personal servants, and the remainder of the staff were to remain in situ and help with the redecoration and restoration.

Dusk was falling when Kitty climbed into Adam's carriage with Georgiana and their abigails. The major rode beside the carriage, whilst Adam took the reins. Her friend kept glancing surreptitiously through the window, presumably in the expectation of seeing Major Brownstone ride by.

They drew to a halt a short while later and the vehicle rocked violently as Adam jumped down. He opened the door and let down the steps. His smile made Kitty's toes curl in her boots.

'Welcome to your future home, my love. I hope you will be happy here.' He reached in and swung her to the ground, whispering in her ear as he set her down. 'If I have my way, sweetheart, you will not return to Pemberley, but remain here with me as my wife.'

'I cannot wait to marry you, but I shall not do so until my parents and other sisters are here to join in the celebration. So you will have to wait at least until the spring for our nuptials.'

His smile was wicked as he replied, 'Shall I indeed? I think not, Miss Bennet. Would you care to place a wager on it?'

'How shocking, Mr King, to suggest that I should do something so reprehensible as gamble with you.' She could not resist the urge to rest her mittened hand on his cheek. 'And to think that you were a man of the cloth until recently. I am shocked at your suggestion.'

Ignoring Georgiana, the two maidservants, and a veritable forest of miscellaneous servants who had come to welcome them, Adam drew her closer and kissed her full on the lips.

THE DUKE'S REFORM
THE DUKE & THE VICAR'S DAUGHTER
BARBARA'S WAR — THE MIDDLE YEARS
BARBARA'S WAR — THE RESOLUTION
LORD ILCHESTER'S INHERITANCE